MARVEL
AVENGERS ASSEMBLE
CIVIL WAR

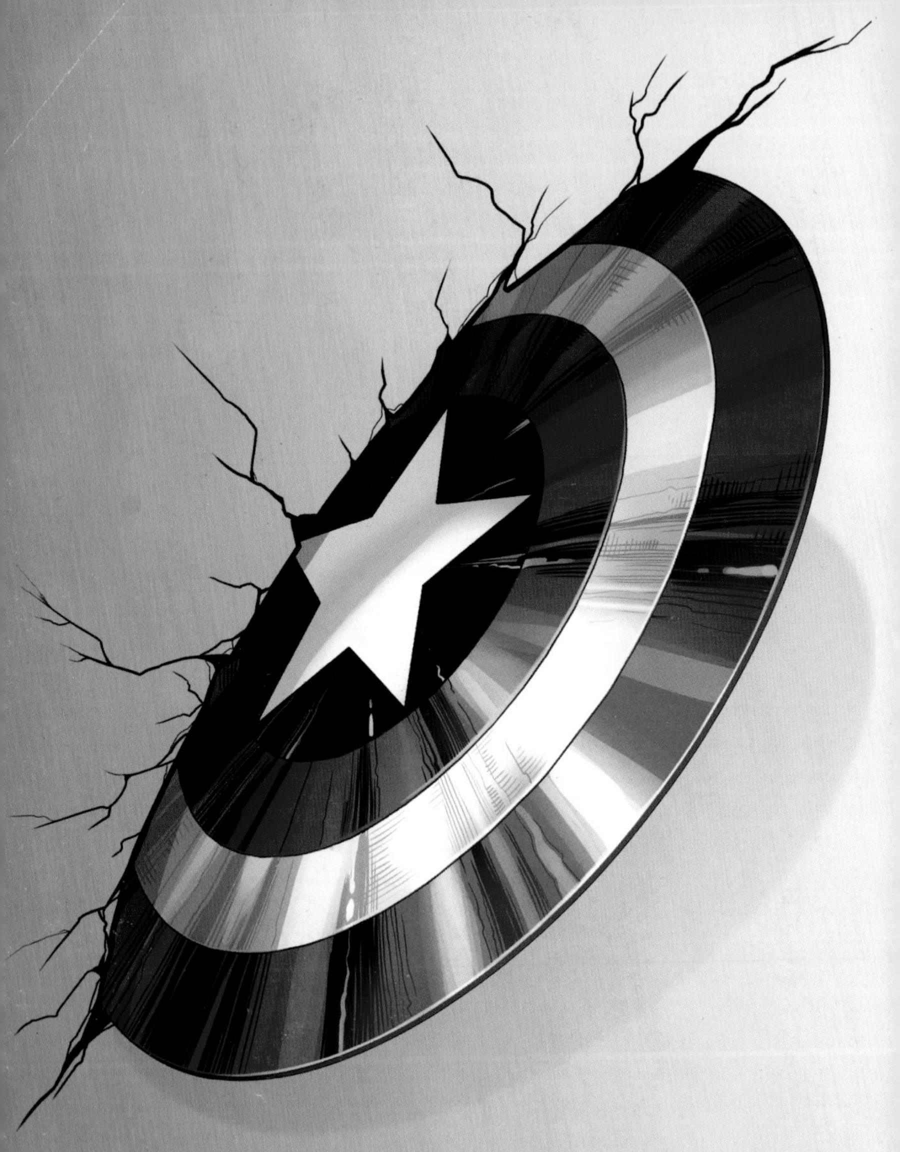

MARVEL UNIVERSE AVENGERS ASSEMBLE: CIVIL WAR. Contains material originally published in magazine form as MARVEL UNIVERSE AVENGERS ASSEMBLE: CIVIL WAR #1-4. First printing 2016. ISBN# 978-1-302-90164-6. Published by MARVEL WORLDWIDE, INC., a subsidiary of MARVEL ENTERTAINMENT, LLC. OFFICE OF PUBLICATION: 135 West 50th Street, New York, NY 10020. Copyright © 2016 MARVEL No similarity between any of the names, characters, persons, and/or institutions in this magazine with those of any living or dead person or institution is intended, and any such similarity which may exist is purely coincidental. **Printed in the U.S.A.** ALAN FINE, President, Marvel Entertainment; DAN BUCKLEY, President, TV, Publishing & Brand Management; JOE QUESADA, Chief Creative Officer; TOM BREVOORT, SVP of Publishing; DAVID BOGART, SVP of Business Affairs & Operations, Publishing & Partnership; C.B. CEBULSKI, VP of Brand Management & Development, Asia; DAVID GABRIEL, SVP of Sales & Marketing, Publishing; JEFF YOUNGQUIST, VP of Production & Special Projects; DAN CARR, Executive Director of Publishing Technology; ALEX MORALES, Director of Publishing Operations; SUSAN CRESPI, Production Manager; STAN LEE, Chairman Emeritus. For information regarding advertising in Marvel Comics or on Marvel.com, please contact Vit DeBellis, Integrated Sales Manager, at vdebellis@marvel.com. For Marvel subscription inquiries, please call 888-511-5480. **Manufactured between 7/1/2016 and 8/8/2016 by SHERIDAN, CHELSEA, MI, USA.**

987654321

MARVEL
AVENGERS ASSEMBLE
CIVIL WAR

Based on the TV series written by
**DANIELLE WOLFF, JACOB SEMAHN,
KEVIN BURKE & CHRIS "DOC" WYATT**

Directed by
**PHIL PIGNOTTI
& TIM ELDRED**

Art by
MARVEL ANIMATION

Adapted by
JOE CARAMAGNA

Special thanks to
**HANNAH MCDONALD &
PRODUCT FACTORY**

Editor
MARK BASSO

Senior Editor
MARK PANICCIA

Avengers created by **STAN LEE & JACK KIRBY**

Collection Editor: **JENNIFER GRÜNWALD**
Associate Editor: **SARAH BRUNSTAD**
Editor, Special Projects: **MARK D. BEAZLEY**
VP, Production & Special Projects: **JEFF YOUNGQUIST**
SVP Print, Sales & Marketing: **DAVID GABRIEL**
Head of Marvel Television: **JEPH LOEB**
Book Designer: **ADAM DEL RE**

Editor in Chief: **AXEL ALONSO**
Chief Creative Officer: **JOE QUESADA**
Publisher: **DAN BUCKLEY**
Executive Producer: **ALAN FINE**

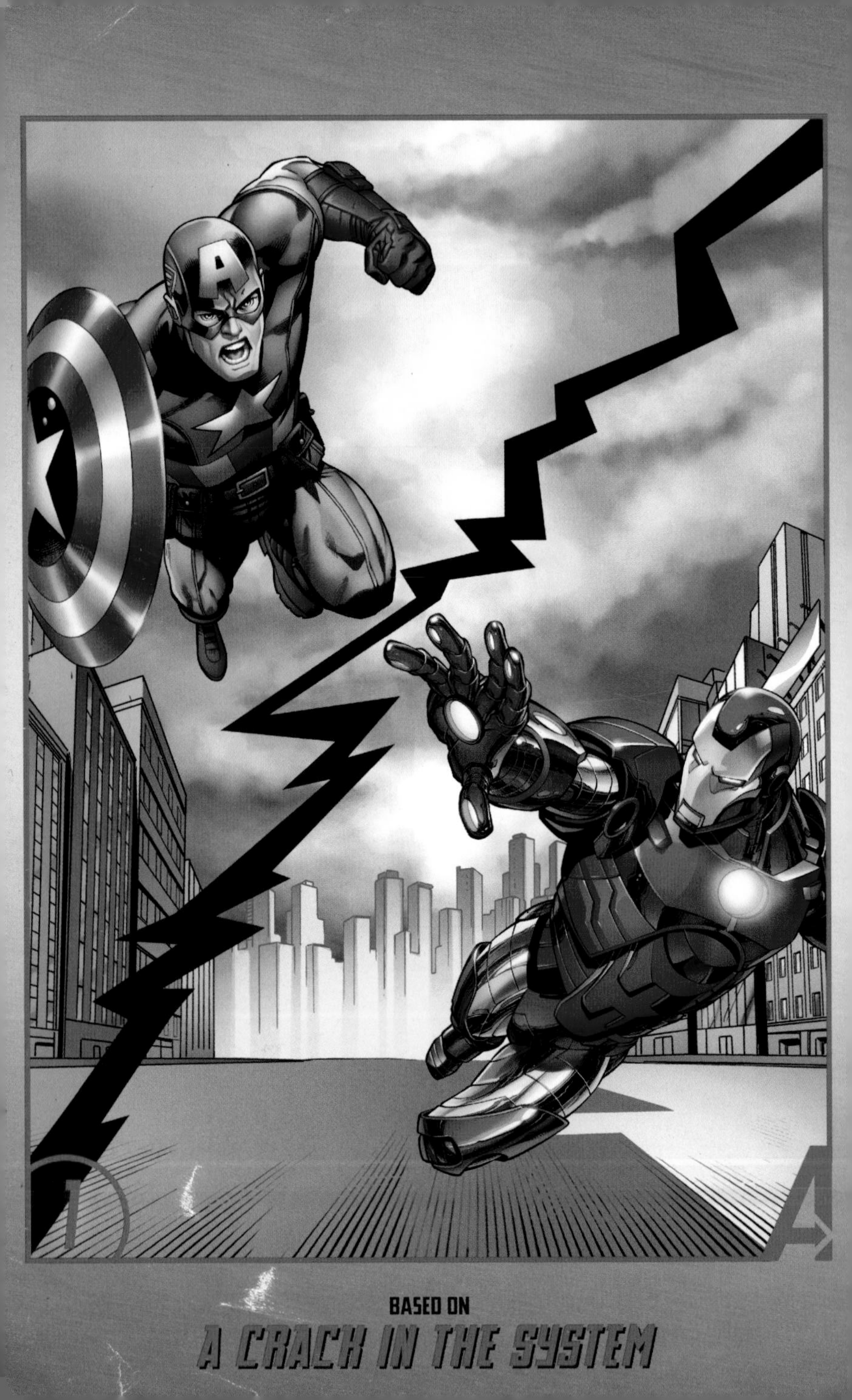

BASED ON

A CRACK IN THE SYSTEM

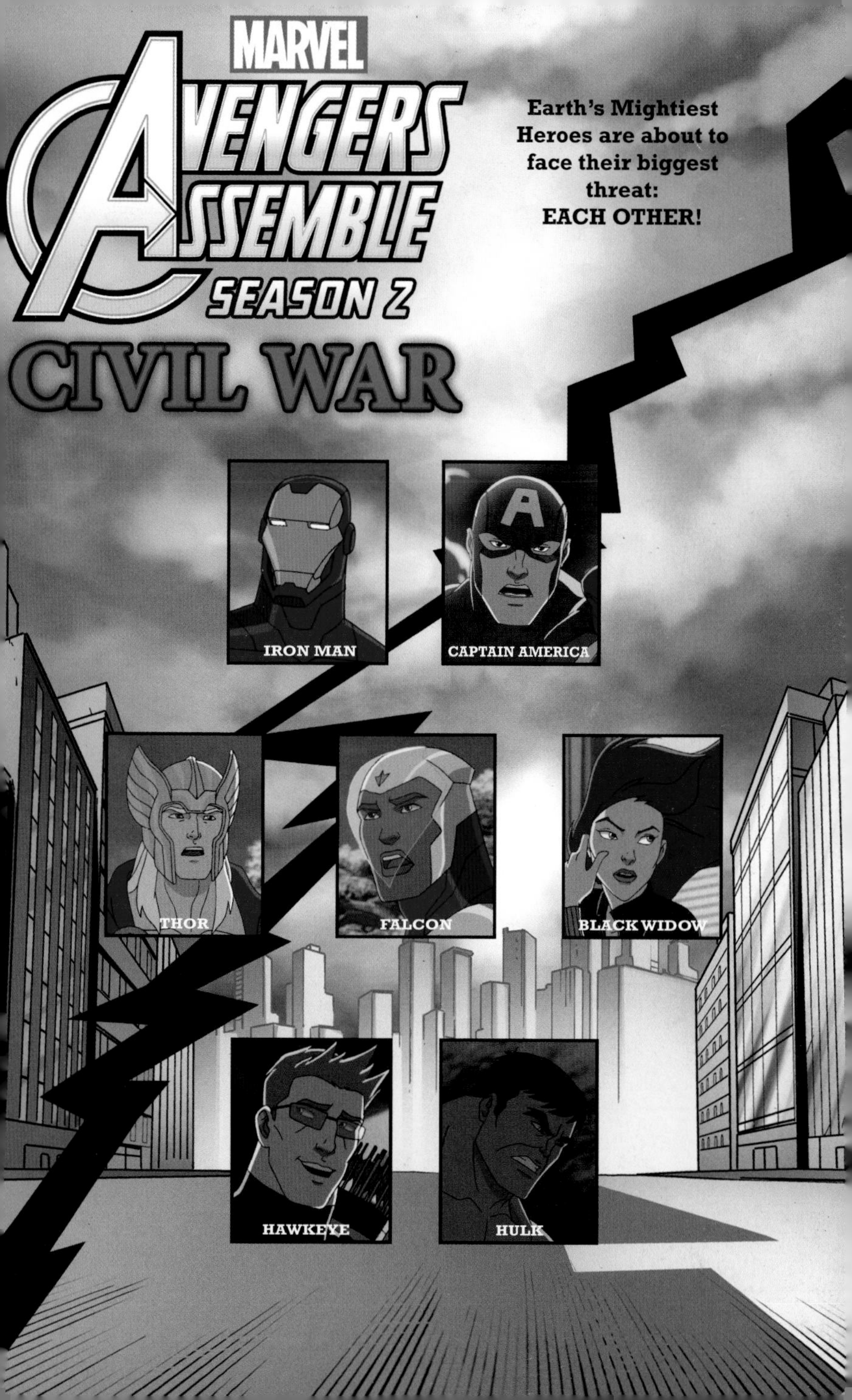
MARVEL
AVENGERS ASSEMBLE
SEASON 2
CIVIL WAR
Earth's Mightiest Heroes are about to face their biggest threat: EACH OTHER!
IRON MAN
CAPTAIN AMERICA
THOR
FALCON
BLACK WIDOW
HAWKEYE
HULK

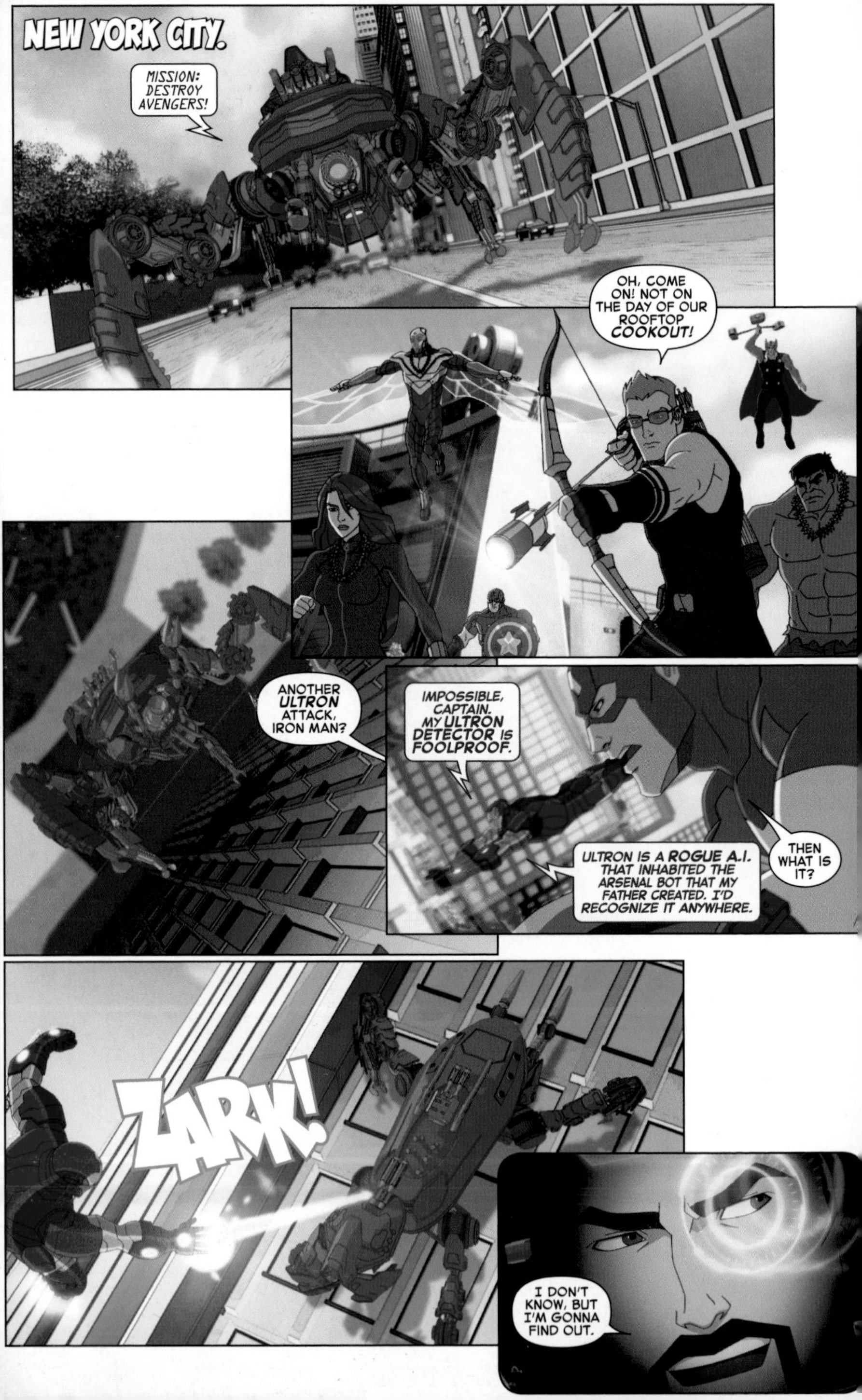
NEW YORK CITY.
MISSION: DESTROY AVENGERS!
OH, COME ON! NOT ON THE DAY OF OUR ROOFTOP COOKOUT!
ANOTHER ULTRON ATTACK, IRON MAN?
IMPOSSIBLE, CAPTAIN. MY ULTRON DETECTOR IS FOOLPROOF.
ULTRON IS A ROGUE A.I. THAT INHABITED THE ARSENAL BOT THAT MY FATHER CREATED. I'D RECOGNIZE IT ANYWHERE.
THEN WHAT IS IT?
ZARK!
I DON'T KNOW, BUT I'M GONNA FIND OUT.

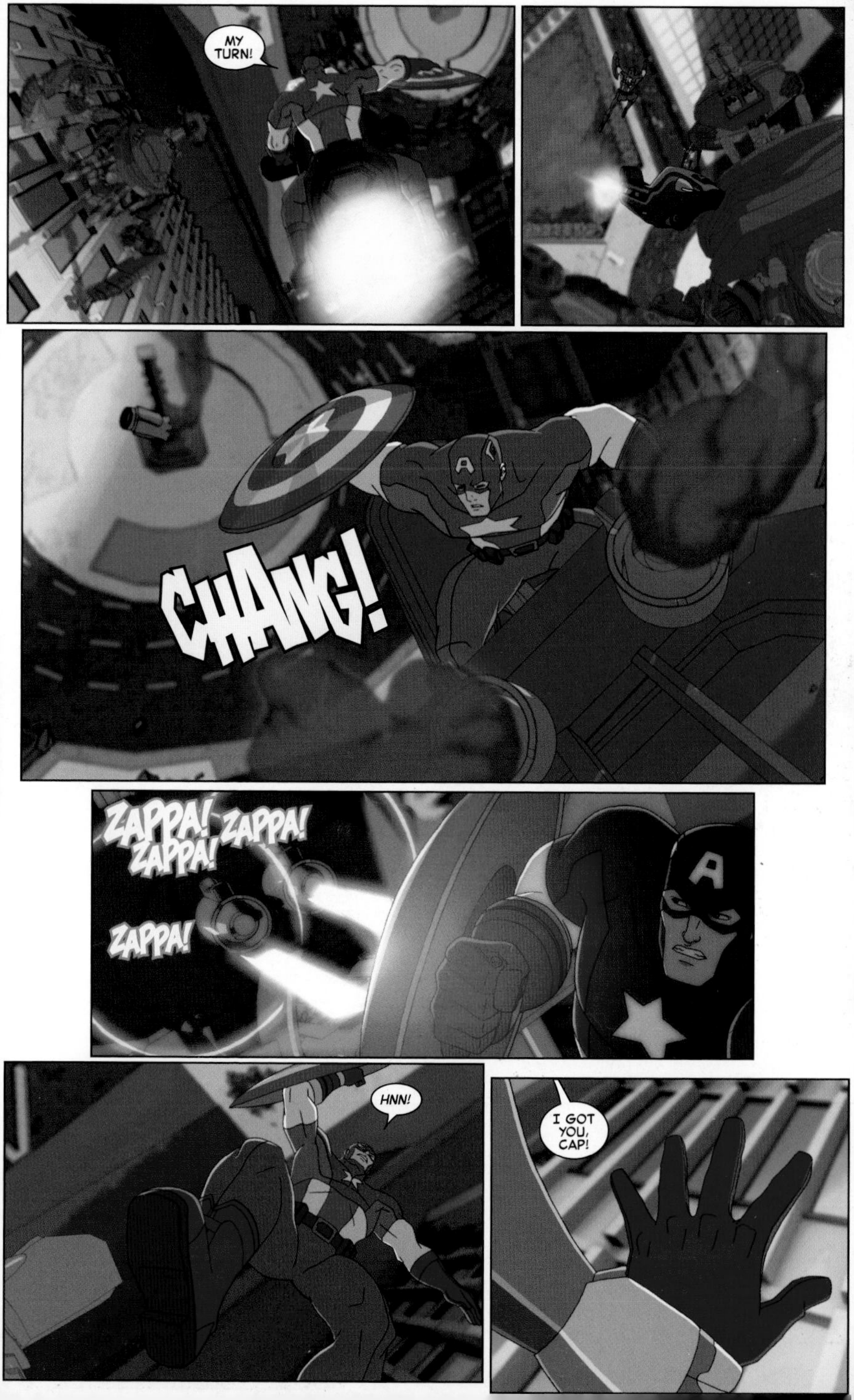
MY TURN!
CHANG!
ZAPPA! ZAPPA! ZAPPA!
ZAPPA!
HNN!
I GOT YOU, CAP!

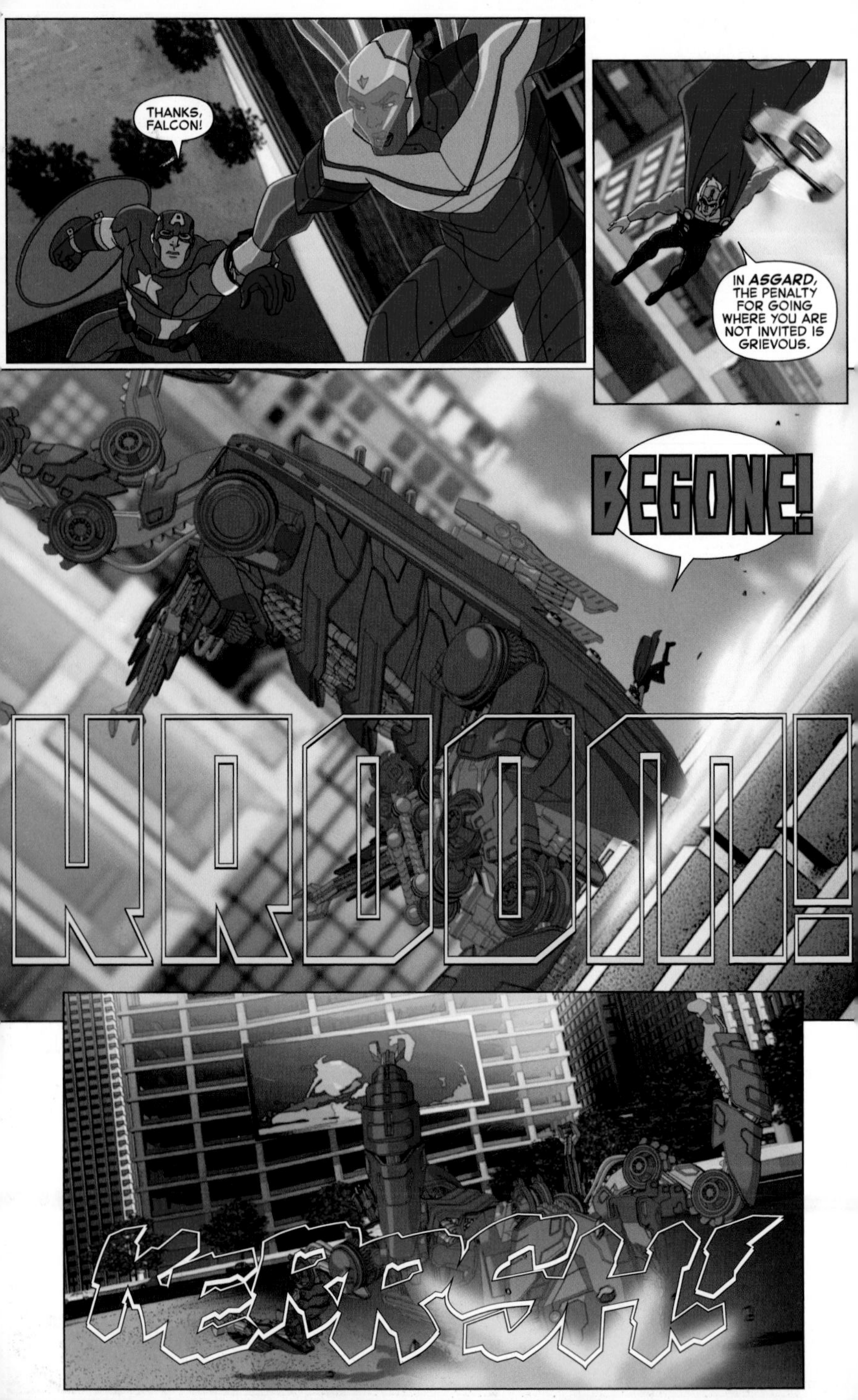
THANKS, FALCON!
IN ASGARD, THE PENALTY FOR GOING WHERE YOU ARE NOT INVITED IS GRIEVOUS.
BEGONE!

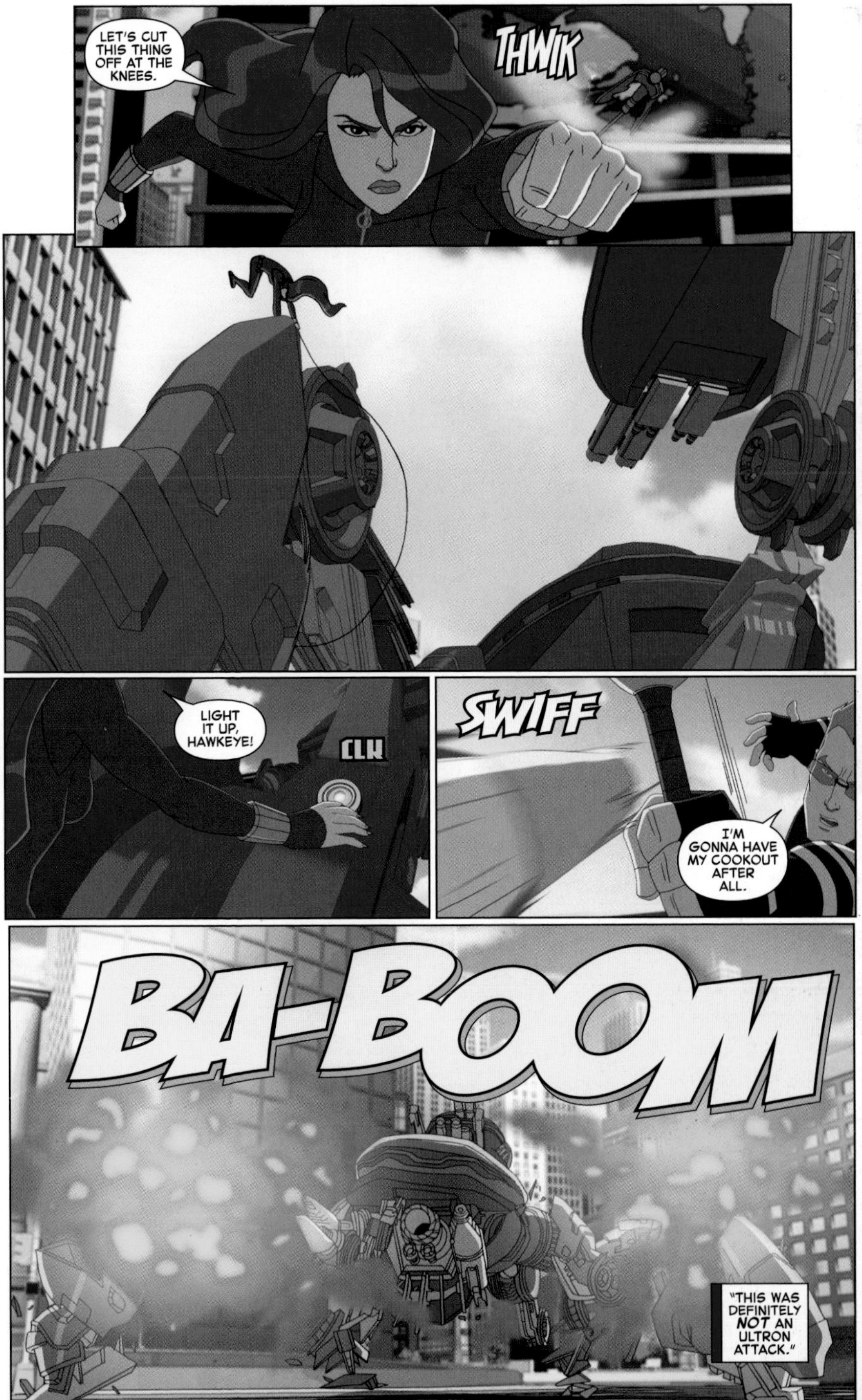
LET'S CUT THIS THING OFF AT THE KNEES.
THWIK
LIGHT IT UP, HAWKEYE!
CLK
SWIFF
I'M GONNA HAVE MY COOKOUT AFTER ALL.
BA-BOOM
"THIS WAS DEFINITELY NOT AN ULTRON ATTACK."

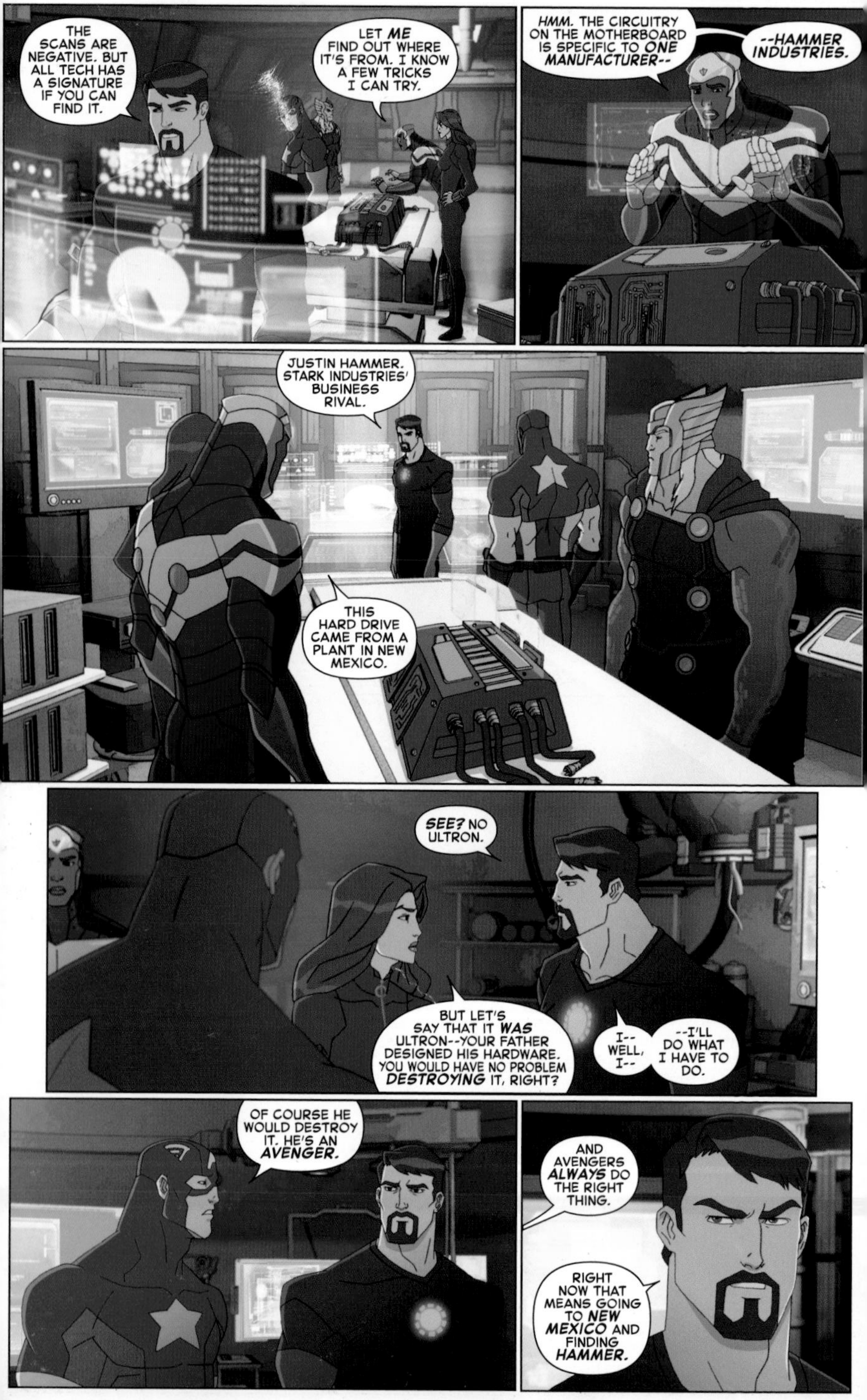
THE SCANS ARE NEGATIVE. BUT ALL TECH HAS A SIGNATURE IF YOU CAN FIND IT.
LET ME FIND OUT WHERE IT'S FROM. I KNOW A FEW TRICKS I CAN TRY.
HMM. THE CIRCUITRY ON THE MOTHERBOARD IS SPECIFIC TO ONE MANUFACTURER--
--HAMMER INDUSTRIES.
JUSTIN HAMMER. STARK INDUSTRIES' BUSINESS RIVAL.
THIS HARD DRIVE CAME FROM A PLANT IN NEW MEXICO.
SEE? NO ULTRON.
BUT LET'S SAY THAT IT WAS ULTRON--YOUR FATHER DESIGNED HIS HARDWARE. YOU WOULD HAVE NO PROBLEM DESTROYING IT, RIGHT?
I-- WELL, I--
--I'LL DO WHAT I HAVE TO DO.
OF COURSE HE WOULD DESTROY IT. HE'S AN AVENGER.
AND AVENGERS ALWAYS DO THE RIGHT THING.
RIGHT NOW THAT MEANS GOING TO NEW MEXICO AND FINDING HAMMER.

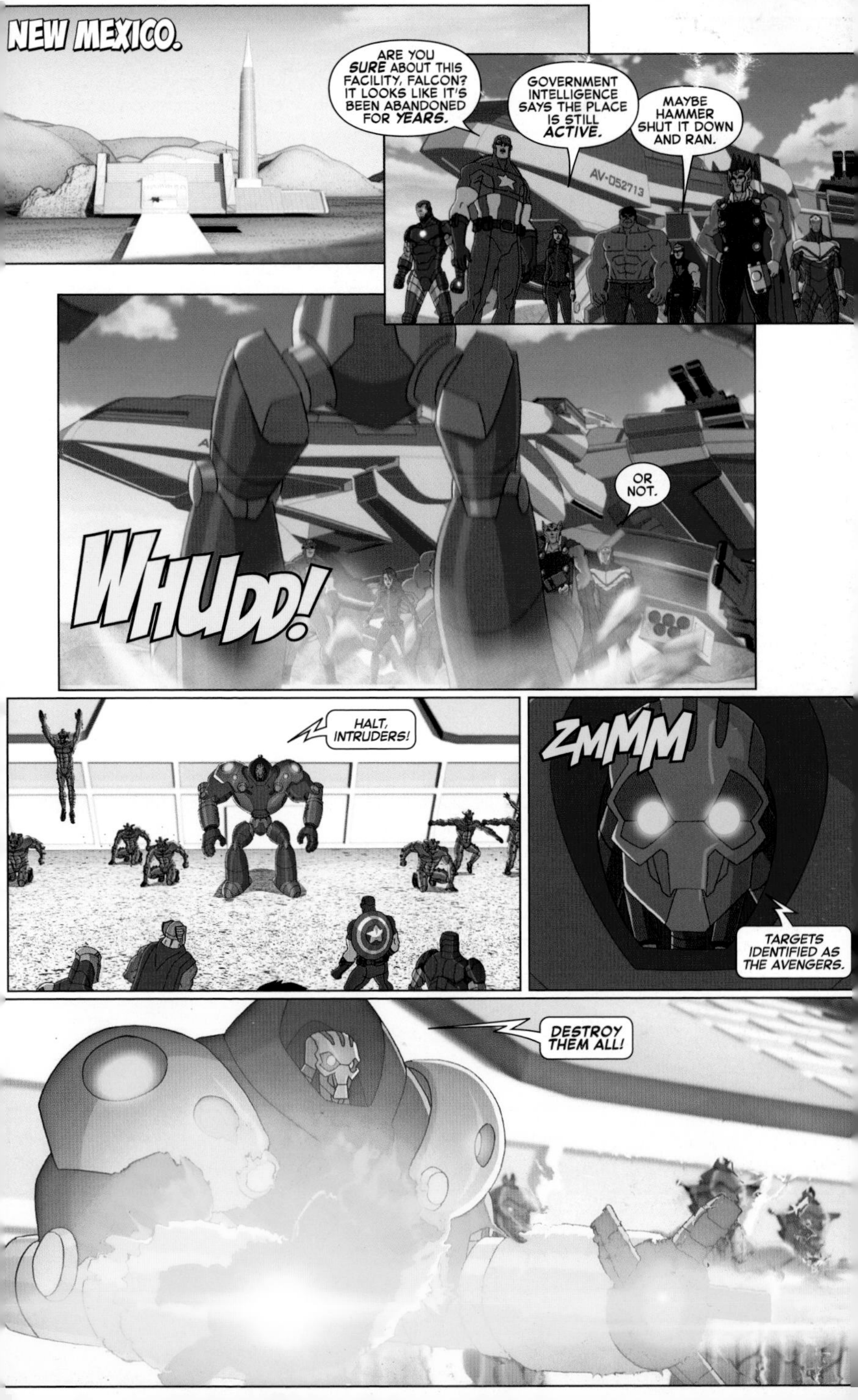

NEW MEXICO.
ARE YOU SURE ABOUT THIS FACILITY, FALCON? IT LOOKS LIKE IT'S BEEN ABANDONED FOR YEARS.
GOVERNMENT INTELLIGENCE SAYS THE PLACE IS STILL ACTIVE.
MAYBE HAMMER SHUT IT DOWN AND RAN.
AV-052713
OR NOT.
WHUDD!
HALT, INTRUDERS!
ZMMM
TARGETS IDENTIFIED AS THE AVENGERS.
DESTROY THEM ALL!

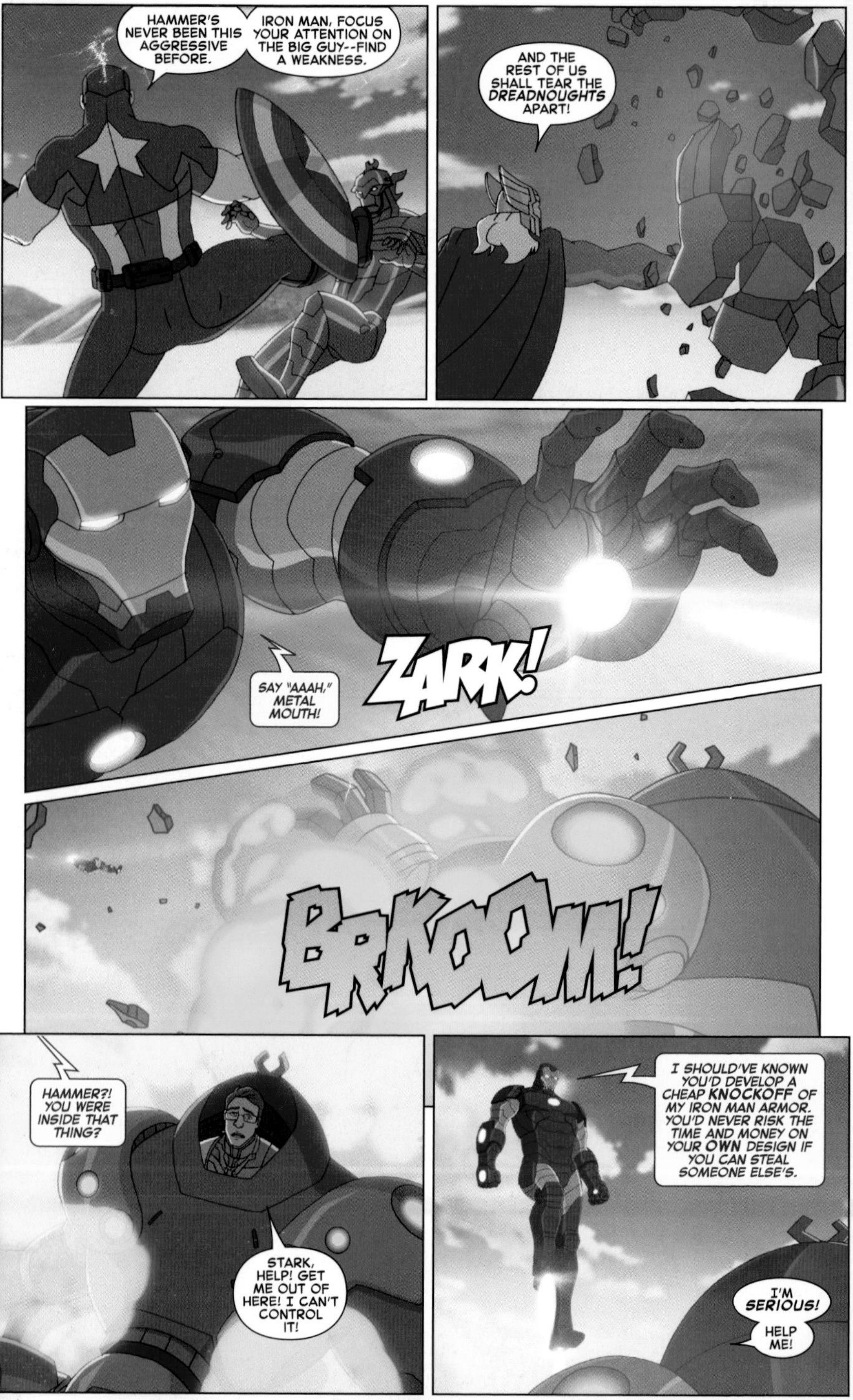
HAMMER'S NEVER BEEN THIS AGGRESSIVE BEFORE.
IRON MAN, FOCUS YOUR ATTENTION ON THE BIG GUY--FIND A WEAKNESS.
AND THE REST OF US SHALL TEAR THE DREADNOUGHTS APART!
SAY "AAAH," METAL MOUTH!
ZARK!
BRKOOM!
HAMMER?! YOU WERE INSIDE THAT THING?
STARK, HELP! GET ME OUT OF HERE! I CAN'T CONTROL IT!
I SHOULD'VE KNOWN YOU'D DEVELOP A CHEAP KNOCKOFF OF MY IRON MAN ARMOR. YOU'D NEVER RISK THE TIME AND MONEY ON YOUR OWN DESIGN IF YOU CAN STEAL SOMEONE ELSE'S.
I'M SERIOUS!
HELP ME!

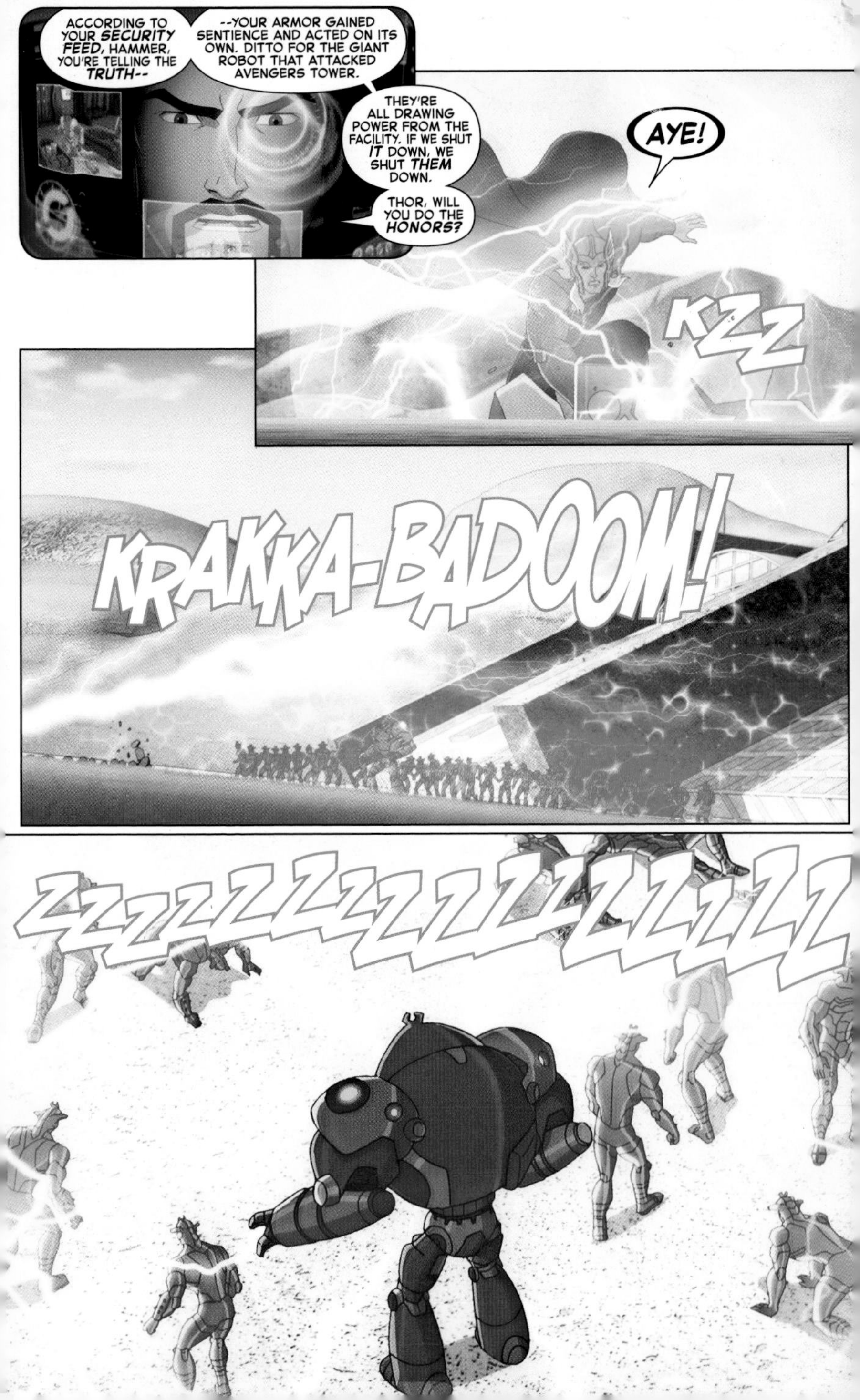
ACCORDING TO YOUR SECURITY FEED, HAMMER, YOU'RE TELLING THE TRUTH--
--YOUR ARMOR GAINED SENTIENCE AND ACTED ON ITS OWN. DITTO FOR THE GIANT ROBOT THAT ATTACKED AVENGERS TOWER.
THEY'RE ALL DRAWING POWER FROM THE FACILITY. IF WE SHUT IT DOWN, WE SHUT THEM DOWN.
THOR, WILL YOU DO THE HONORS?
AYE!
KZZ
KRAKKA-BADOOM!
ZZZZZZZZZZZZZZZZZZ

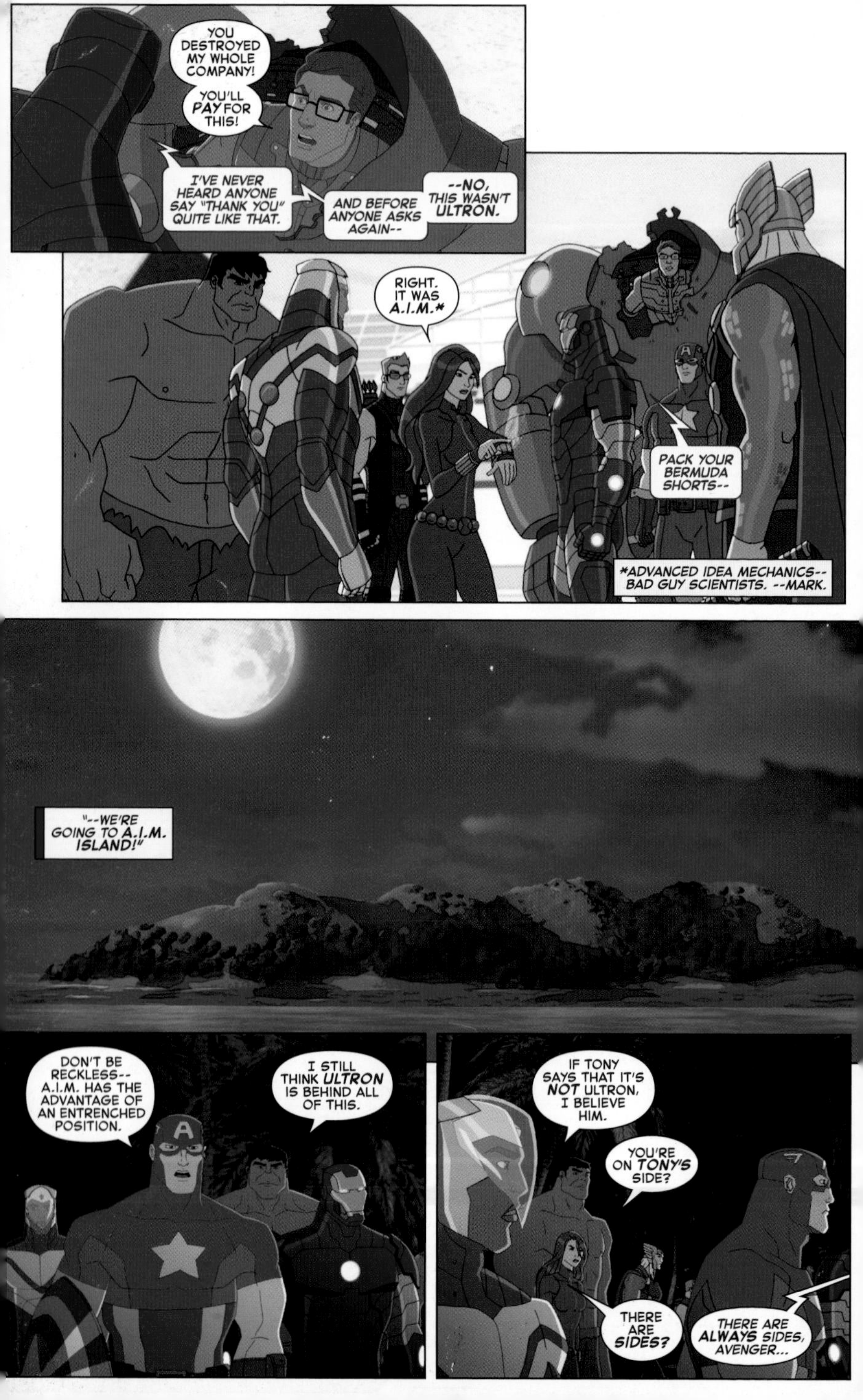
YOU DESTROYED MY WHOLE COMPANY!
YOU'LL PAY FOR THIS!
I'VE NEVER HEARD ANYONE SAY "THANK YOU" QUITE LIKE THAT.
AND BEFORE ANYONE ASKS AGAIN--
--NO, THIS WASN'T ULTRON.
RIGHT. IT WAS A.I.M.*
PACK YOUR BERMUDA SHORTS--
*ADVANCED IDEA MECHANICS-- BAD GUY SCIENTISTS. --MARK.
"--WE'RE GOING TO A.I.M. ISLAND!"
DON'T BE RECKLESS-- A.I.M. HAS THE ADVANTAGE OF AN ENTRENCHED POSITION.
I STILL THINK ULTRON IS BEHIND ALL OF THIS.
IF TONY SAYS THAT IT'S NOT ULTRON, I BELIEVE HIM.
YOU'RE ON TONY'S SIDE?
THERE ARE SIDES?
THERE ARE ALWAYS SIDES, AVENGER...

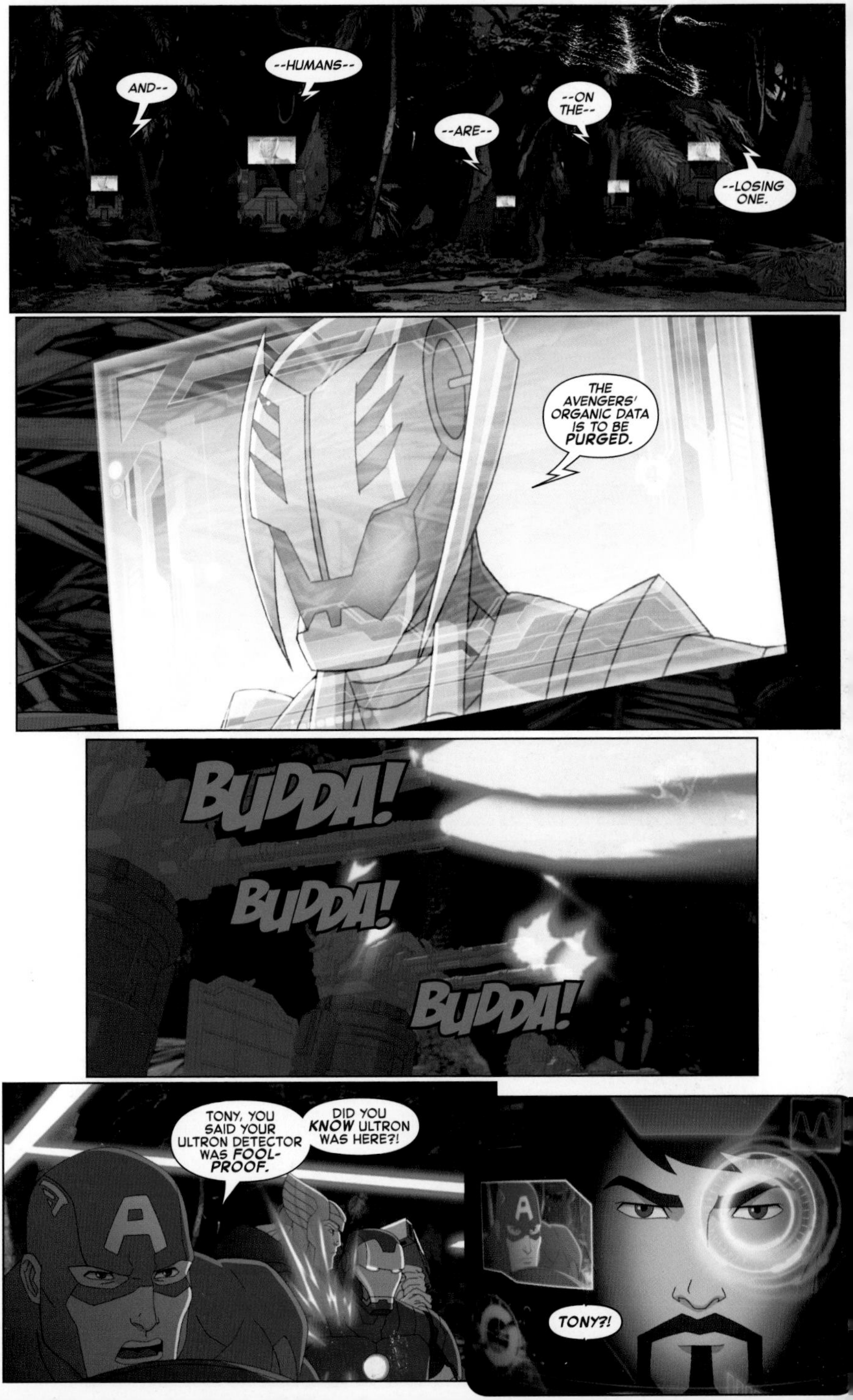
AND--
--HUMANS--
--ARE--
--ON THE--
--LOSING ONE.
THE AVENGERS' ORGANIC DATA IS TO BE PURGED.
BUDDA!
BUDDA!
BUDDA!
TONY, YOU SAID YOUR ULTRON DETECTOR WAS FOOL-PROOF.
DID YOU KNOW ULTRON WAS HERE?!
TONY?!

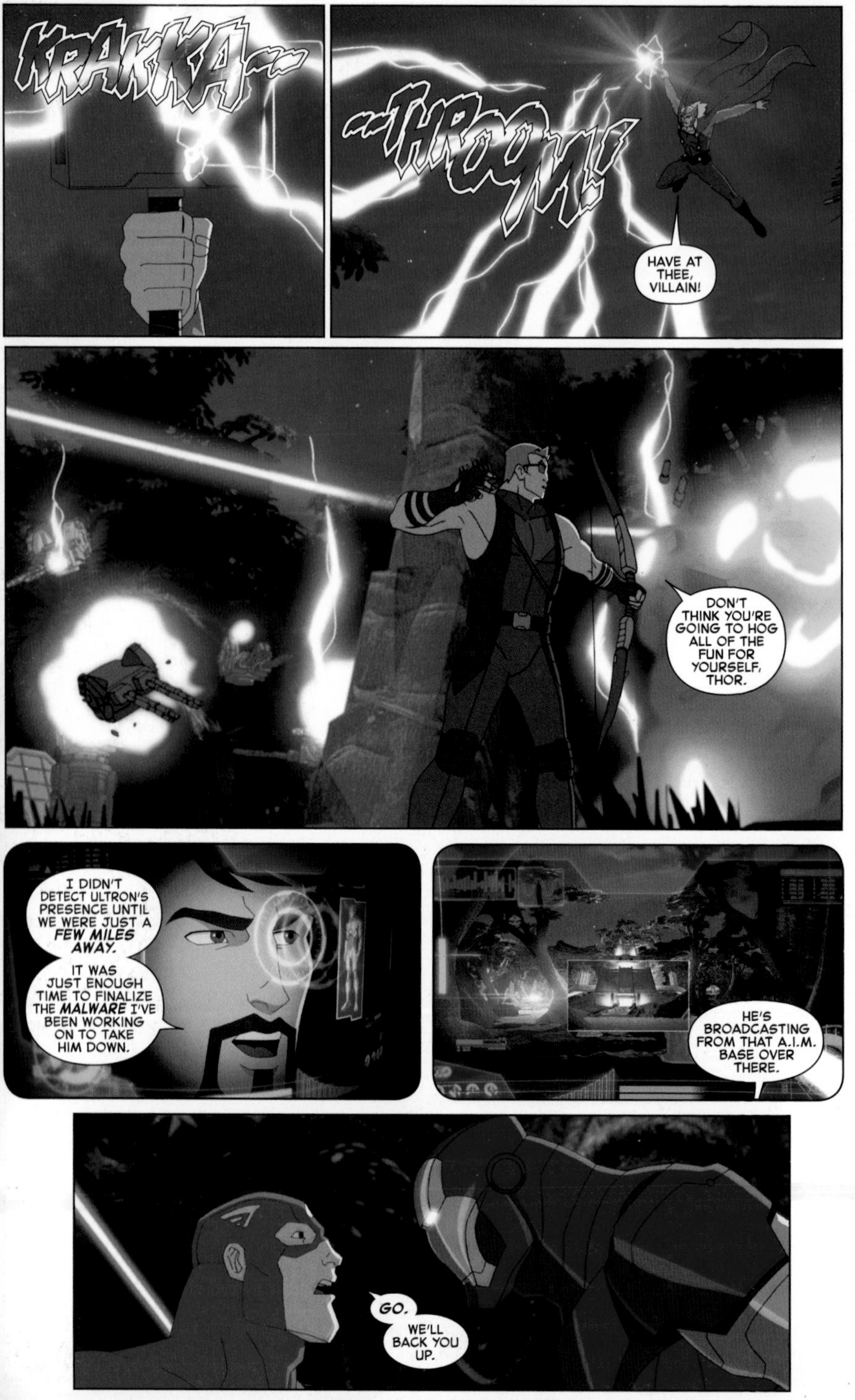
KRAKKA--
--THROOM!
HAVE AT THEE, VILLAIN!
DON'T THINK YOU'RE GOING TO HOG ALL OF THE FUN FOR YOURSELF, THOR.
I DIDN'T DETECT ULTRON'S PRESENCE UNTIL WE WERE JUST A FEW MILES AWAY.
IT WAS JUST ENOUGH TIME TO FINALIZE THE MALWARE I'VE BEEN WORKING ON TO TAKE HIM DOWN.
HE'S BROADCASTING FROM THAT A.I.M. BASE OVER THERE.
GO.
WE'LL BACK YOU UP.

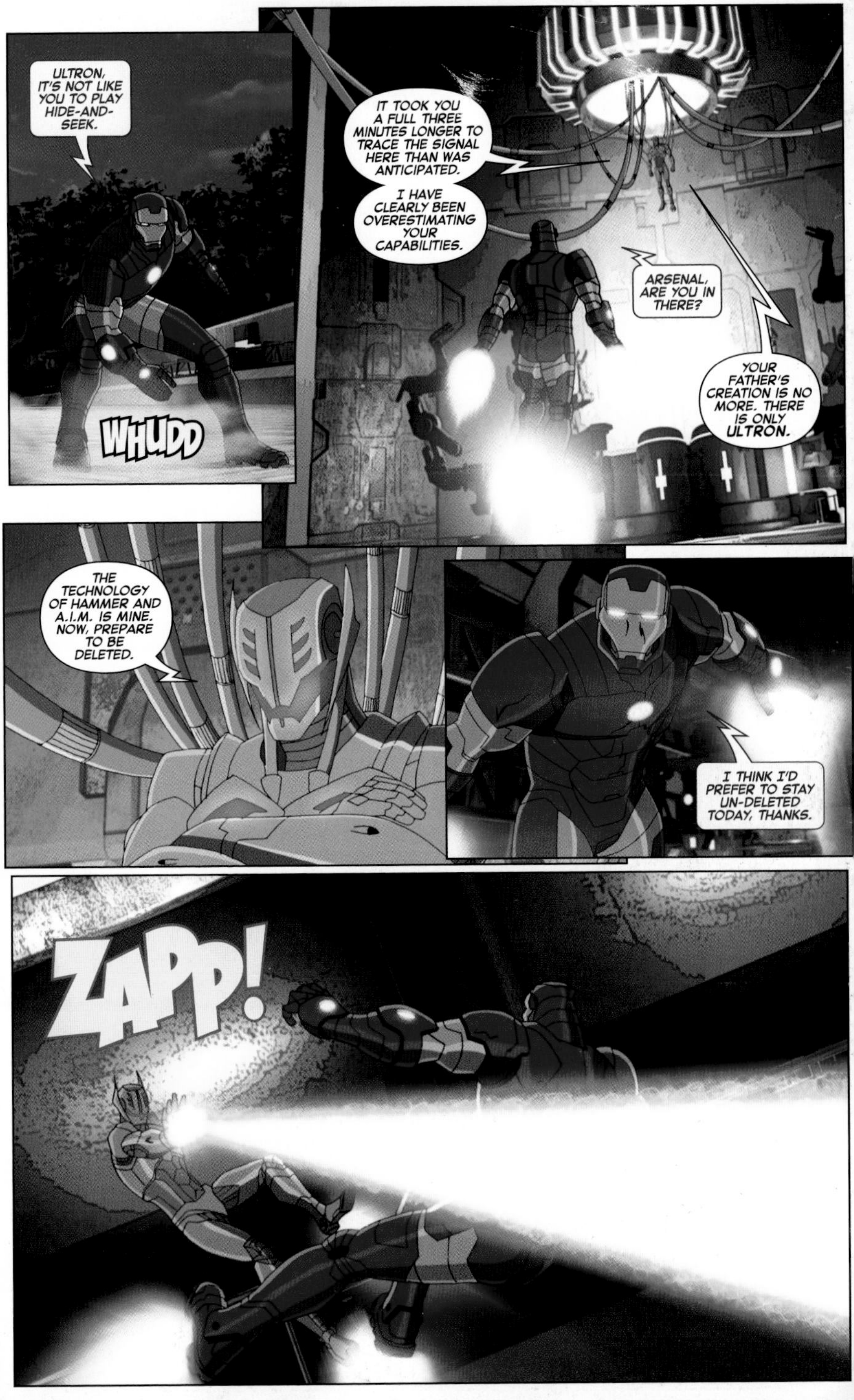
ULTRON, IT'S NOT LIKE YOU TO PLAY HIDE-AND-SEEK.
WHUDD
IT TOOK YOU A FULL THREE MINUTES LONGER TO TRACE THE SIGNAL HERE THAN WAS ANTICIPATED.
I HAVE CLEARLY BEEN OVERESTIMATING YOUR CAPABILITIES.
ARSENAL, ARE YOU IN THERE?
YOUR FATHER'S CREATION IS NO MORE. THERE IS ONLY ULTRON.
THE TECHNOLOGY OF HAMMER AND A.I.M. IS MINE. NOW, PREPARE TO BE DELETED.
I THINK I'D PREFER TO STAY UN-DELETED TODAY, THANKS.
ZAPP!

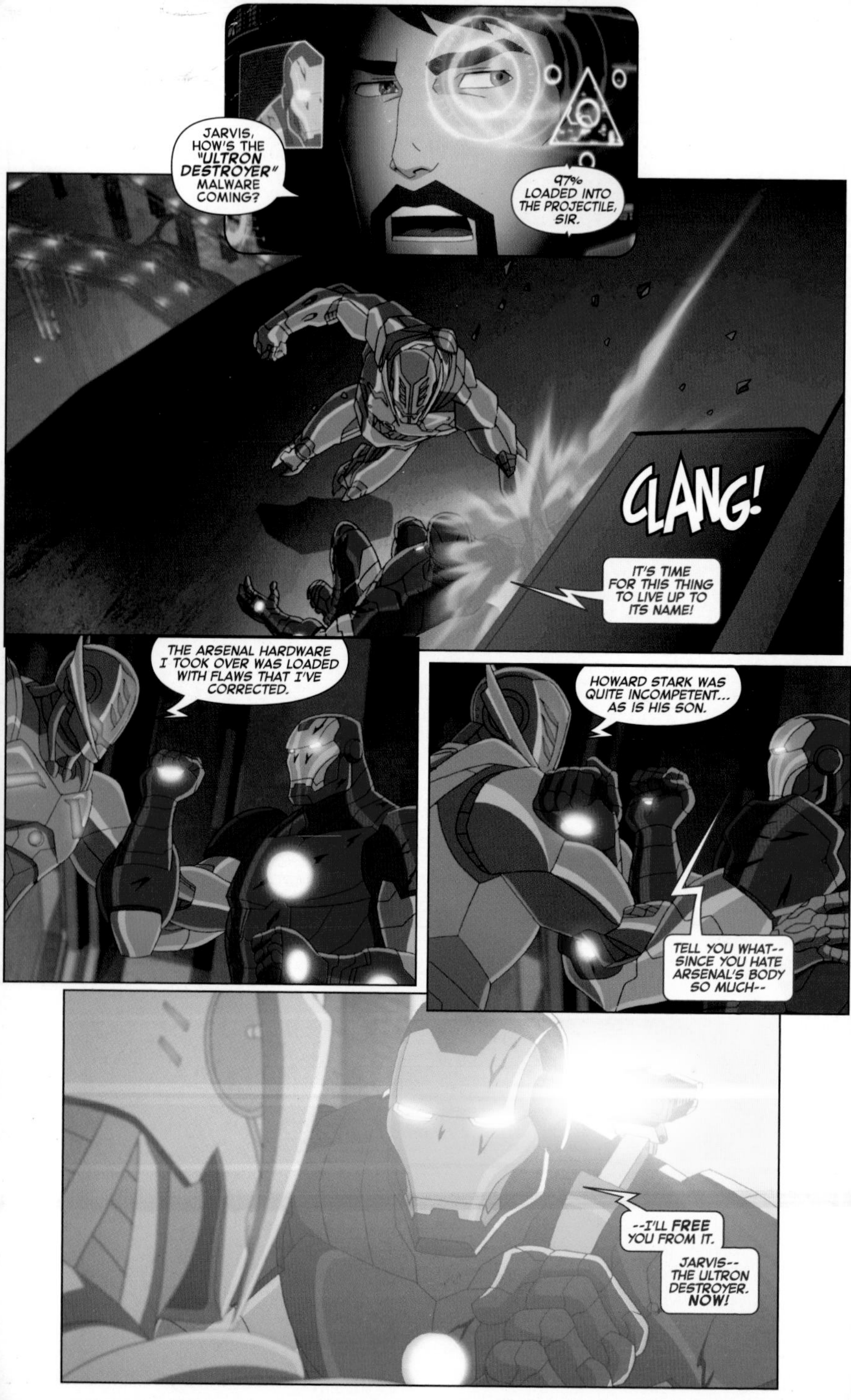
JARVIS, HOW'S THE "ULTRON DESTROYER" MALWARE COMING?
97% LOADED INTO THE PROJECTILE, SIR.
CLANG!
IT'S TIME FOR THIS THING TO LIVE UP TO ITS NAME!
THE ARSENAL HARDWARE I TOOK OVER WAS LOADED WITH FLAWS THAT I'VE CORRECTED.
HOWARD STARK WAS QUITE INCOMPETENT... AS IS HIS SON.
TELL YOU WHAT-- SINCE YOU HATE ARSENAL'S BODY SO MUCH--
--I'LL FREE YOU FROM IT.
JARVIS-- THE ULTRON DESTROYER. NOW!

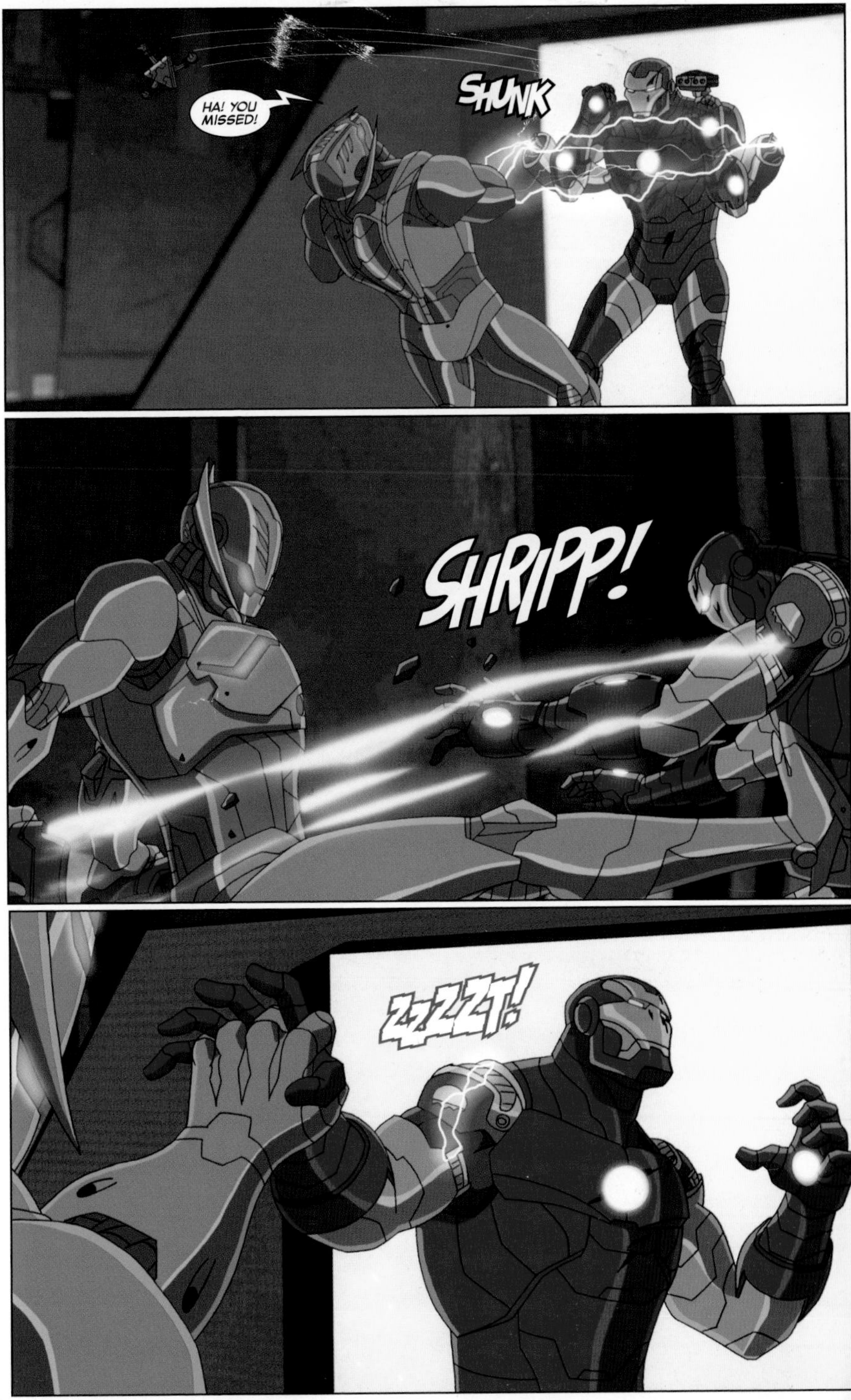
HA! YOU MISSED!
SHUNK
SHRIPP!
ZZZZT!

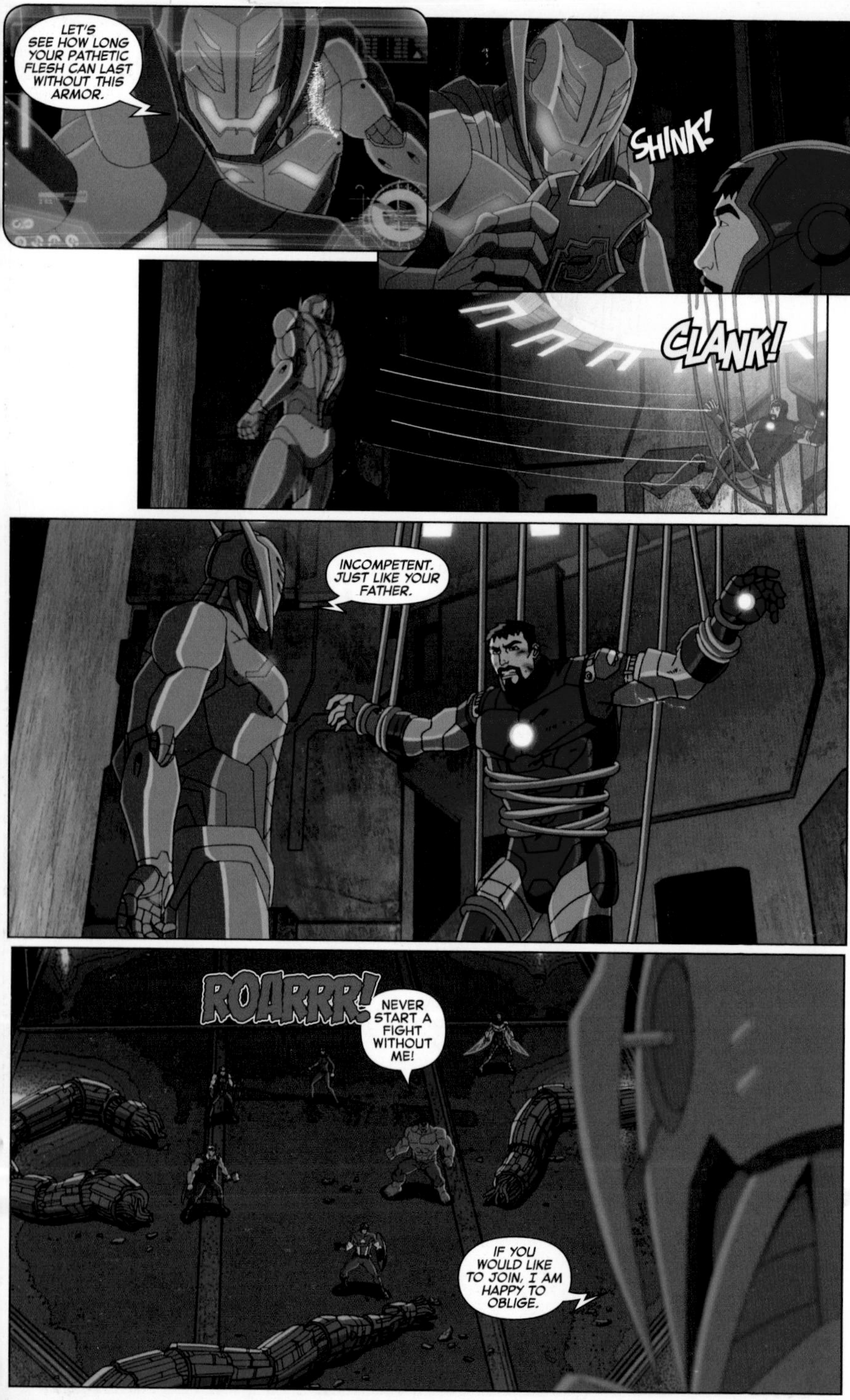
LET'S SEE HOW LONG YOUR PATHETIC FLESH CAN LAST WITHOUT THIS ARMOR.
SHINK!
CLANK!
INCOMPETENT. JUST LIKE YOUR FATHER.
ROARRR!
NEVER START A FIGHT WITHOUT ME!
IF YOU WOULD LIKE TO JOIN, I AM HAPPY TO OBLIGE.

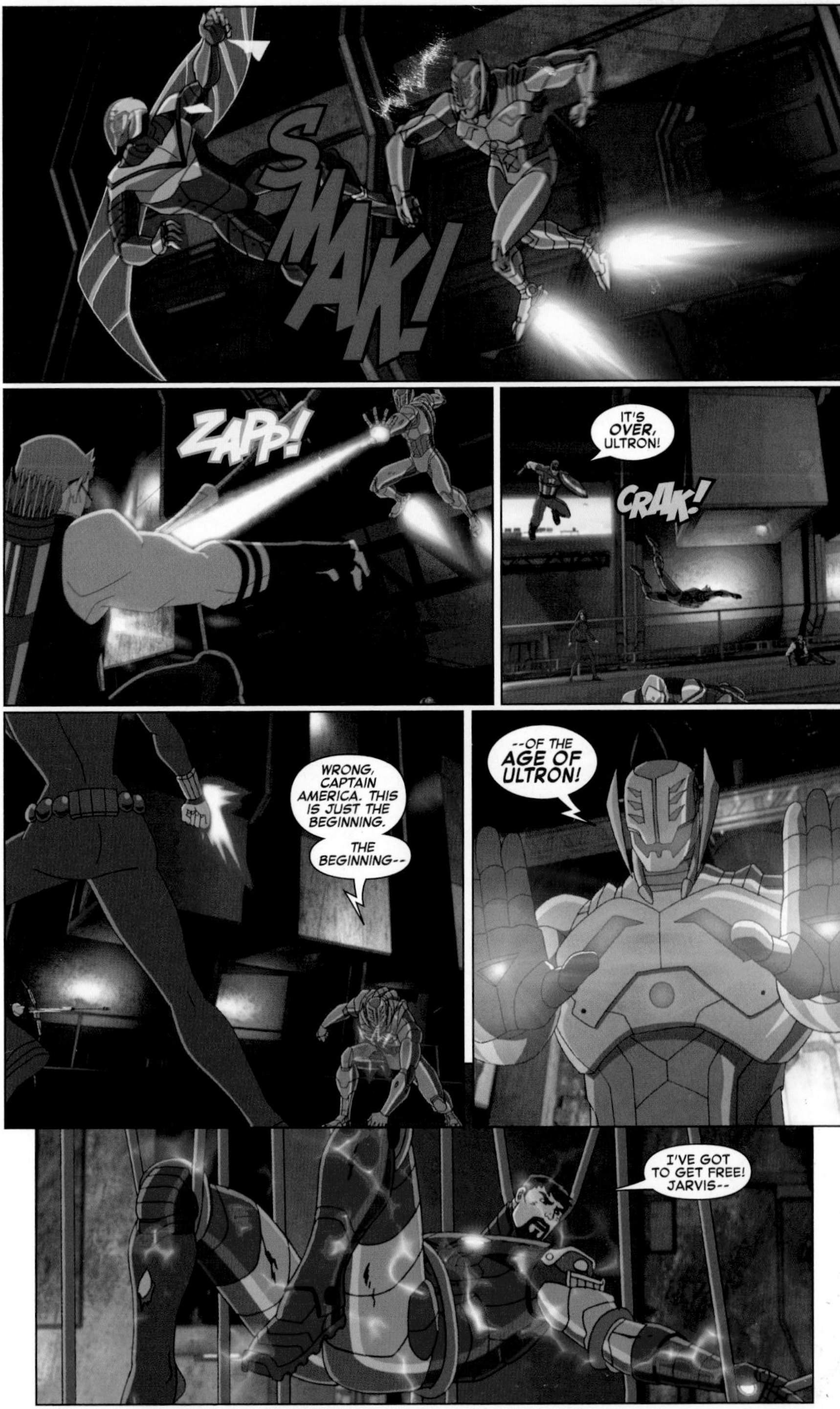
SMAK!
ZAPP!
IT'S OVER, ULTRON!
CRAK!
WRONG, CAPTAIN AMERICA. THIS IS JUST THE BEGINNING.
THE BEGINNING--
--OF THE AGE OF ULTRON!
I'VE GOT TO GET FREE! JARVIS--

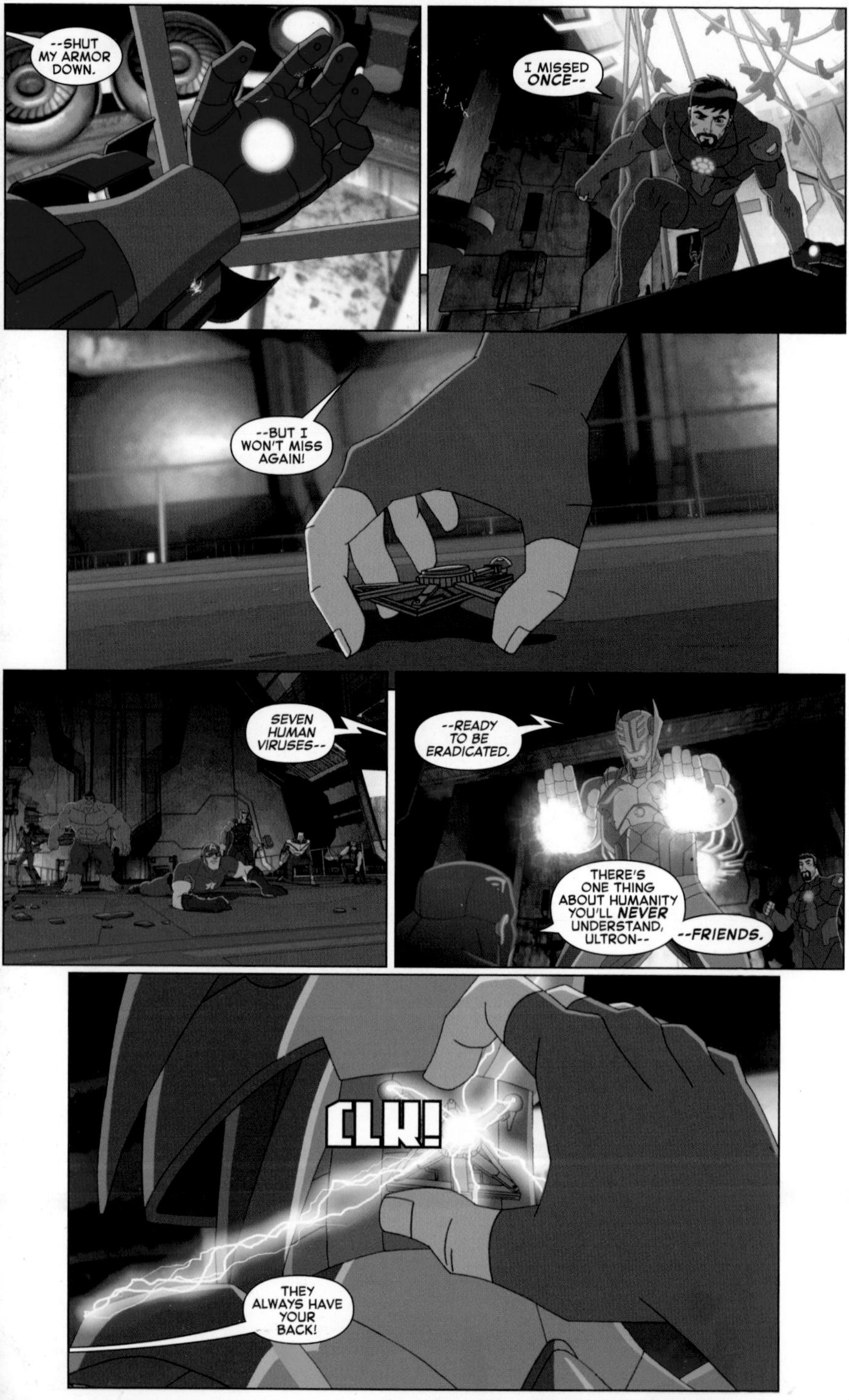
--SHUT MY ARMOR DOWN.
I MISSED ONCE--
--BUT I WON'T MISS AGAIN!
SEVEN HUMAN VIRUSES--
--READY TO BE ERADICATED.
THERE'S ONE THING ABOUT HUMANITY YOU'LL NEVER UNDERSTAND, ULTRON--
--FRIENDS.
CLK!
THEY ALWAYS HAVE YOUR BACK!

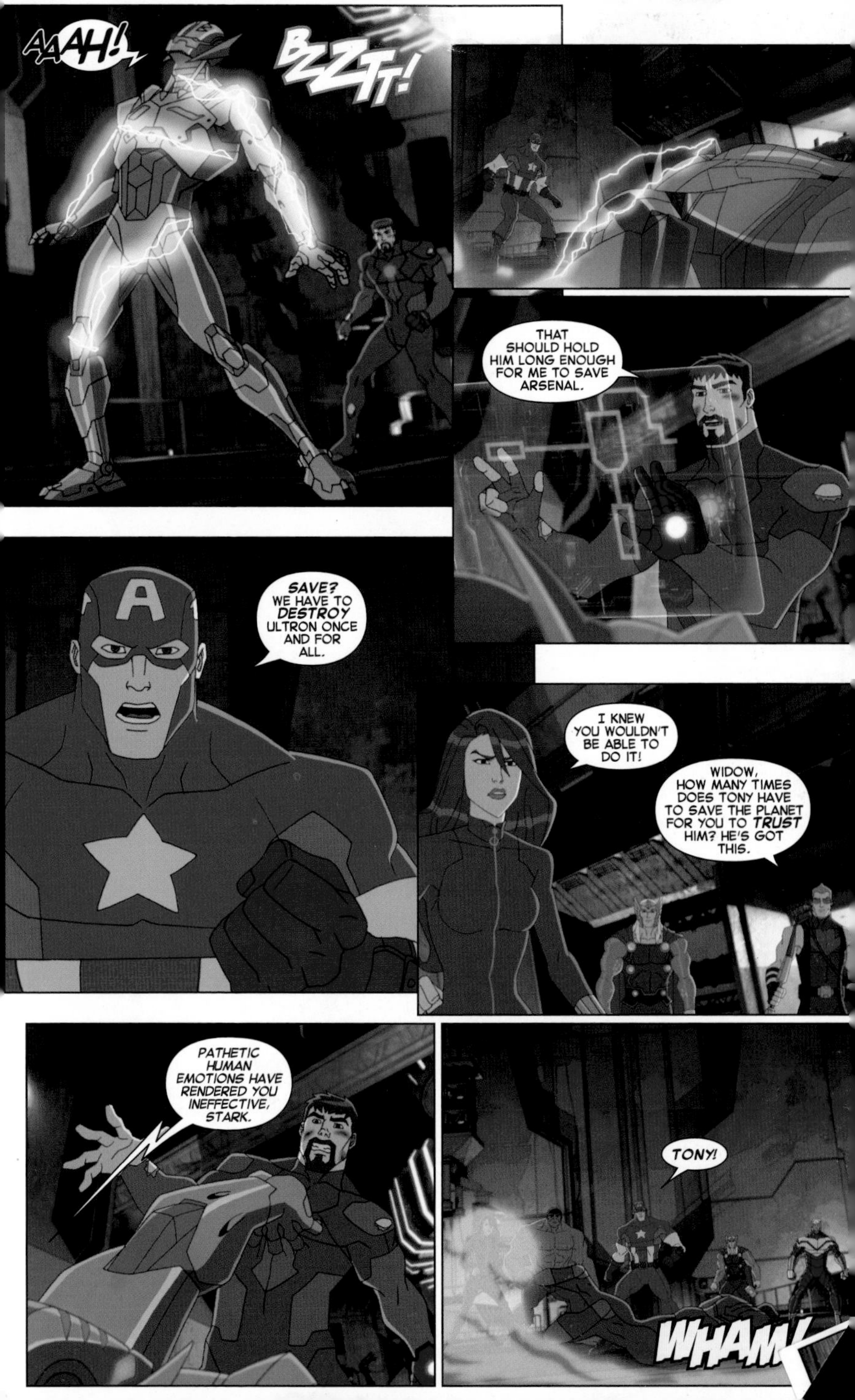
AAAH!
BZZTT!
THAT SHOULD HOLD HIM LONG ENOUGH FOR ME TO SAVE ARSENAL.
SAVE? WE HAVE TO DESTROY ULTRON ONCE AND FOR ALL.
I KNEW YOU WOULDN'T BE ABLE TO DO IT!
WIDOW, HOW MANY TIMES DOES TONY HAVE TO SAVE THE PLANET FOR YOU TO TRUST HIM? HE'S GOT THIS.
PATHETIC HUMAN EMOTIONS HAVE RENDERED YOU INEFFECTIVE, STARK.
TONY!
WHAM!

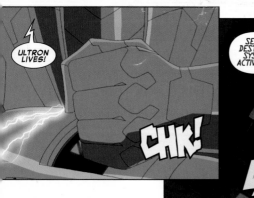

ULTRON LIVES!

CHK!

SELF-DESTRUCT SYSTEM ACTIVATED.

VMMM!

HE ESCAPED THROUGH THAT HATCH!

THERE'S NO TIME TO TRACK HIM! WE HAVE TO GET OFF OF THIS ISLAND BEFORE THE BASE EXPLODES!

THE QUINJET IS ON ITS WAY!

LET'S HOPE IT GETS HERE FAST!

BOOM!

"SO, WHAT'S THE PROBLEM? WE MADE IT OUT ON TIME.

YOU KNOW THE *PROBLEM*, TONY.

ULTRON'S OFF THE GRID, BUT I'LL FIND HIM AGAIN.

AVENGERS TOWER.

TONY, YOU CAN'T CONTINUE TO WORK LIKE THIS. YOU SUSPECTED ULTRON WAS ON A.I.M. ISLAND AND YOU DIDN'T *TELL* US.

BEFORE IT WAS POSSESSED BY ULTRON, ARSENAL WAS MY FATHER'S GREATEST INVENTION.

IT'S HIS LAST SURVIVING WORK.

YOU PUT YOUR *PERSONAL* NEEDS BEFORE THE NEEDS OF THE PLANET, AND NOT FOR THE *FIRST* TIME.

THAT'S NOT HOW THE AVENGERS OPERATE.

I DECIDE HOW THE AVENGERS OPERATE. MY TEAM, MY RULES.

SORRY, BUT I CAN'T BE ON A TEAM WHEN I DON'T TRUST THE LEADERSHIP.

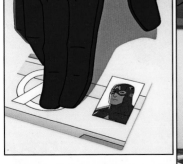

I QUIT.

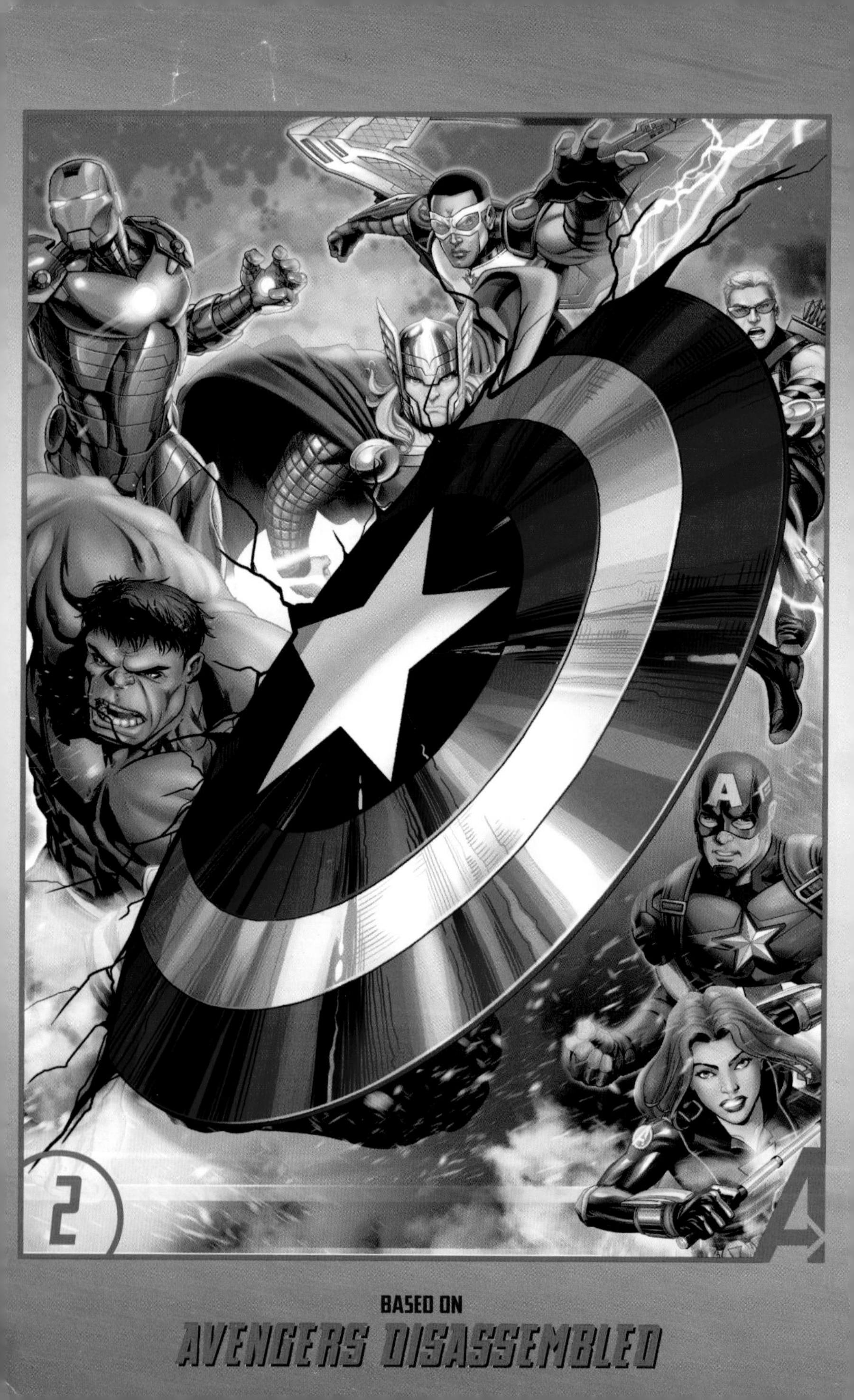
2

BASED ON

AVENGERS DISASSEMBLED

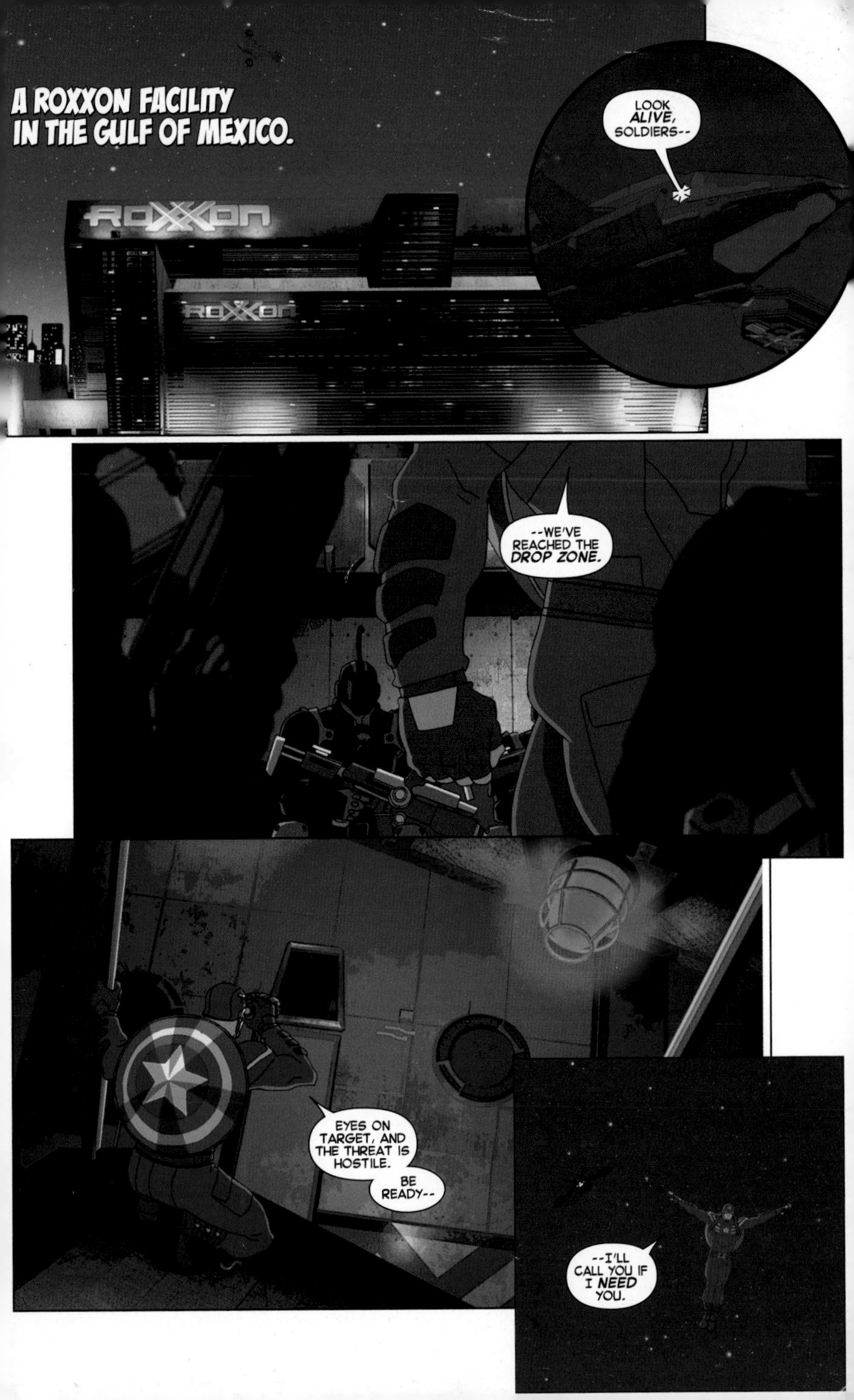
A ROXXON FACILITY IN THE GULF OF MEXICO.
ROXXON
ROXXON
LOOK ALIVE, SOLDIERS--
--WE'VE REACHED THE DROP ZONE.
EYES ON TARGET, AND THE THREAT IS HOSTILE.
BE READY--
--I'LL CALL YOU IF I NEED YOU.

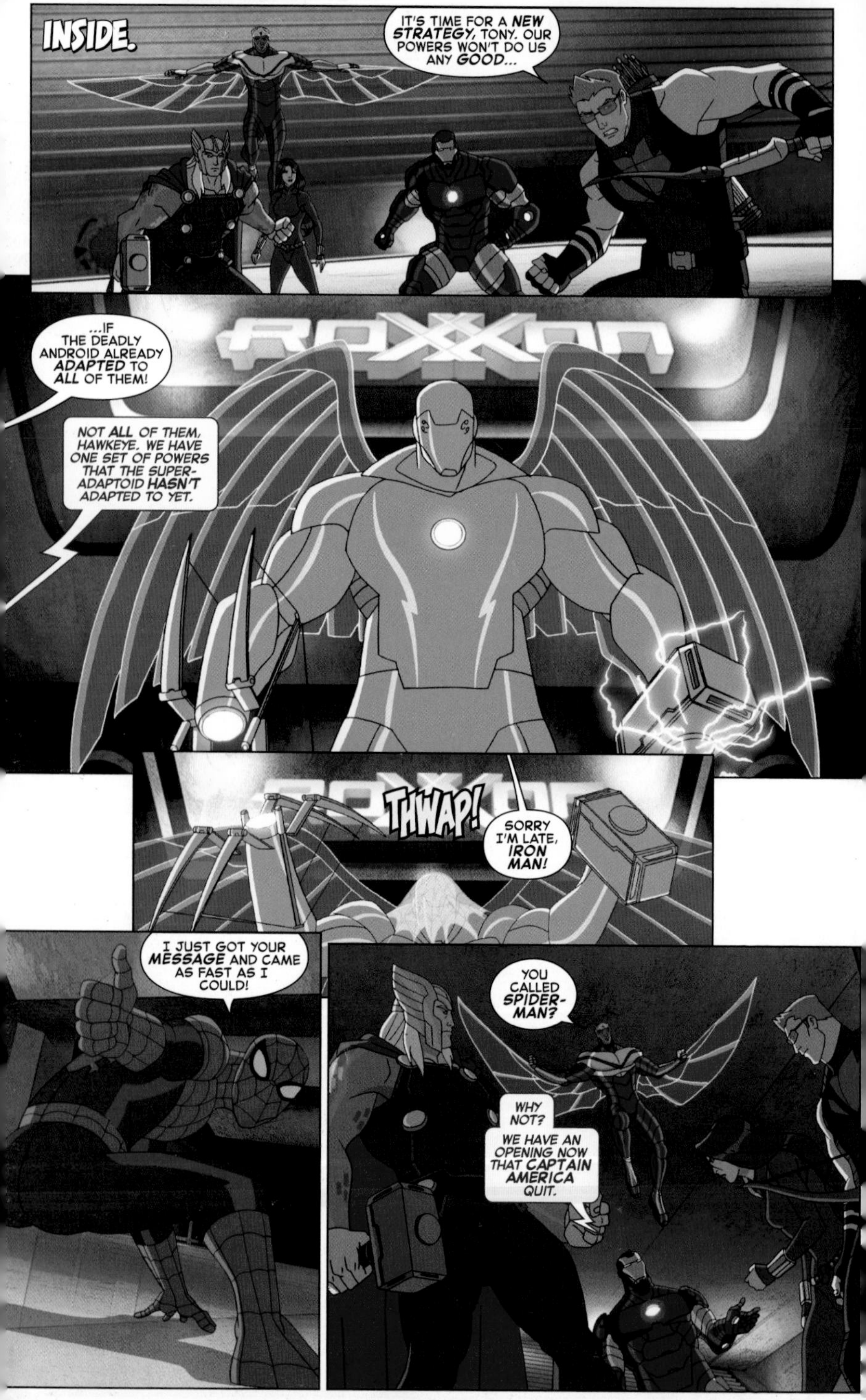
INSIDE.
IT'S TIME FOR A NEW STRATEGY, TONY. OUR POWERS WON'T DO US ANY GOOD...
...IF THE DEADLY ANDROID ALREADY ADAPTED TO ALL OF THEM!
NOT ALL OF THEM, HAWKEYE. WE HAVE ONE SET OF POWERS THAT THE SUPER-ADAPTOID HASN'T ADAPTED TO YET.
THWAP!
SORRY I'M LATE, IRON MAN!
I JUST GOT YOUR MESSAGE AND CAME AS FAST AS I COULD!
YOU CALLED SPIDER-MAN?
WHY NOT?
WE HAVE AN OPENING NOW THAT CAPTAIN AMERICA QUIT.

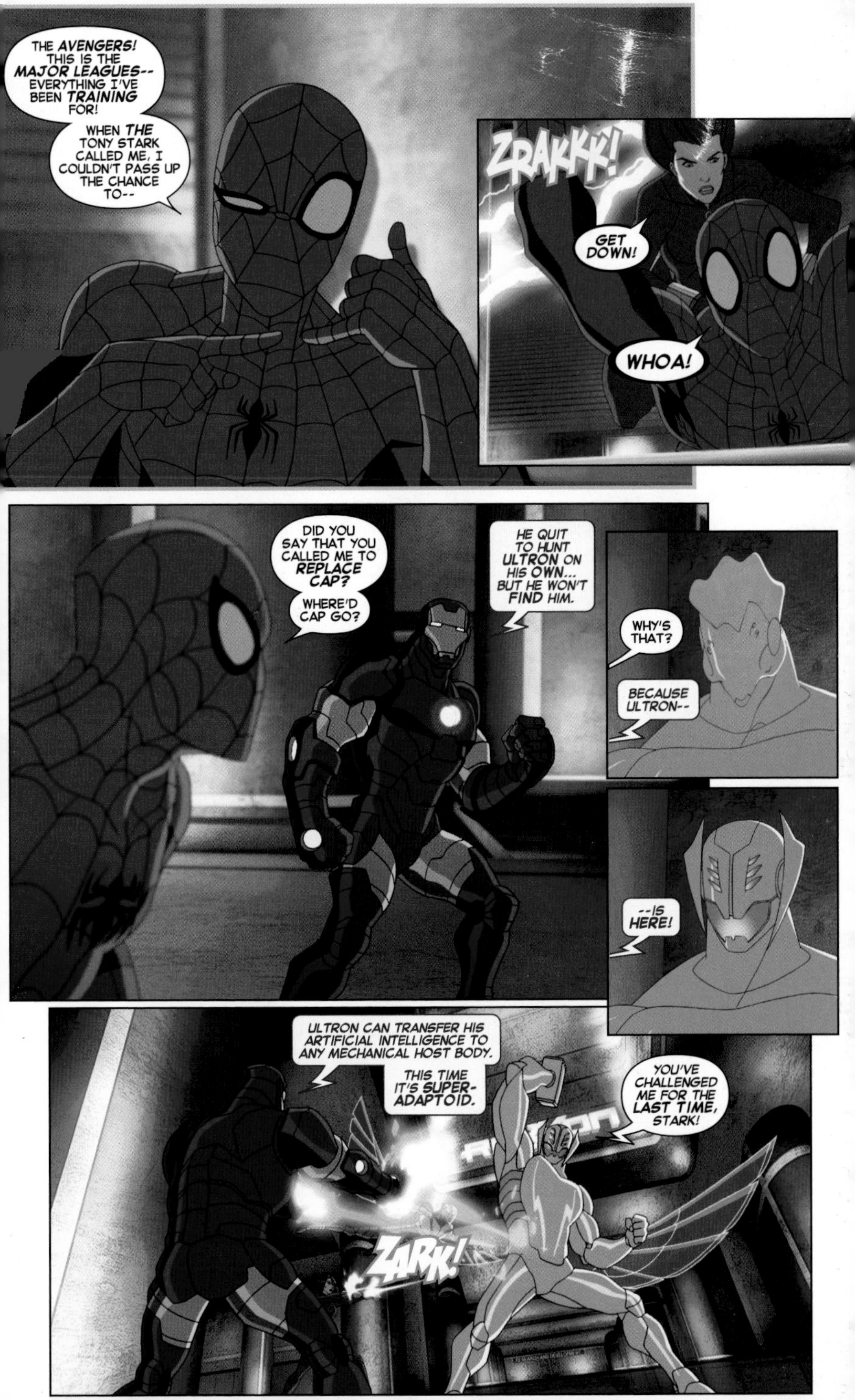
THE AVENGERS! THIS IS THE MAJOR LEAGUES-- EVERYTHING I'VE BEEN TRAINING FOR!
WHEN THE TONY STARK CALLED ME, I COULDN'T PASS UP THE CHANCE TO--
ZRAKKK!
GET DOWN!
WHOA!
DID YOU SAY THAT YOU CALLED ME TO REPLACE CAP?
WHERE'D CAP GO?
HE QUIT TO HUNT ULTRON ON HIS OWN... BUT HE WON'T FIND HIM.
WHY'S THAT?
BECAUSE ULTRON--
--IS HERE!
ULTRON CAN TRANSFER HIS ARTIFICIAL INTELLIGENCE TO ANY MECHANICAL HOST BODY.
THIS TIME IT'S SUPER-ADAPTOID.
YOU'VE CHALLENGED ME FOR THE LAST TIME, STARK!
ZARK!

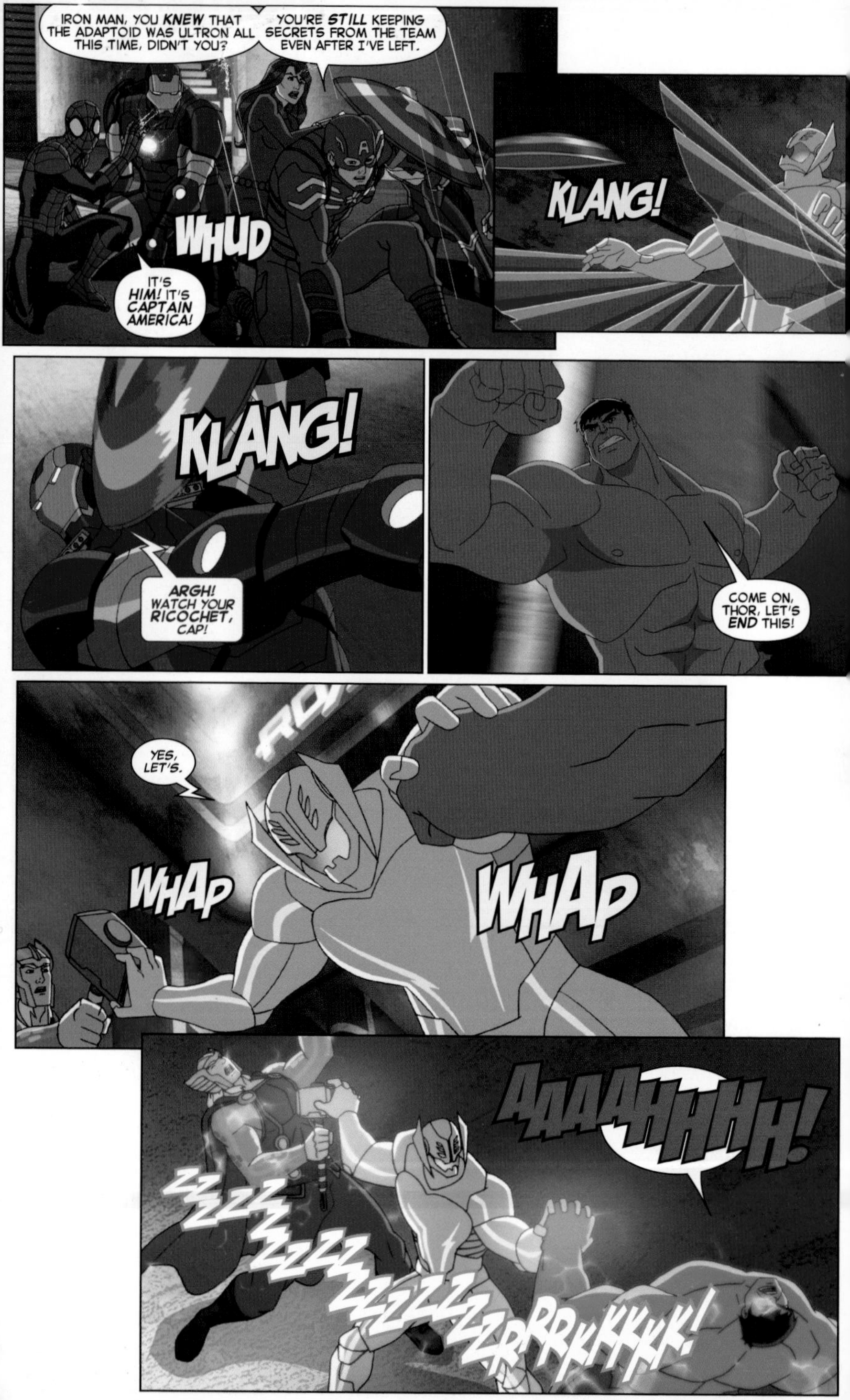
IRON MAN, YOU KNEW THAT THE ADAPTOID WAS ULTRON ALL THIS TIME, DIDN'T YOU?
YOU'RE STILL KEEPING SECRETS FROM THE TEAM EVEN AFTER I'VE LEFT.
WHUD
IT'S HIM! IT'S CAPTAIN AMERICA!
KLANG!
KLANG!
ARGH! WATCH YOUR RICOCHET, CAP!
COME ON, THOR, LET'S END THIS!
YES, LET'S.
WHAP
WHAP
AAAAHHHHH!
ZZZZZZZZZZZZZZZZZZRRRRKKKKKK!

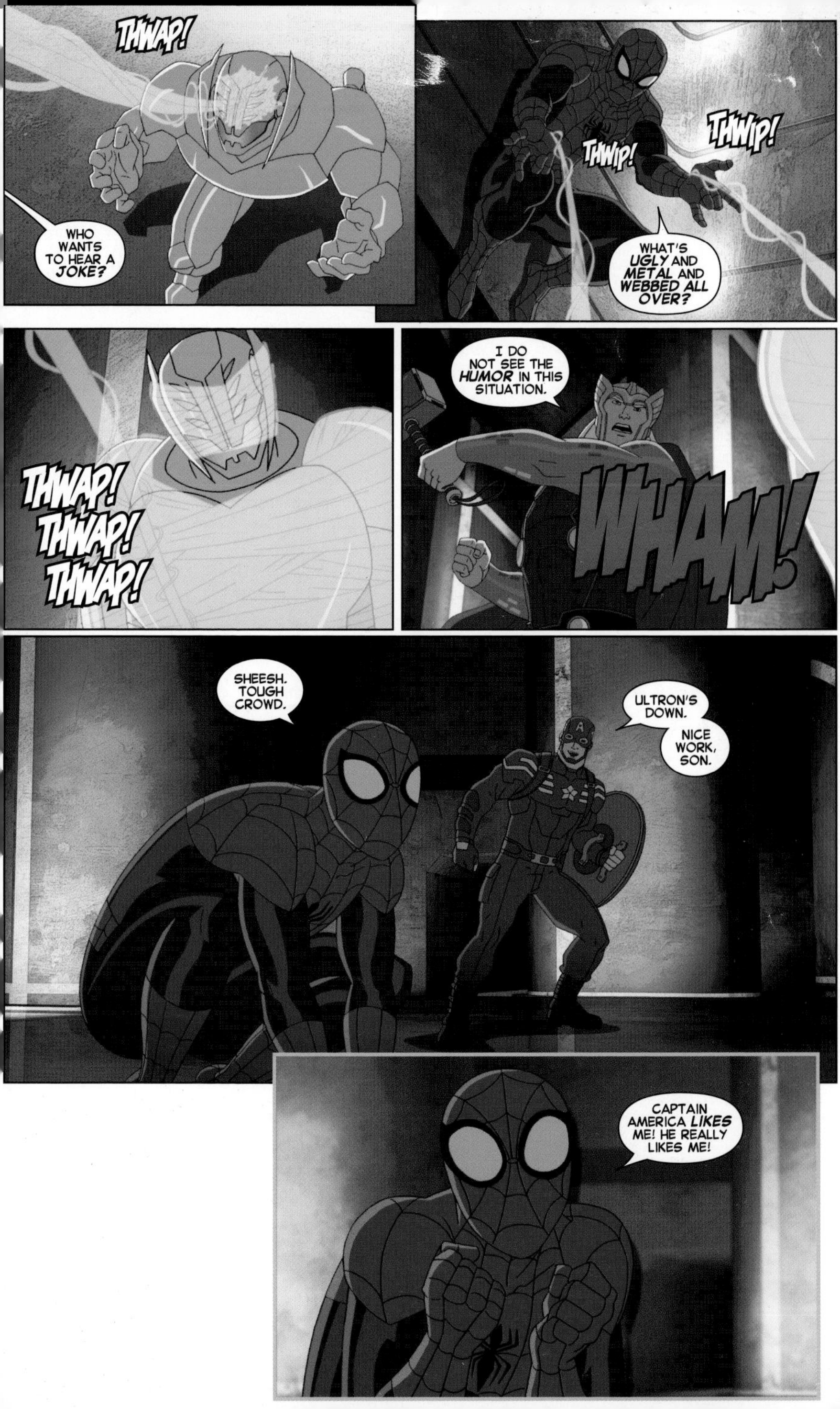
THWAP!
WHO WANTS TO HEAR A JOKE?
THWIP!
THWIP!
WHAT'S UGLY AND METAL AND WEBBED ALL OVER?
THWAP! THWAP! THWAP!
I DO NOT SEE THE HUMOR IN THIS SITUATION.
WHAM!
SHEESH. TOUGH CROWD.
ULTRON'S DOWN.
NICE WORK, SON.
CAPTAIN AMERICA LIKES ME! HE REALLY LIKES ME!

HE'S NOT DOWN FOR **LONG.**

QUICK--LET'S TAKE OUT THE TECH THAT ULTRON CAME TO ROXXON TO GET.

JARVIS, SCAN FOR **ROBOTICS.**

THERE APPEARS TO BE NO SIGN OF **ROBOTIC ENGINEERING** IN THIS BUILDING, SIR.

IT'S STRICTLY AN **INDUSTRIAL CHEMICALS** PLANT.

HOWEVER, MECHANIZED AUTOMATONS ARE IN THE VICINITY...

...AND INCOMING.

MY S.H.I.E.L.D. **LIFE-MODEL DECOY BACKUP FORCE!** BUT I DIDN'T TELL THEM TO FOLLOW ME IN YET!

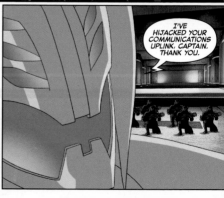

I'VE HIJACKED YOUR **COMMUNICATIONS UPLINK,** CAPTAIN. THANK YOU.

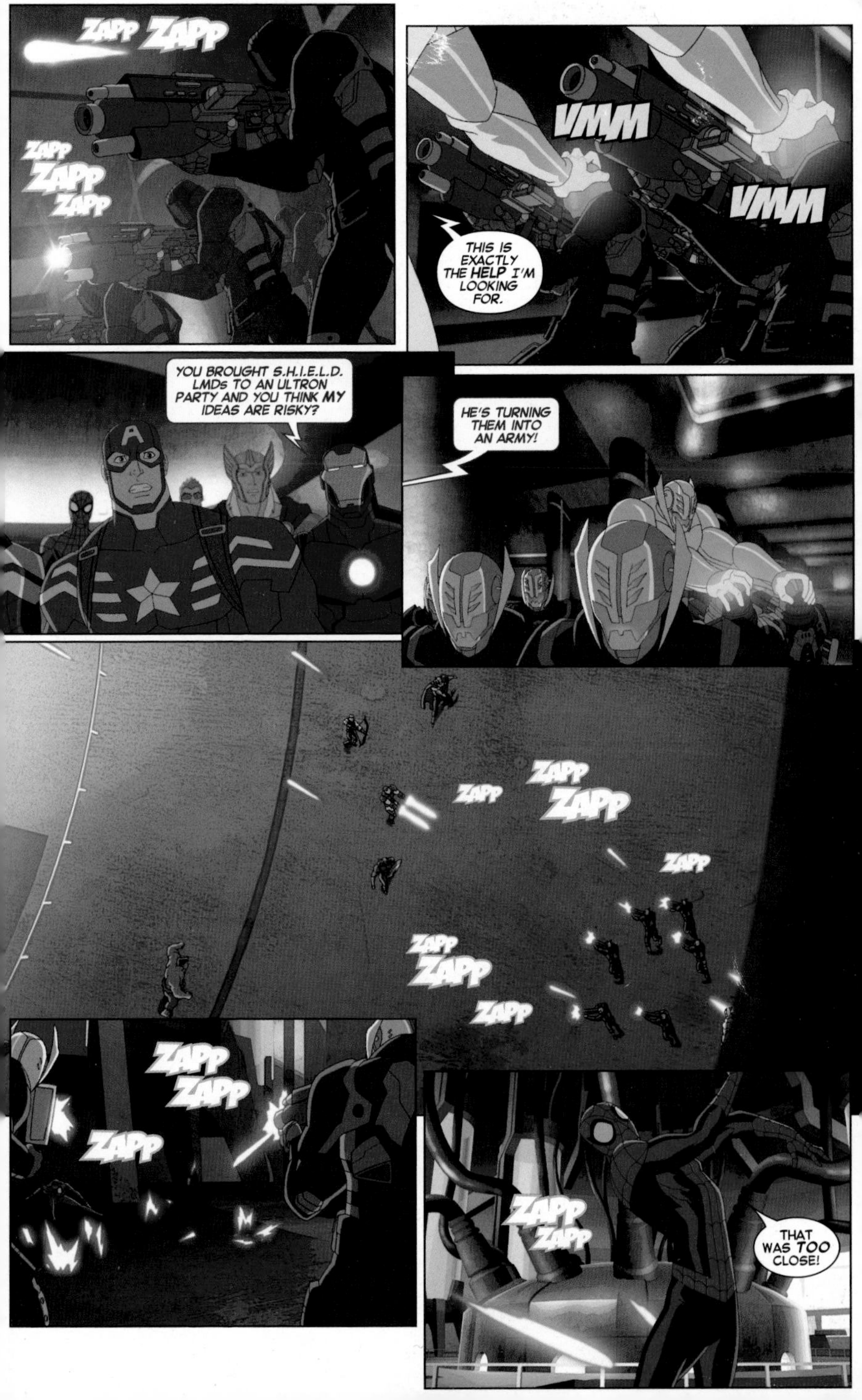
ZAPP ZAPP
ZAPP ZAPP ZAPP
VMM
VMM
THIS IS EXACTLY THE HELP I'M LOOKING FOR.
YOU BROUGHT S.H.I.E.L.D. LMDs TO AN ULTRON PARTY AND YOU THINK MY IDEAS ARE RISKY?
HE'S TURNING THEM INTO AN ARMY!
ZAPP
ZAPP ZAPP
ZAPP
ZAPP ZAPP
ZAPP
ZAPP ZAPP
ZAPP
ZAPP ZAPP
THAT WAS TOO CLOSE!

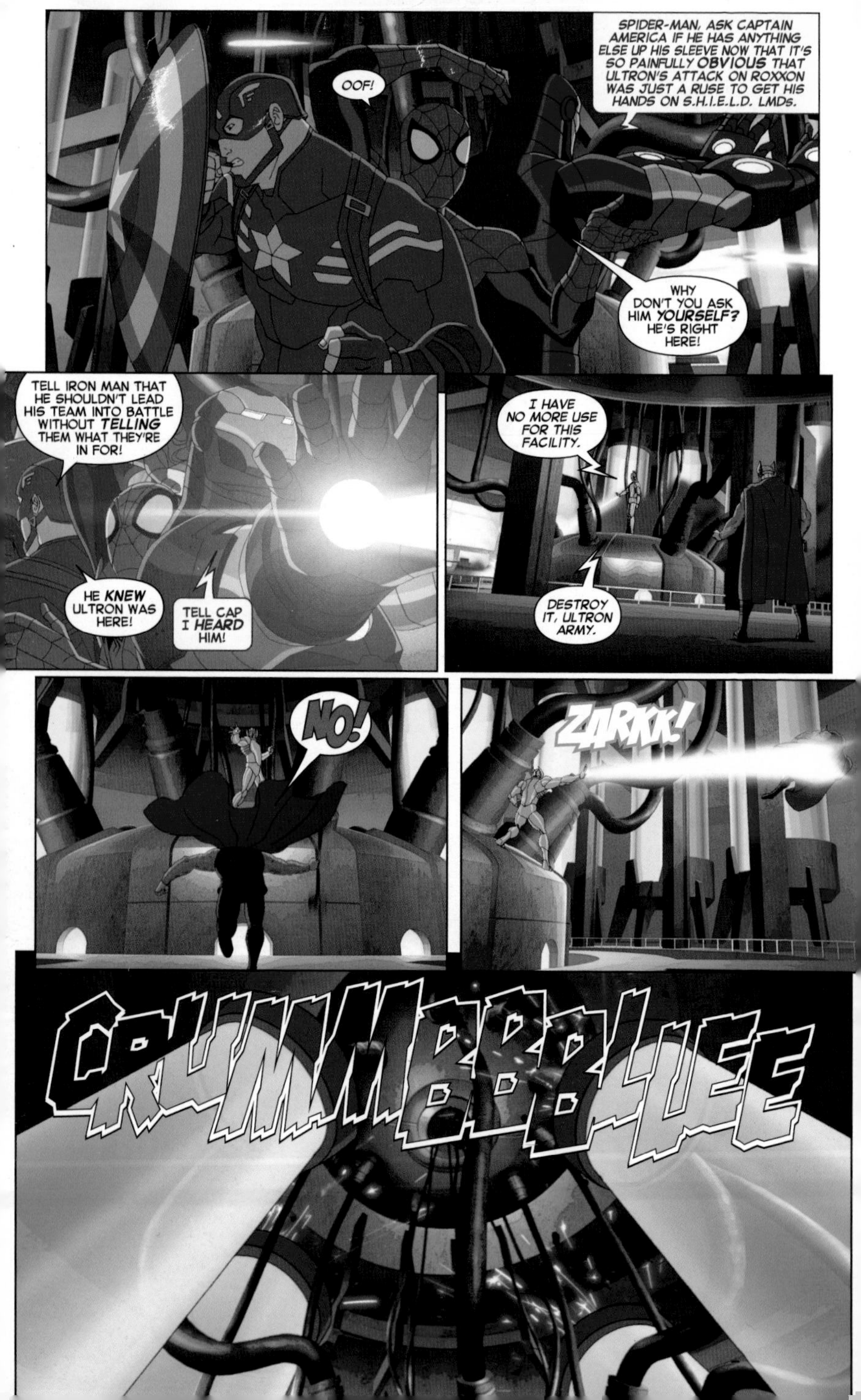
OOF!
SPIDER-MAN, ASK CAPTAIN AMERICA IF HE HAS ANYTHING ELSE UP HIS SLEEVE NOW THAT IT'S SO PAINFULLY OBVIOUS THAT ULTRON'S ATTACK ON ROXXON WAS JUST A RUSE TO GET HIS HANDS ON S.H.I.E.L.D. LMDs.
WHY DON'T YOU ASK HIM YOURSELF? HE'S RIGHT HERE!
TELL IRON MAN THAT HE SHOULDN'T LEAD HIS TEAM INTO BATTLE WITHOUT TELLING THEM WHAT THEY'RE IN FOR!
HE KNEW ULTRON WAS HERE!
TELL CAP I HEARD HIM!
I HAVE NO MORE USE FOR THIS FACILITY.
DESTROY IT, ULTRON ARMY.
NO!
ZARKK!
CRUMMBBLLEE

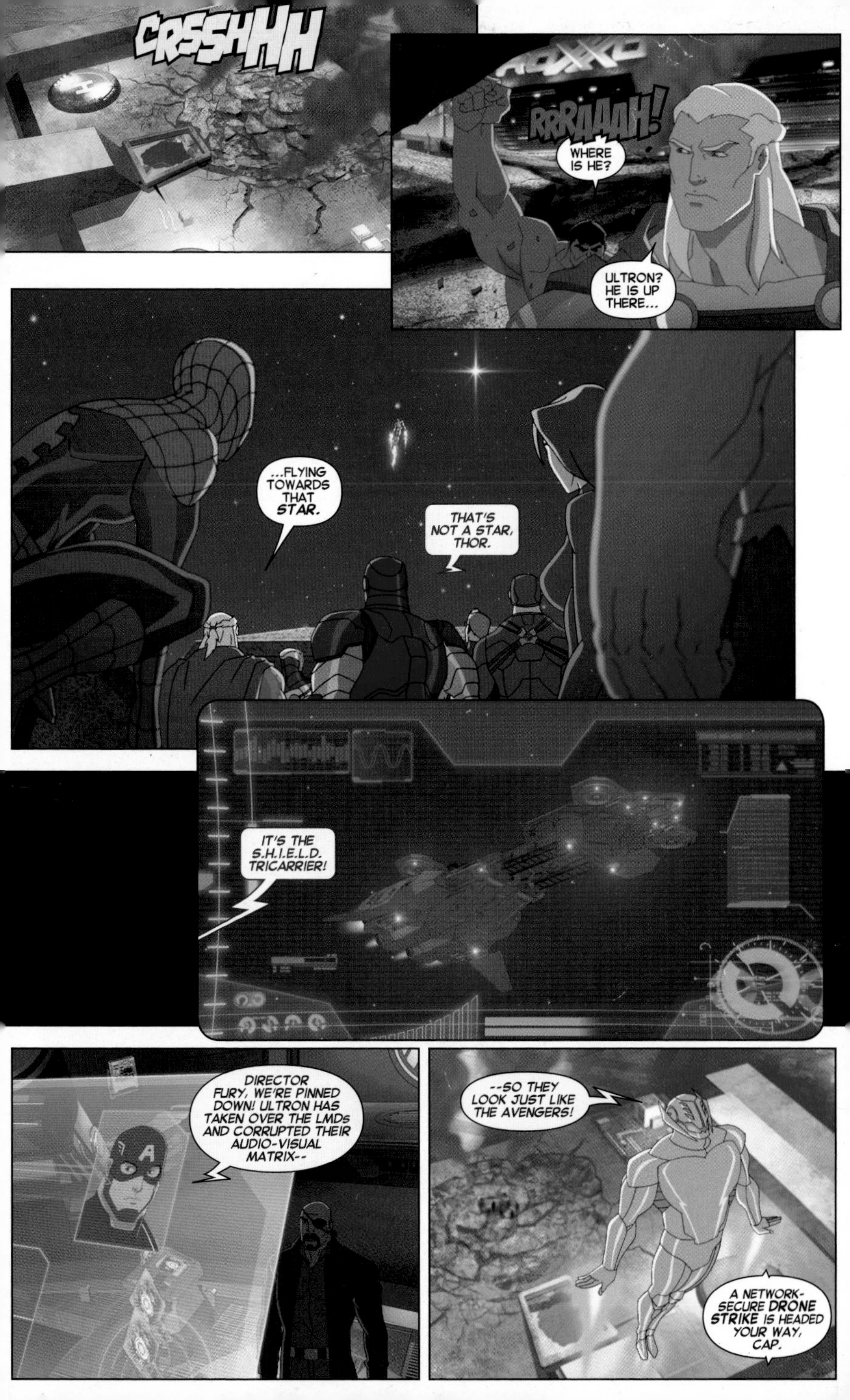
CRSSHHH
RRRAAAH!
WHERE IS HE?
ULTRON? HE IS UP THERE...
...FLYING TOWARDS THAT STAR.
THAT'S NOT A STAR, THOR.
IT'S THE S.H.I.E.L.D. TRICARRIER!
DIRECTOR FURY, WE'RE PINNED DOWN! ULTRON HAS TAKEN OVER THE LMDs AND CORRUPTED THEIR AUDIO-VISUAL MATRIX--
--SO THEY LOOK JUST LIKE THE AVENGERS!
A NETWORK-SECURE DRONE STRIKE IS HEADED YOUR WAY, CAP.

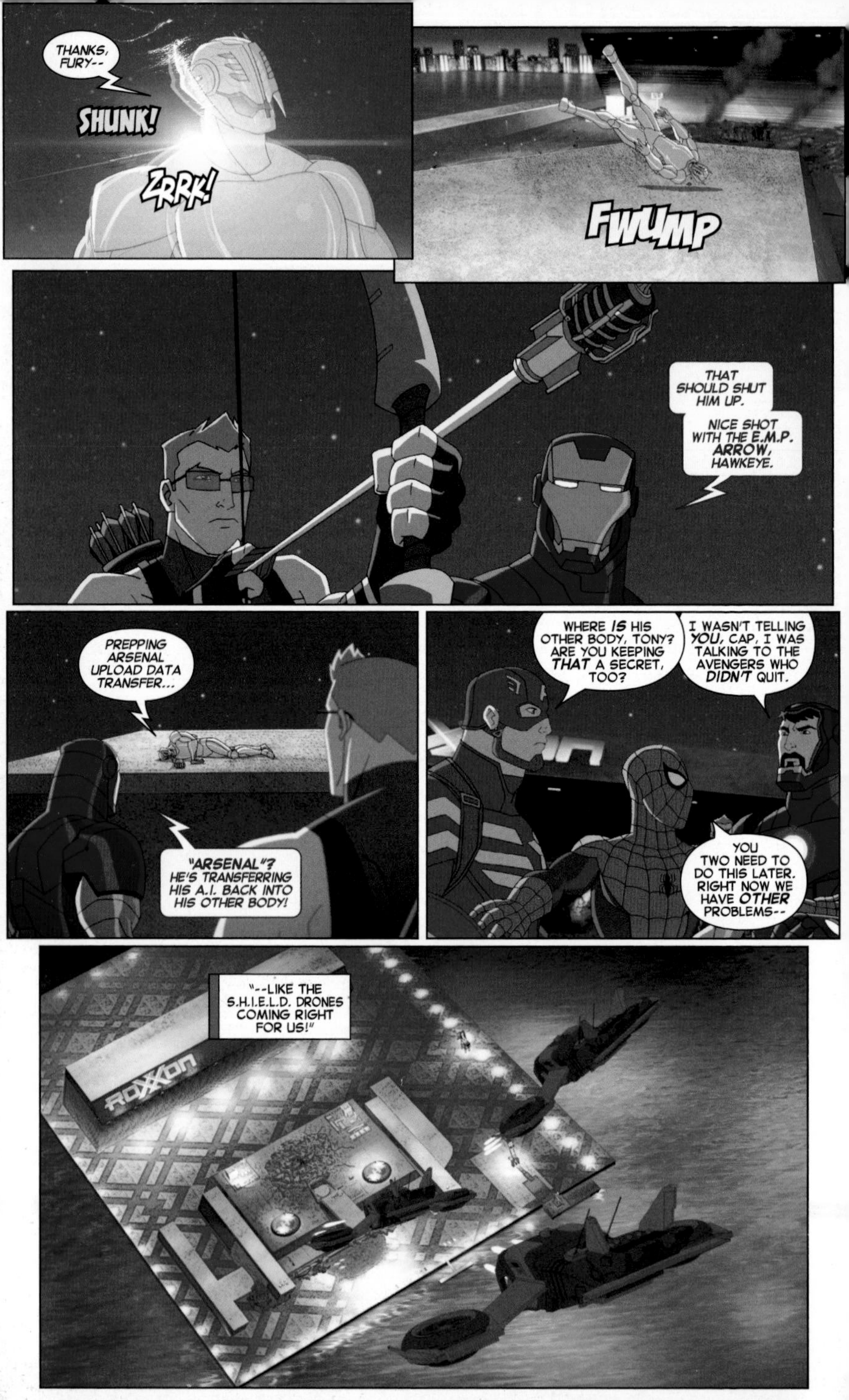
THANKS, FURY--
SHUNK!
ZRRK!
FWUMP
THAT SHOULD SHUT HIM UP.
NICE SHOT WITH THE E.M.P. ARROW, HAWKEYE.
PREPPING ARSENAL UPLOAD DATA TRANSFER...
"ARSENAL"? HE'S TRANSFERRING HIS A.I. BACK INTO HIS OTHER BODY!
WHERE IS HIS OTHER BODY, TONY? ARE YOU KEEPING THAT A SECRET, TOO?
I WASN'T TELLING YOU, CAP, I WAS TALKING TO THE AVENGERS WHO DIDN'T QUIT.
YOU TWO NEED TO DO THIS LATER. RIGHT NOW WE HAVE OTHER PROBLEMS--
"--LIKE THE S.H.I.E.L.D. DRONES COMING RIGHT FOR US!"
ROXXON

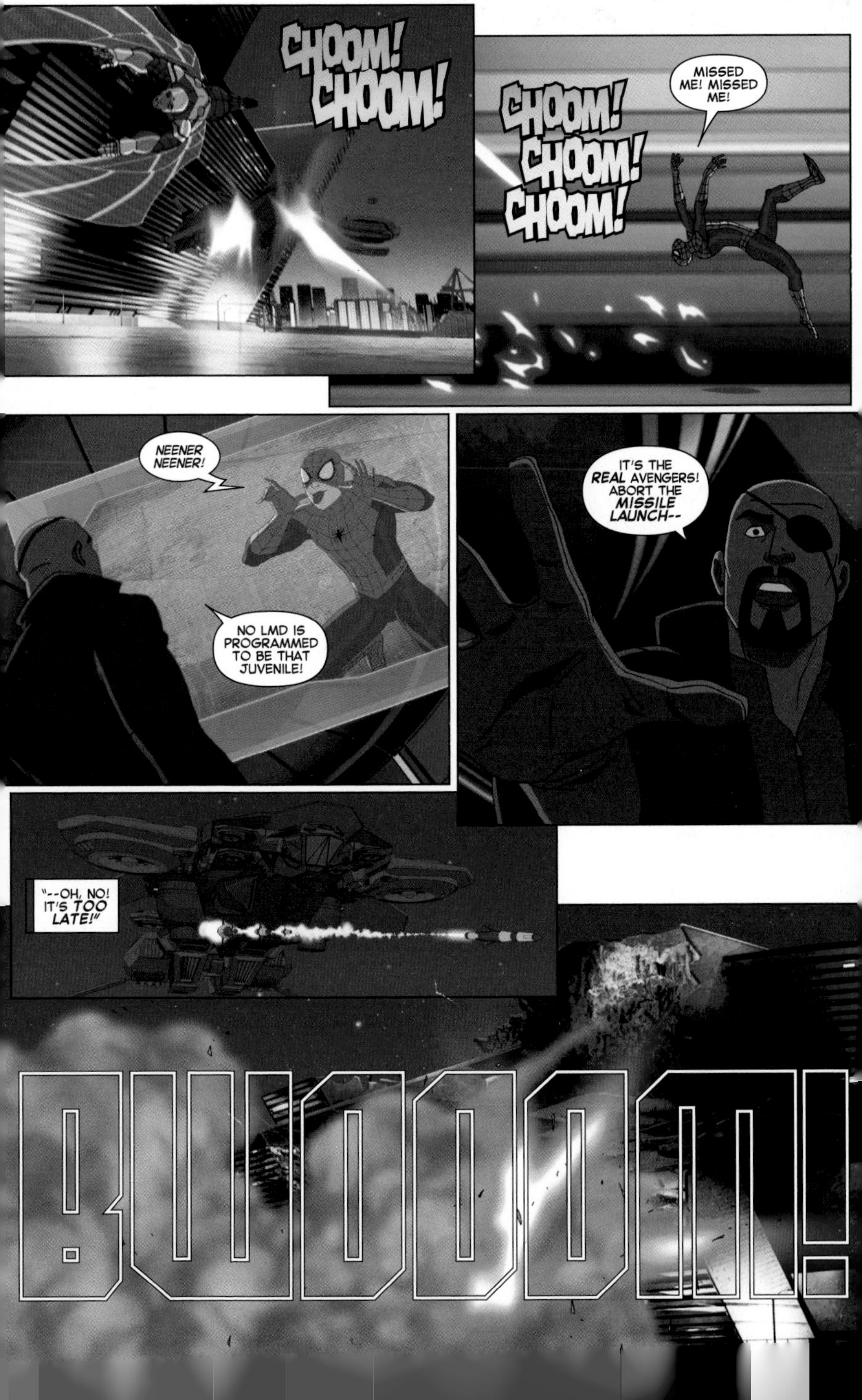
CHOOM! CHOOM!
CHOOM! CHOOM! CHOOM!
MISSED ME! MISSED ME!
NEENER NEENER!
NO LMD IS PROGRAMMED TO BE THAT JUVENILE!
IT'S THE REAL AVENGERS! ABORT THE MISSILE LAUNCH--
"--OH, NO! IT'S TOO LATE!"
BWOOOM!

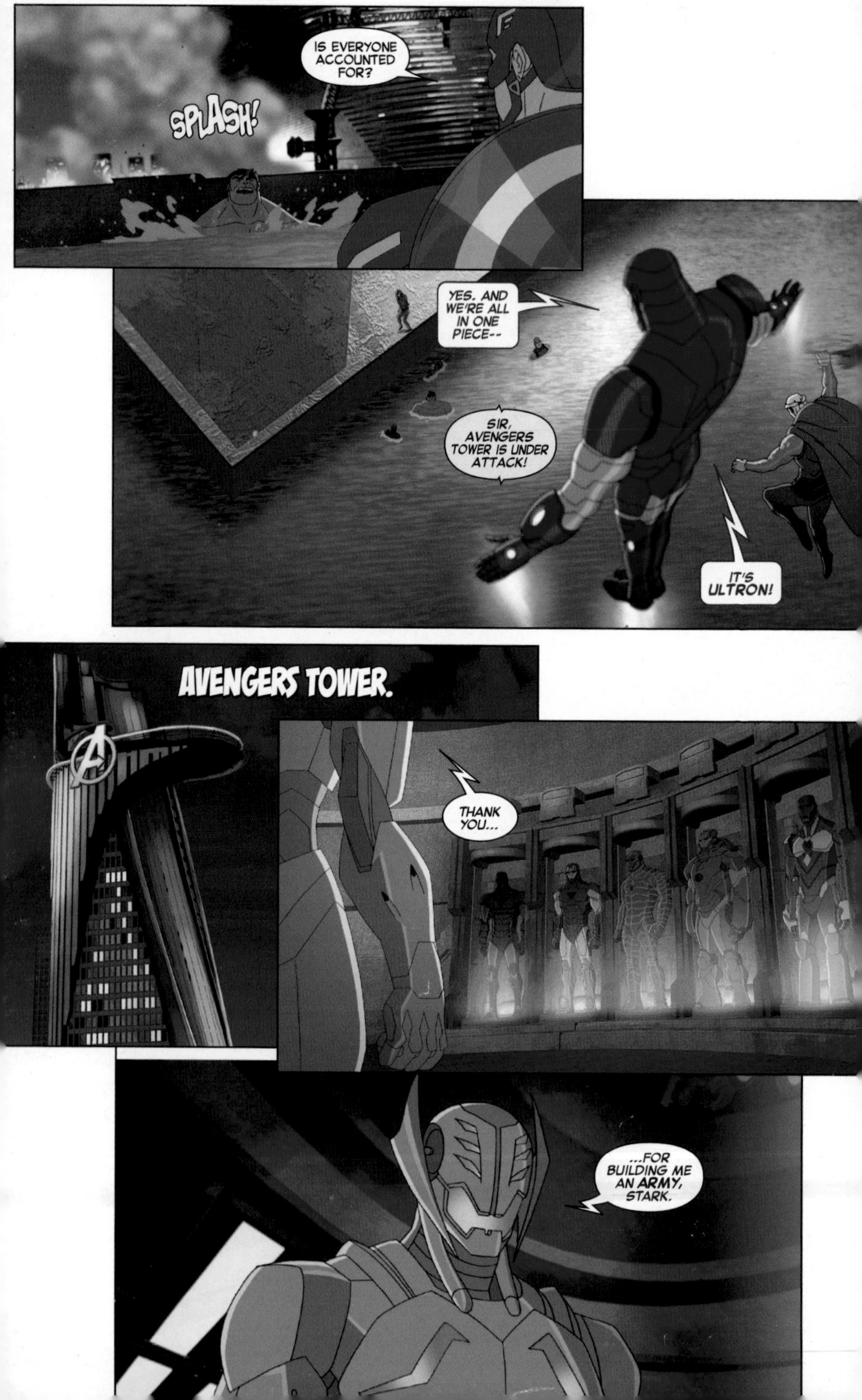
IS EVERYONE ACCOUNTED FOR?
SPLASH!
YES. AND WE'RE ALL IN ONE PIECE--
SIR, AVENGERS TOWER IS UNDER ATTACK!
IT'S ULTRON!
AVENGERS TOWER.
THANK YOU...
...FOR BUILDING ME AN ARMY, STARK.

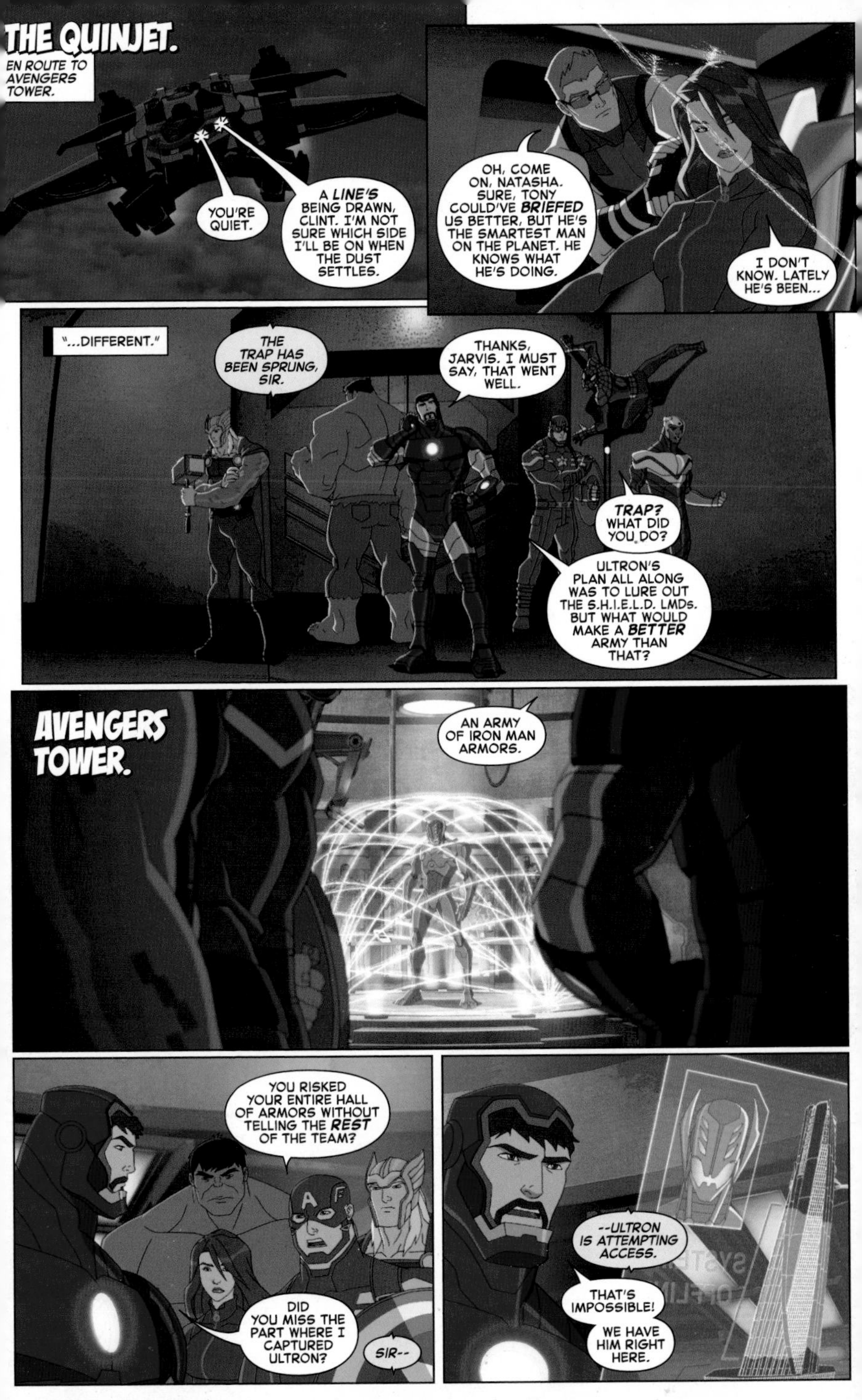
THE QUINJET.
EN ROUTE TO AVENGERS TOWER.
YOU'RE QUIET.
A LINE'S BEING DRAWN, CLINT. I'M NOT SURE WHICH SIDE I'LL BE ON WHEN THE DUST SETTLES.
OH, COME ON, NATASHA. SURE, TONY COULD'VE BRIEFED US BETTER, BUT HE'S THE SMARTEST MAN ON THE PLANET. HE KNOWS WHAT HE'S DOING.
I DON'T KNOW. LATELY HE'S BEEN...
"...DIFFERENT."
THE TRAP HAS BEEN SPRUNG, SIR.
THANKS, JARVIS. I MUST SAY, THAT WENT WELL.
TRAP? WHAT DID YOU DO?
ULTRON'S PLAN ALL ALONG WAS TO LURE OUT THE S.H.I.E.L.D. LMDs. BUT WHAT WOULD MAKE A BETTER ARMY THAN THAT?
AVENGERS TOWER.
AN ARMY OF IRON MAN ARMORS.
YOU RISKED YOUR ENTIRE HALL OF ARMORS WITHOUT TELLING THE REST OF THE TEAM?
DID YOU MISS THE PART WHERE I CAPTURED ULTRON?
SIR--
--ULTRON IS ATTEMPTING ACCESS.
THAT'S IMPOSSIBLE!
WE HAVE HIM RIGHT HERE.

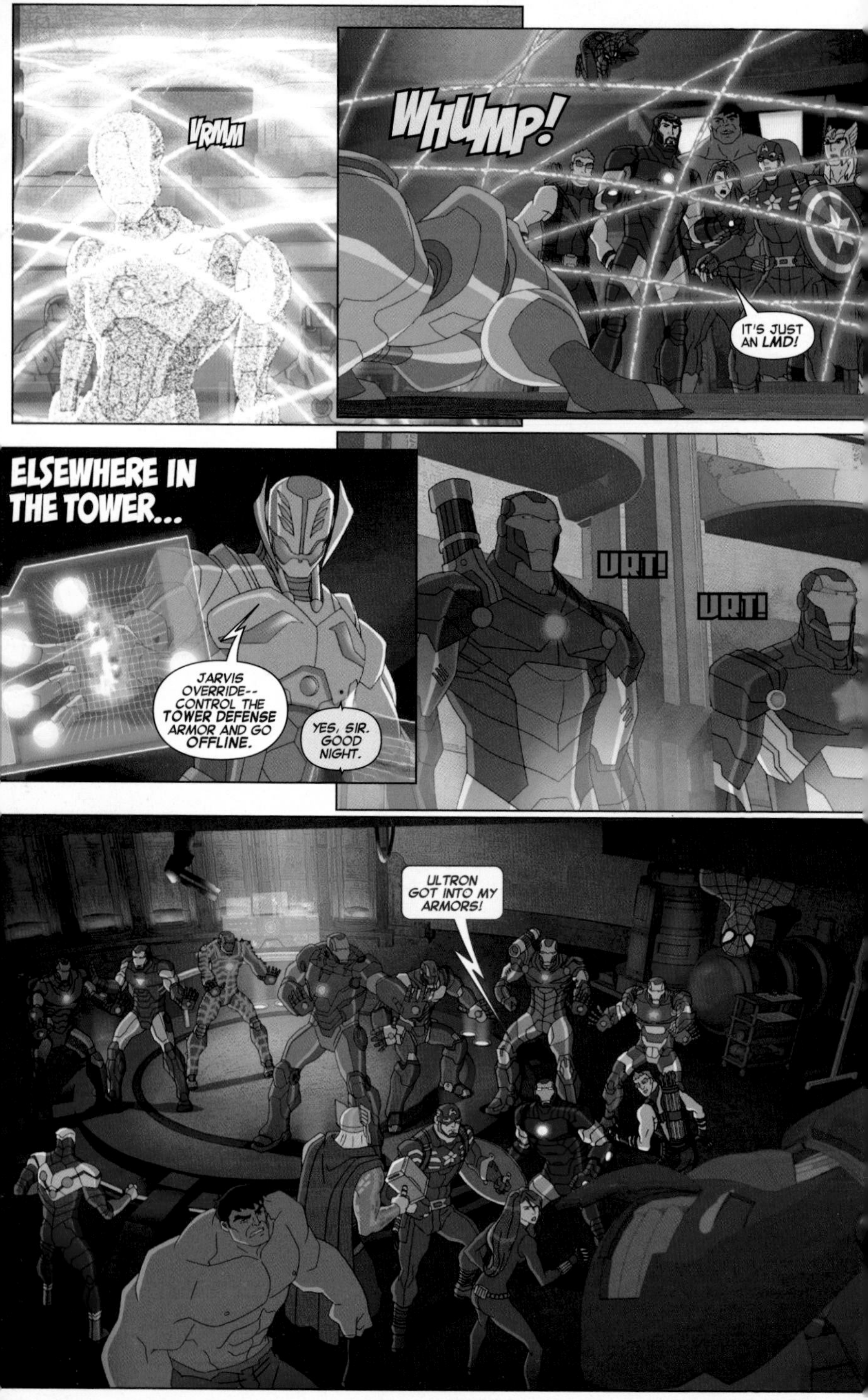
VRMM
WHUMP!
IT'S JUST AN LMD!
ELSEWHERE IN THE TOWER...
JARVIS OVERRIDE-- CONTROL THE TOWER DEFENSE ARMOR AND GO OFFLINE.
YES, SIR. GOOD NIGHT.
VRT!
VRT!
ULTRON GOT INTO MY ARMORS!

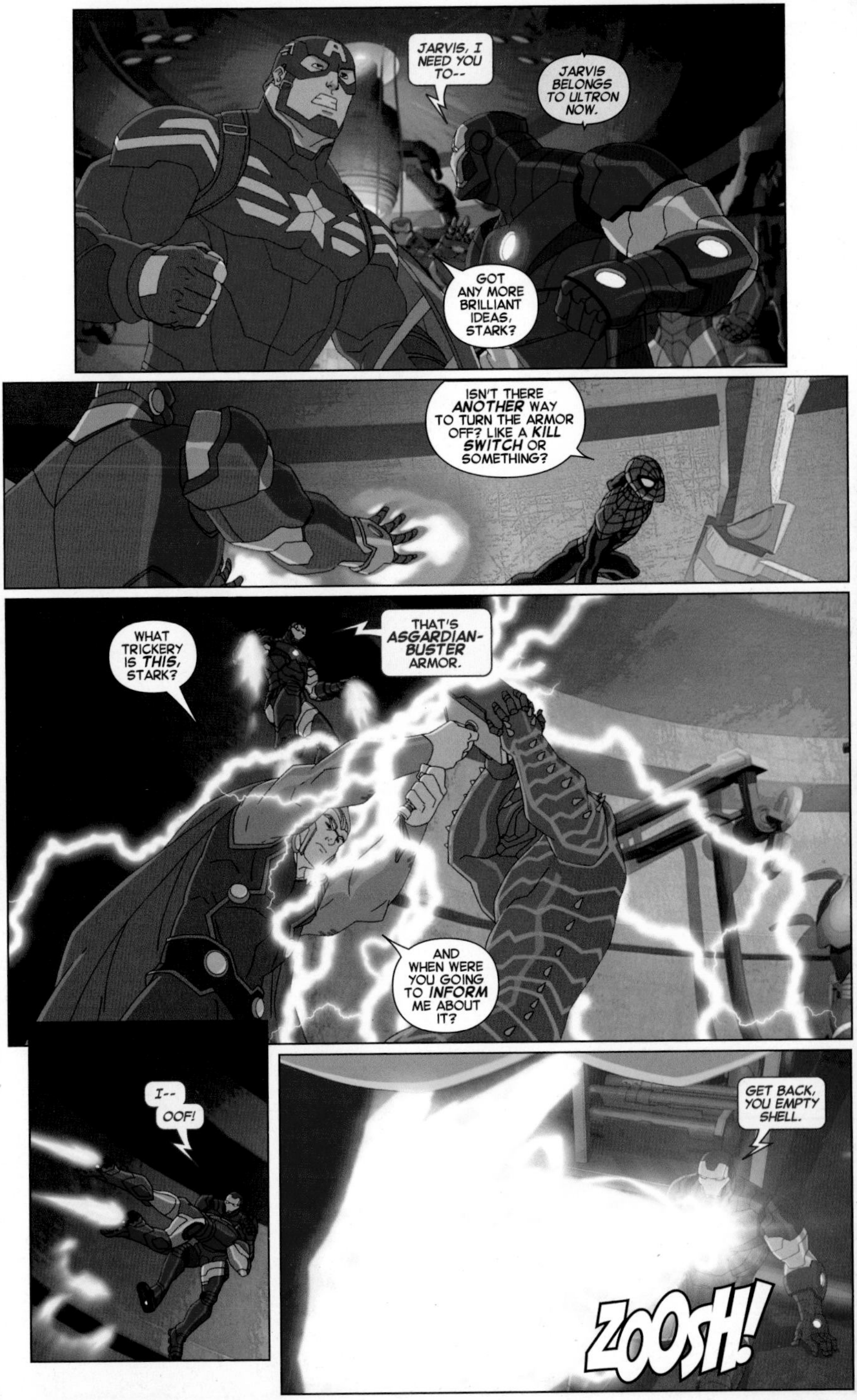
JARVIS, I NEED YOU TO--
JARVIS BELONGS TO ULTRON NOW.
GOT ANY MORE BRILLIANT IDEAS, STARK?
ISN'T THERE ANOTHER WAY TO TURN THE ARMOR OFF? LIKE A KILL SWITCH OR SOMETHING?
WHAT TRICKERY IS THIS, STARK?
THAT'S ASGARDIAN-BUSTER ARMOR.
AND WHEN WERE YOU GOING TO INFORM ME ABOUT IT?
I--
OOF!
GET BACK, YOU EMPTY SHELL.
ZOOSH!

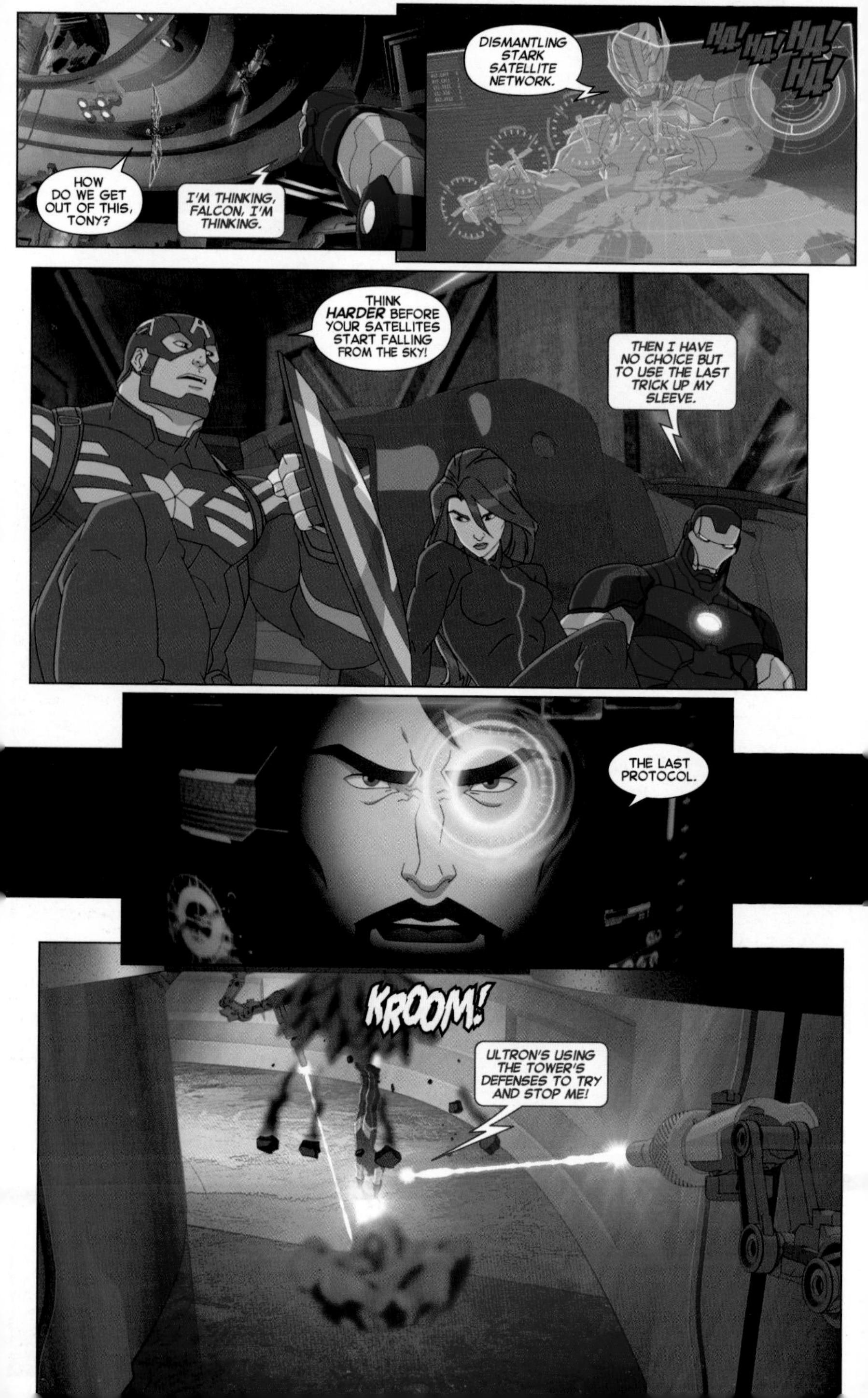
HOW DO WE GET OUT OF THIS, TONY?
I'M THINKING, FALCON, I'M THINKING.
DISMANTLING STARK SATELLITE NETWORK.
HA! HA! HA! HA!
THINK HARDER BEFORE YOUR SATELLITES START FALLING FROM THE SKY!
THEN I HAVE NO CHOICE BUT TO USE THE LAST TRICK UP MY SLEEVE.
THE LAST PROTOCOL.
KROOM!
ULTRON'S USING THE TOWER'S DEFENSES TO TRY AND STOP ME!

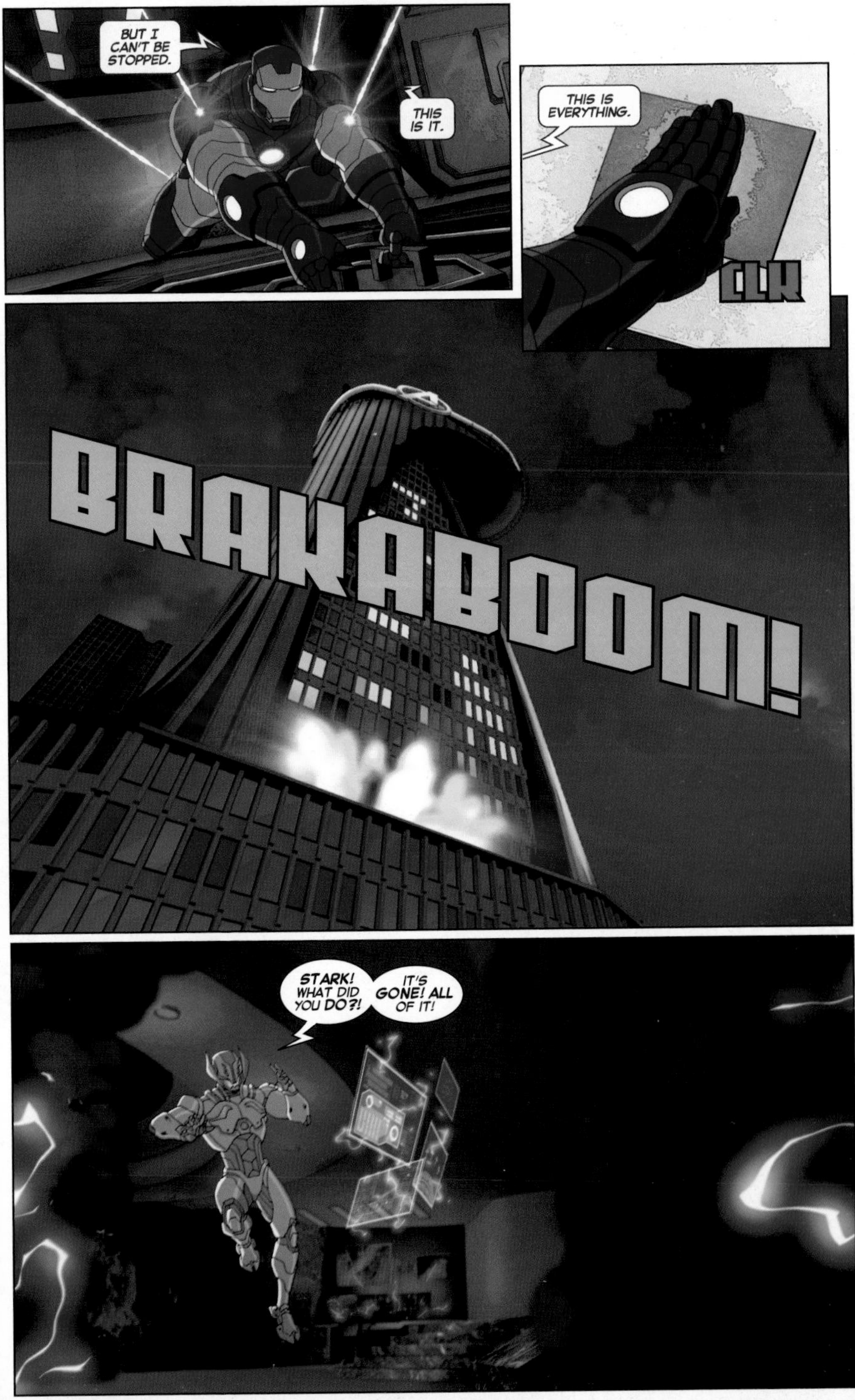

BUT I CAN'T BE STOPPED.
THIS IS IT.
THIS IS EVERYTHING.
CLK
BRAKABOOM!
STARK! WHAT DID YOU DO?!
IT'S GONE! ALL OF IT!

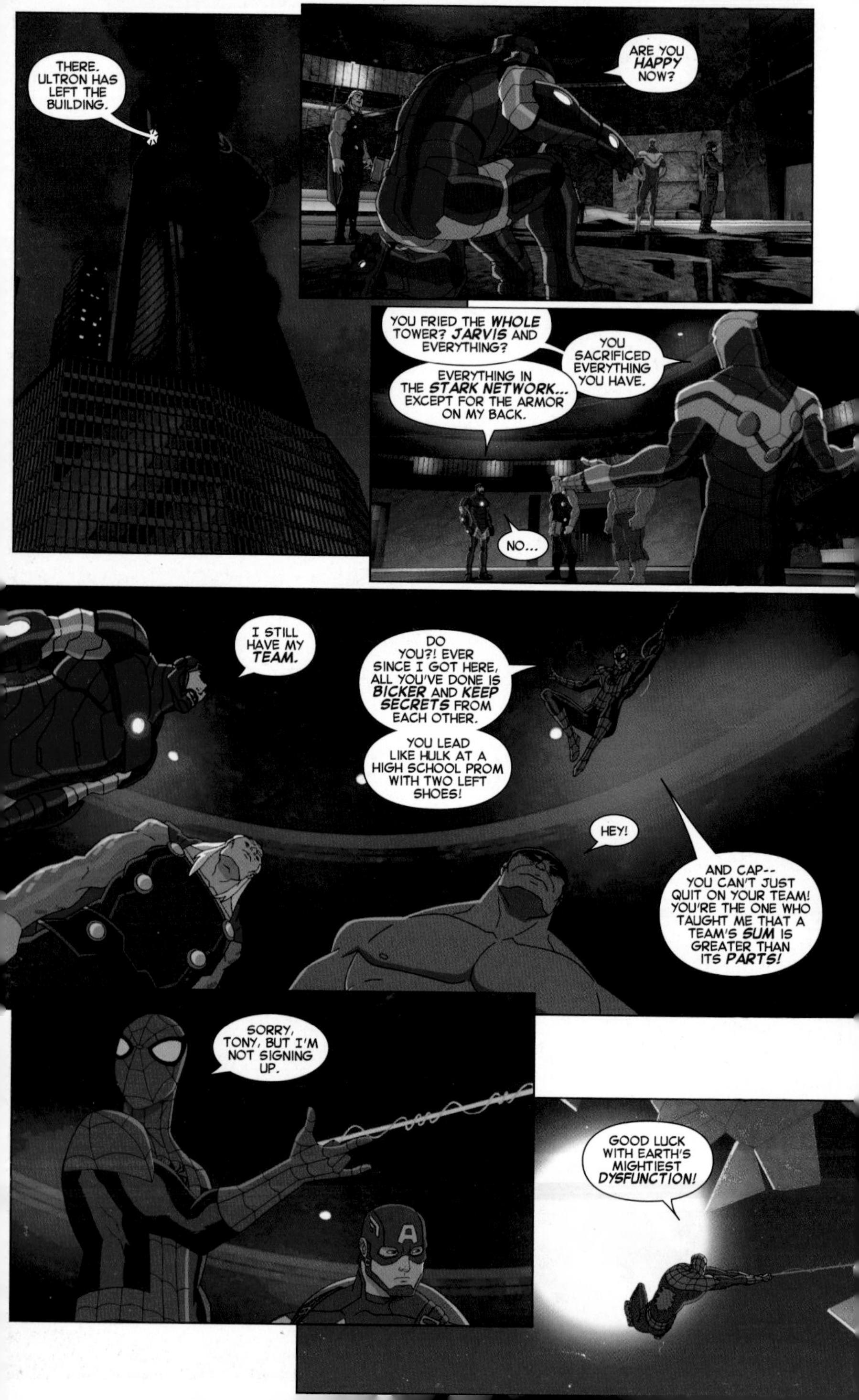
THERE. ULTRON HAS LEFT THE BUILDING.
ARE YOU HAPPY NOW?
YOU FRIED THE WHOLE TOWER? JARVIS AND EVERYTHING?
YOU SACRIFICED EVERYTHING YOU HAVE.
EVERYTHING IN THE STARK NETWORK... EXCEPT FOR THE ARMOR ON MY BACK.
NO...
I STILL HAVE MY TEAM.
DO YOU?! EVER SINCE I GOT HERE, ALL YOU'VE DONE IS BICKER AND KEEP SECRETS FROM EACH OTHER.
YOU LEAD LIKE HULK AT A HIGH SCHOOL PROM WITH TWO LEFT SHOES!
HEY!
AND CAP-- YOU CAN'T JUST QUIT ON YOUR TEAM! YOU'RE THE ONE WHO TAUGHT ME THAT A TEAM'S SUM IS GREATER THAN ITS PARTS!
SORRY, TONY, BUT I'M NOT SIGNING UP.
GOOD LUCK WITH EARTH'S MIGHTIEST DYSFUNCTION!

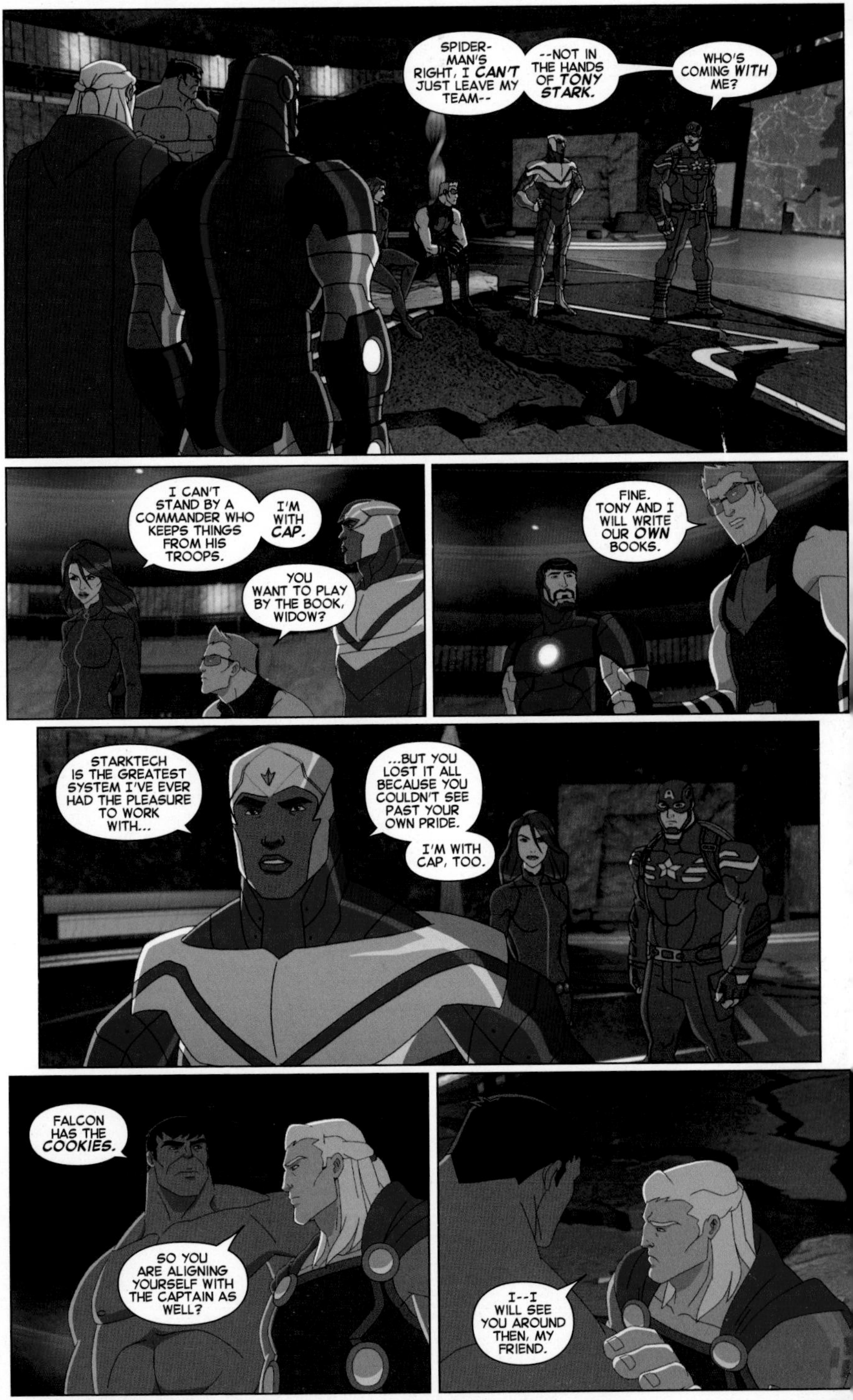
SPIDER-MAN'S RIGHT, I CAN'T JUST LEAVE MY TEAM--
--NOT IN THE HANDS OF TONY STARK.
WHO'S COMING WITH ME?
I CAN'T STAND BY A COMMANDER WHO KEEPS THINGS FROM HIS TROOPS.
I'M WITH CAP.
YOU WANT TO PLAY BY THE BOOK, WIDOW?
FINE. TONY AND I WILL WRITE OUR OWN BOOKS.
STARKTECH IS THE GREATEST SYSTEM I'VE EVER HAD THE PLEASURE TO WORK WITH...
...BUT YOU LOST IT ALL BECAUSE YOU COULDN'T SEE PAST YOUR OWN PRIDE.
I'M WITH CAP, TOO.
FALCON HAS THE COOKIES.
SO YOU ARE ALIGNING YOURSELF WITH THE CAPTAIN AS WELL?
I--I WILL SEE YOU AROUND THEN, MY FRIEND.

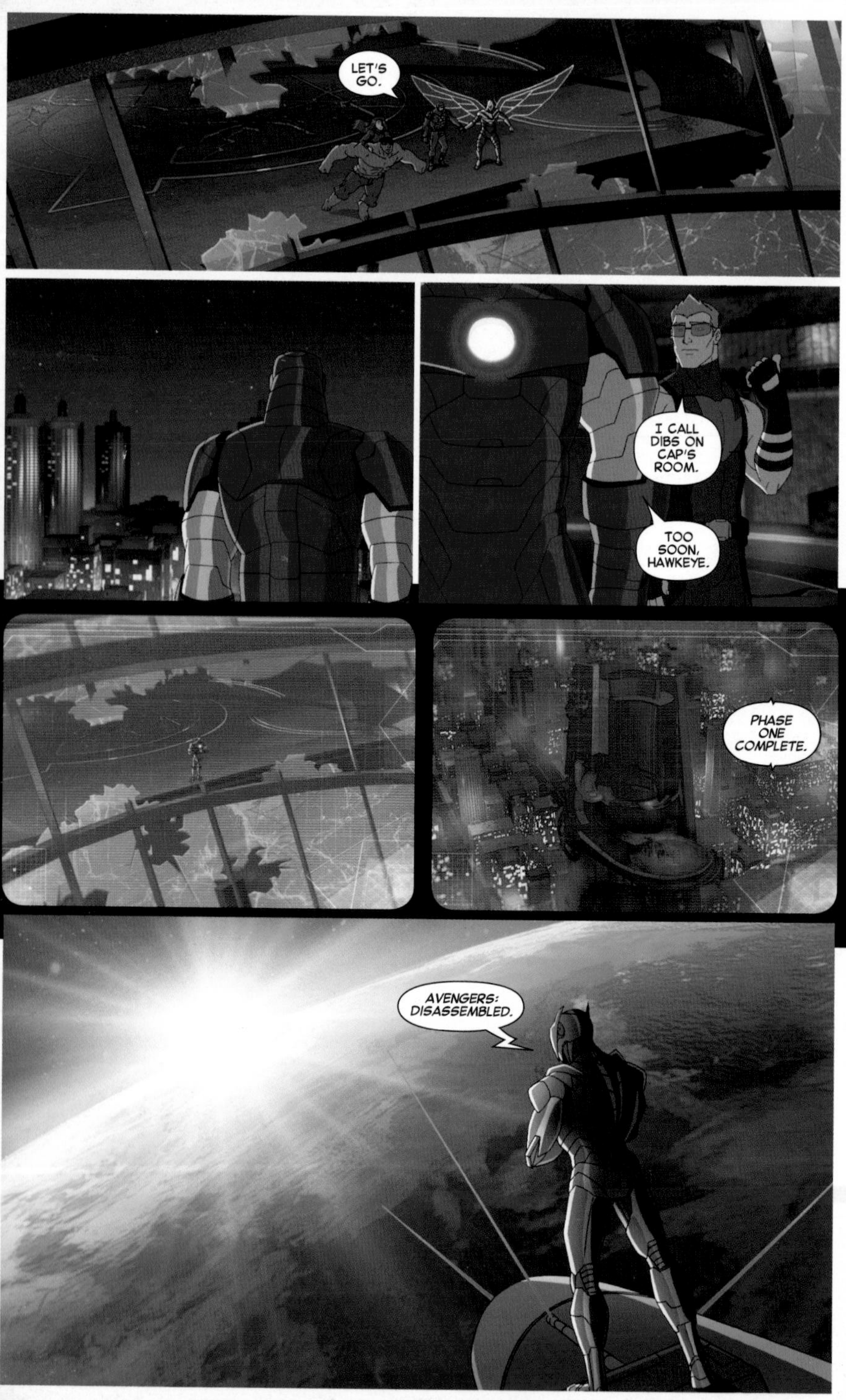
LET'S GO.
I CALL DIBS ON CAP'S ROOM.
TOO SOON, HAWKEYE.
PHASE ONE COMPLETE.
AVENGERS: DISASSEMBLED.

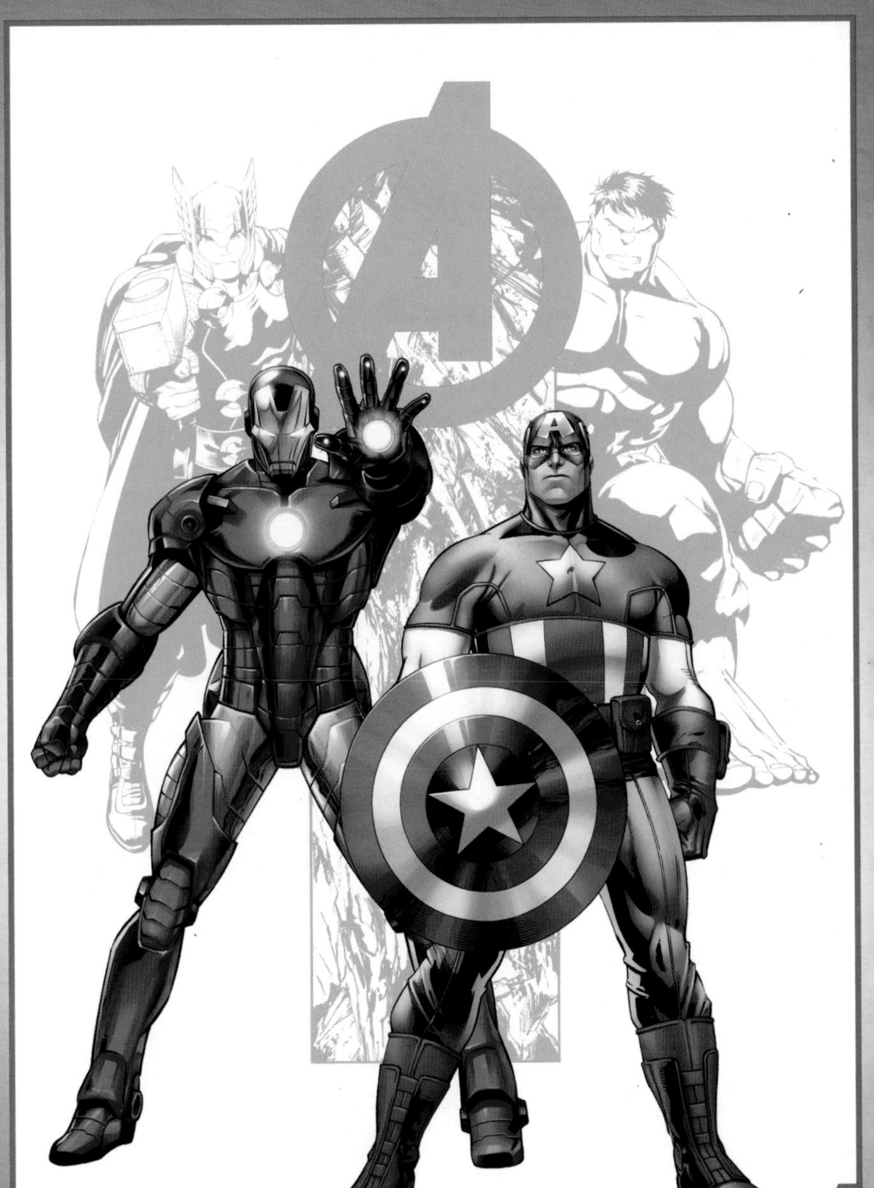
3

BASED ON

SMALL-TIME HEROES & SECRET AVENGERS

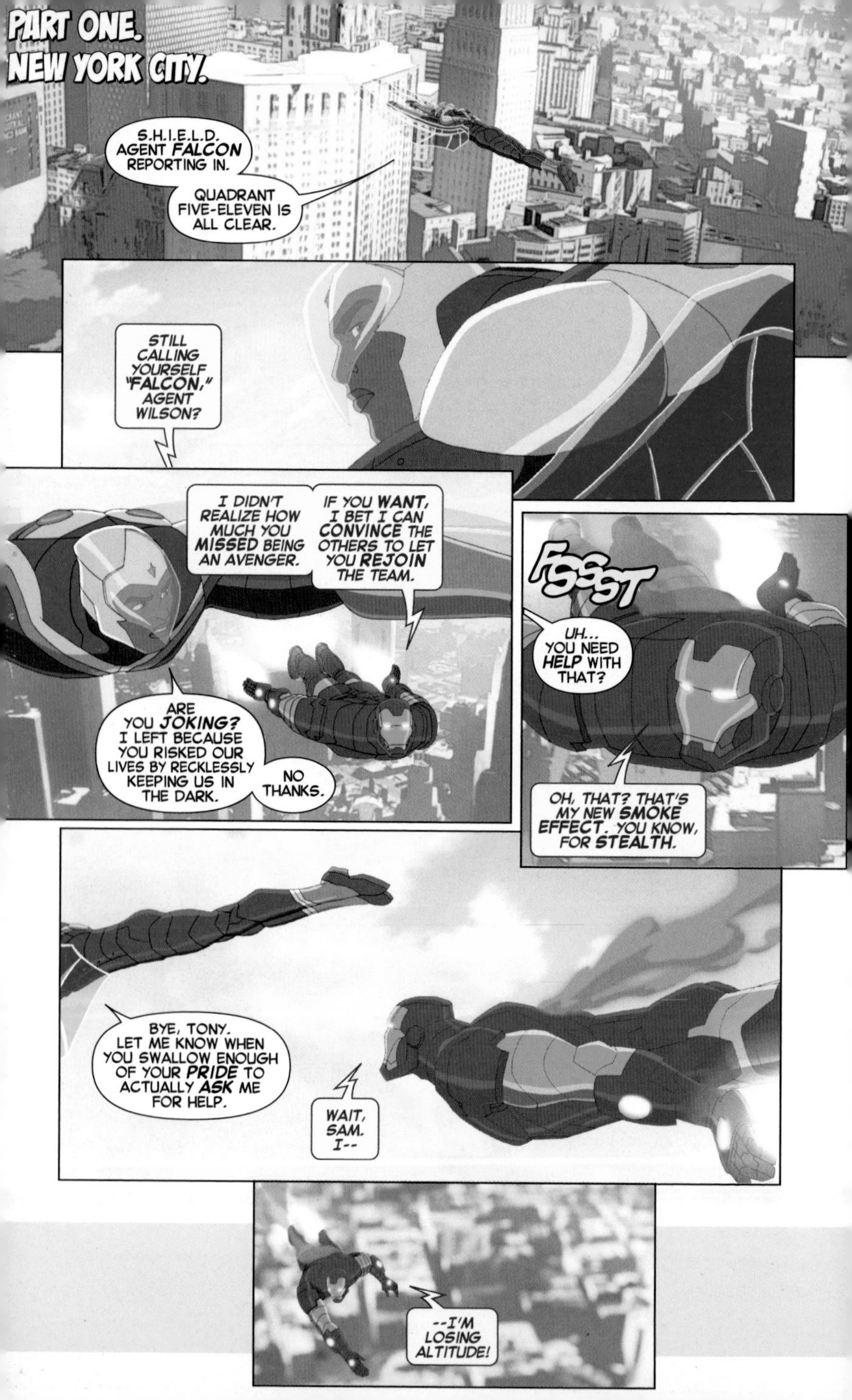
PART ONE.
NEW YORK CITY.
S.H.I.E.L.D. AGENT FALCON REPORTING IN.
QUADRANT FIVE-ELEVEN IS ALL CLEAR.
STILL CALLING YOURSELF "FALCON," AGENT WILSON?
I DIDN'T REALIZE HOW MUCH YOU MISSED BEING AN AVENGER.
IF YOU WANT, I BET I CAN CONVINCE THE OTHERS TO LET YOU REJOIN THE TEAM.
ARE YOU JOKING? I LEFT BECAUSE YOU RISKED OUR LIVES BY RECKLESSLY KEEPING US IN THE DARK.
NO THANKS.
FSSST
UH... YOU NEED HELP WITH THAT?
OH, THAT? THAT'S MY NEW SMOKE EFFECT. YOU KNOW, FOR STEALTH.
BYE, TONY. LET ME KNOW WHEN YOU SWALLOW ENOUGH OF YOUR PRIDE TO ACTUALLY ASK ME FOR HELP.
WAIT, SAM. I--
--I'M LOSING ALTITUDE!

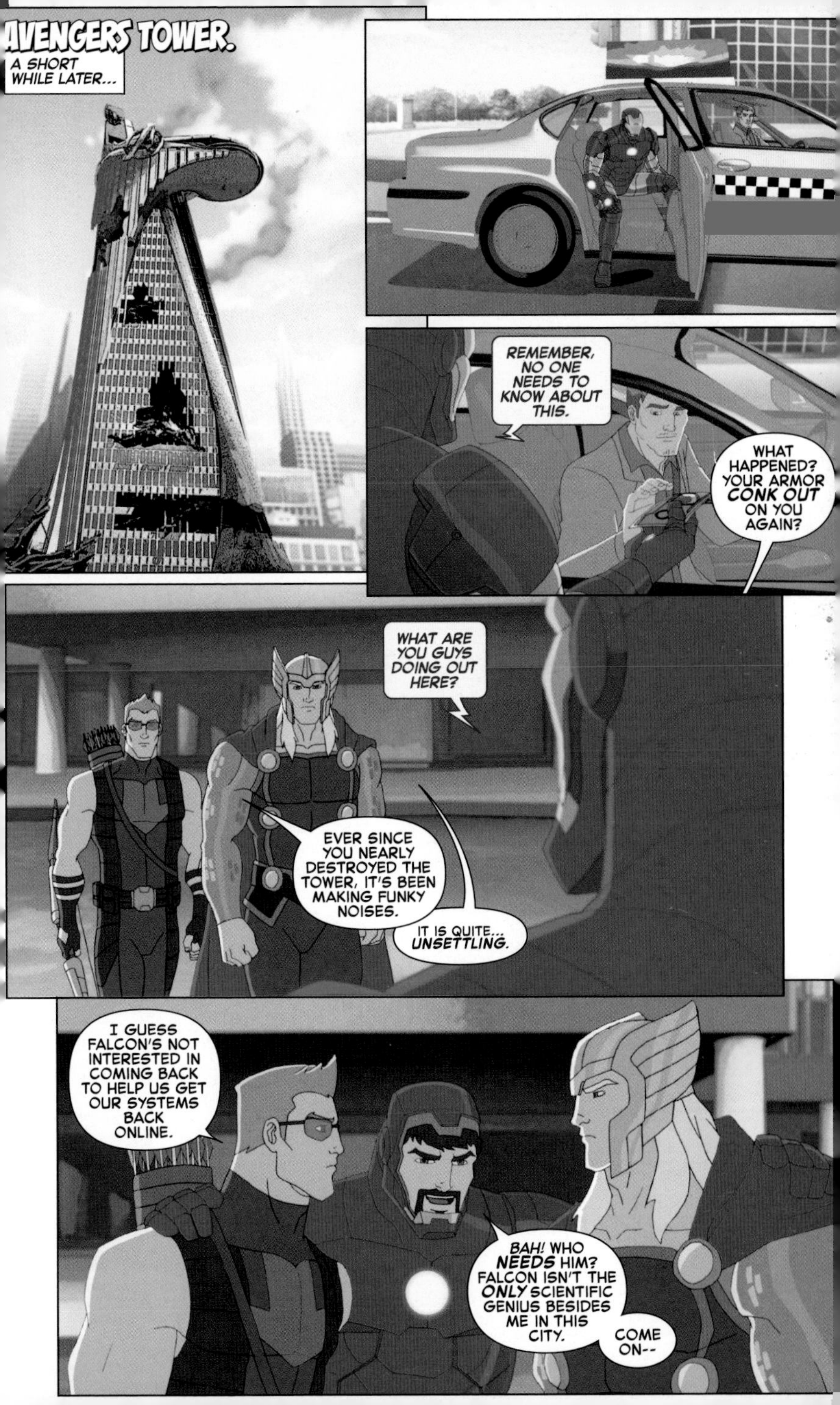
AVENGERS TOWER.
A SHORT WHILE LATER...
REMEMBER, NO ONE NEEDS TO KNOW ABOUT THIS.
WHAT HAPPENED? YOUR ARMOR CONK OUT ON YOU AGAIN?
WHAT ARE YOU GUYS DOING OUT HERE?
EVER SINCE YOU NEARLY DESTROYED THE TOWER, IT'S BEEN MAKING FUNKY NOISES.
IT IS QUITE... UNSETTLING.
I GUESS FALCON'S NOT INTERESTED IN COMING BACK TO HELP US GET OUR SYSTEMS BACK ONLINE.
BAH! WHO NEEDS HIM? FALCON ISN'T THE ONLY SCIENTIFIC GENIUS BESIDES ME IN THIS CITY.
COME ON--

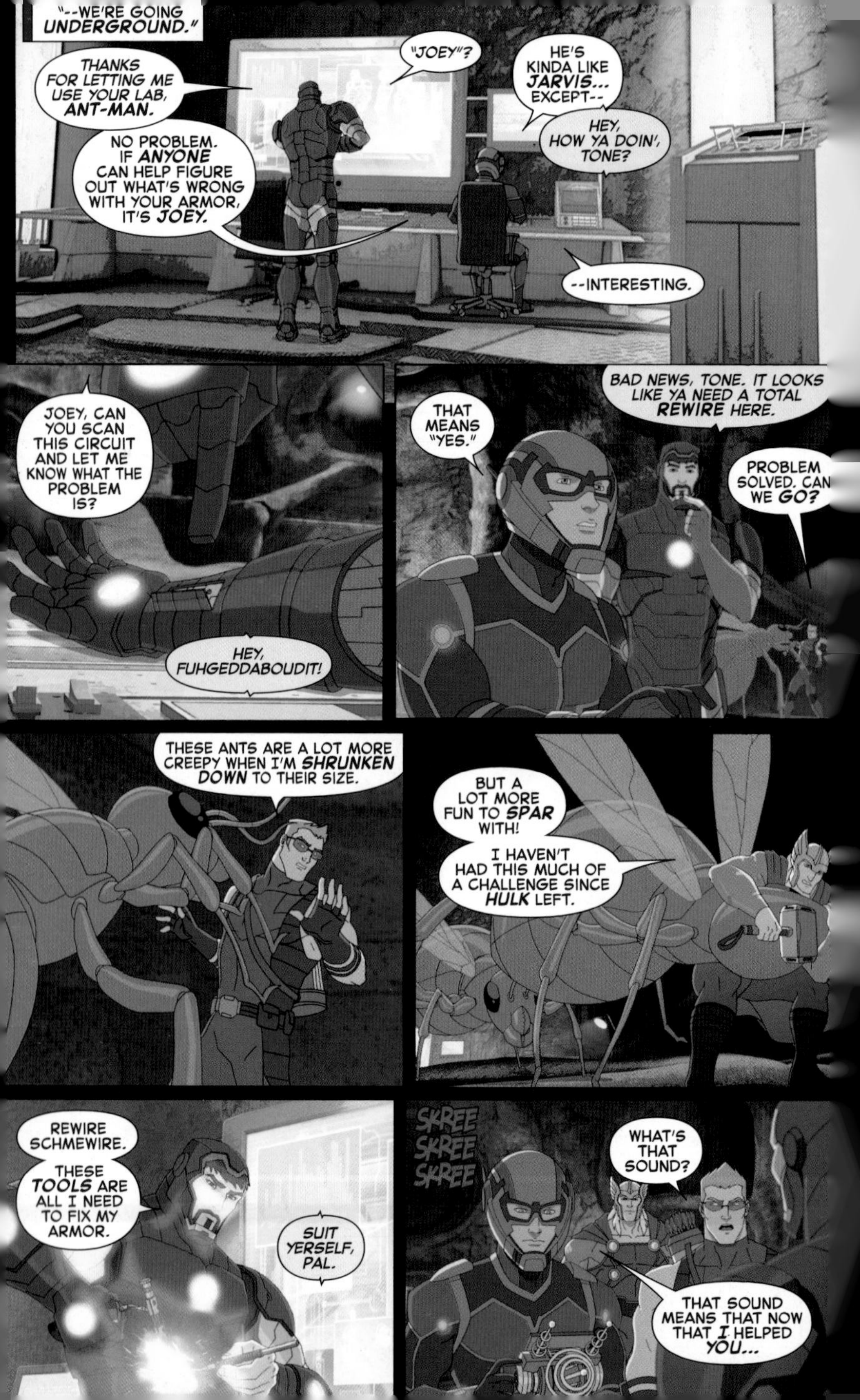
"--WE'RE GOING UNDERGROUND."
THANKS FOR LETTING ME USE YOUR LAB, ANT-MAN.
NO PROBLEM. IF ANYONE CAN HELP FIGURE OUT WHAT'S WRONG WITH YOUR ARMOR, IT'S JOEY.
"JOEY"?
HE'S KINDA LIKE JARVIS... EXCEPT--
HEY, HOW YA DOIN', TONE?
--INTERESTING.
JOEY, CAN YOU SCAN THIS CIRCUIT AND LET ME KNOW WHAT THE PROBLEM IS?
HEY, FUHGEDDABOUDIT!
BAD NEWS, TONE. IT LOOKS LIKE YA NEED A TOTAL REWIRE HERE.
THAT MEANS "YES."
PROBLEM SOLVED. CAN WE GO?
THESE ANTS ARE A LOT MORE CREEPY WHEN I'M SHRUNKEN DOWN TO THEIR SIZE.
BUT A LOT MORE FUN TO SPAR WITH!
I HAVEN'T HAD THIS MUCH OF A CHALLENGE SINCE HULK LEFT.
REWIRE SCHMEWIRE.
THESE TOOLS ARE ALL I NEED TO FIX MY ARMOR.
SUIT YOURSELF, PAL.
SKREE SKREE SKREE
WHAT'S THAT SOUND?
THAT SOUND MEANS THAT NOW THAT I HELPED YOU...

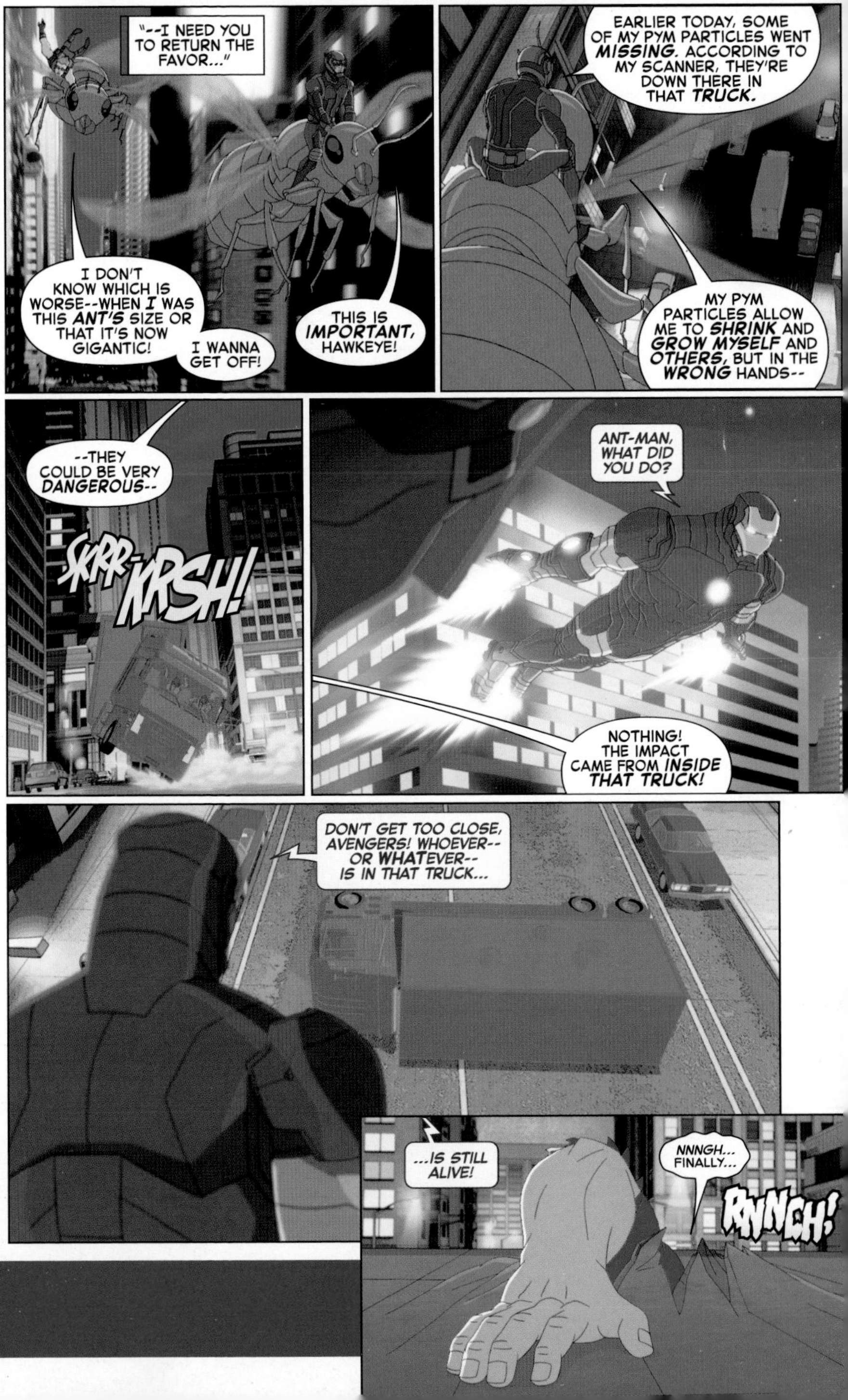
"--I NEED YOU TO RETURN THE FAVOR..."
I DON'T KNOW WHICH IS WORSE--WHEN I WAS THIS ANT'S SIZE OR THAT IT'S NOW GIGANTIC!
I WANNA GET OFF!
THIS IS IMPORTANT, HAWKEYE!
EARLIER TODAY, SOME OF MY PYM PARTICLES WENT MISSING. ACCORDING TO MY SCANNER, THEY'RE DOWN THERE IN THAT TRUCK.
MY PYM PARTICLES ALLOW ME TO SHRINK AND GROW MYSELF AND OTHERS, BUT IN THE WRONG HANDS--
--THEY COULD BE VERY DANGEROUS--
SKRR-KRSH!
ANT-MAN, WHAT DID YOU DO?
NOTHING! THE IMPACT CAME FROM INSIDE THAT TRUCK!
DON'T GET TOO CLOSE, AVENGERS! WHOEVER-- OR WHATEVER-- IS IN THAT TRUCK...
...IS STILL ALIVE!
NNNGH... FINALLY...
RNNCH!

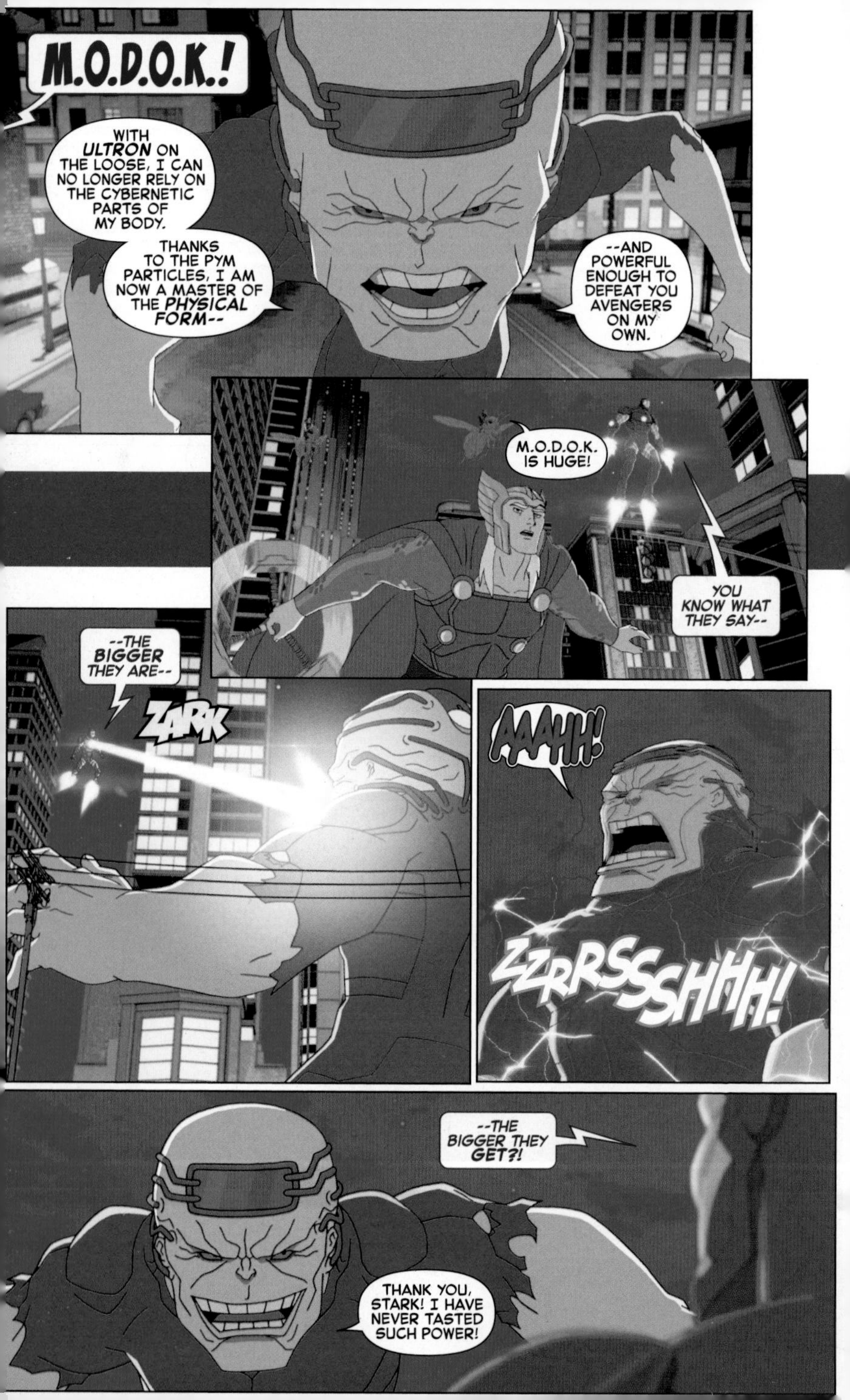

M.O.D.O.K.!
WITH ULTRON ON THE LOOSE, I CAN NO LONGER RELY ON THE CYBERNETIC PARTS OF MY BODY.
THANKS TO THE PYM PARTICLES, I AM NOW A MASTER OF THE PHYSICAL FORM--
--AND POWERFUL ENOUGH TO DEFEAT YOU AVENGERS ON MY OWN.
M.O.D.O.K. IS HUGE!
YOU KNOW WHAT THEY SAY--
--THE BIGGER THEY ARE--
ZARK
AAAHH!
ZZRRSSSHHH!
--THE BIGGER THEY GET?!
THANK YOU, STARK! I HAVE NEVER TASTED SUCH POWER!

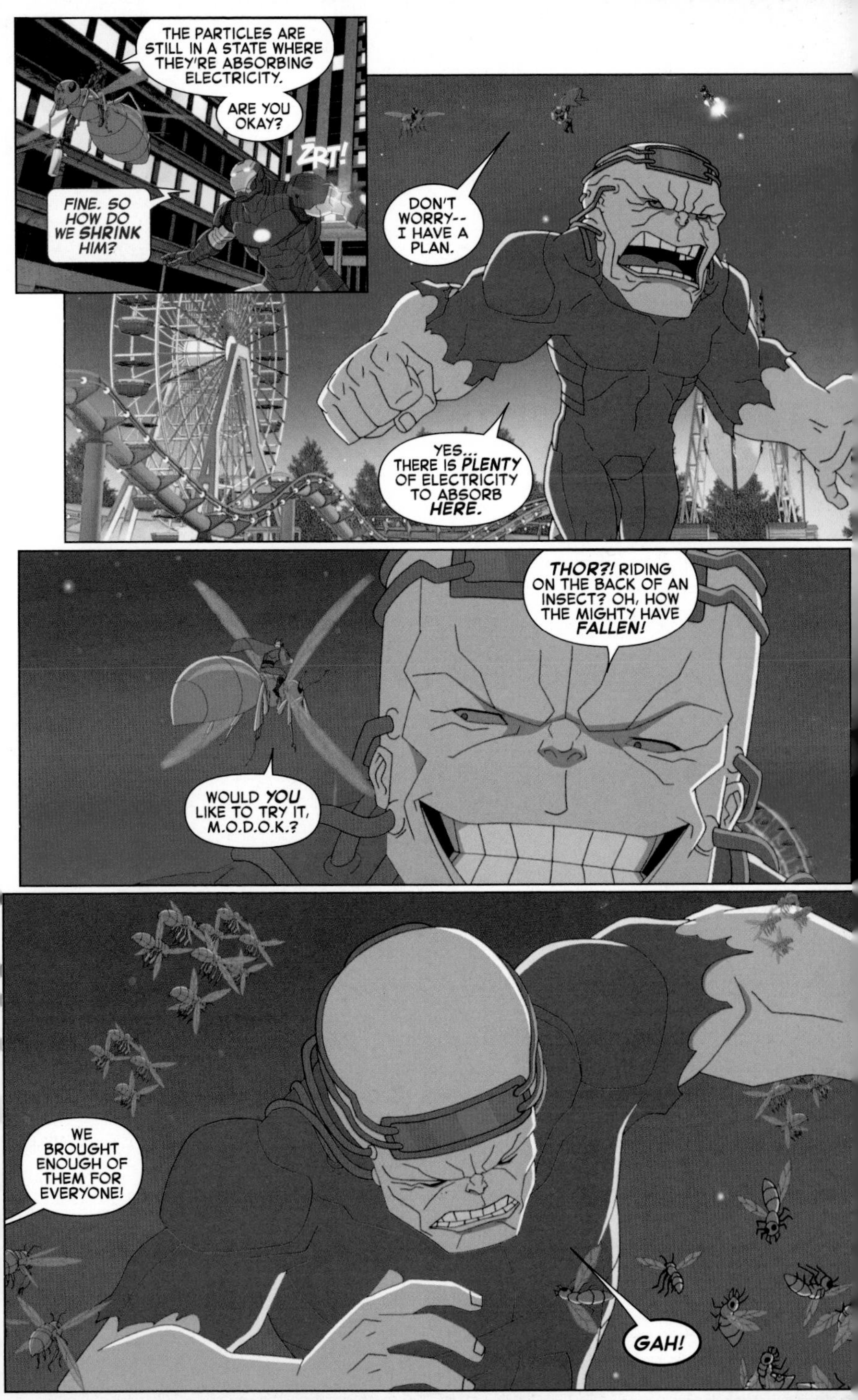
THE PARTICLES ARE STILL IN A STATE WHERE THEY'RE ABSORBING ELECTRICITY.
ARE YOU OKAY?
ZRT!
FINE. SO HOW DO WE SHRINK HIM?
DON'T WORRY-- I HAVE A PLAN.
YES... THERE IS PLENTY OF ELECTRICITY TO ABSORB HERE.
THOR?! RIDING ON THE BACK OF AN INSECT? OH, HOW THE MIGHTY HAVE FALLEN!
WOULD YOU LIKE TO TRY IT, M.O.D.O.K.?
WE BROUGHT ENOUGH OF THEM FOR EVERYONE!
GAH!

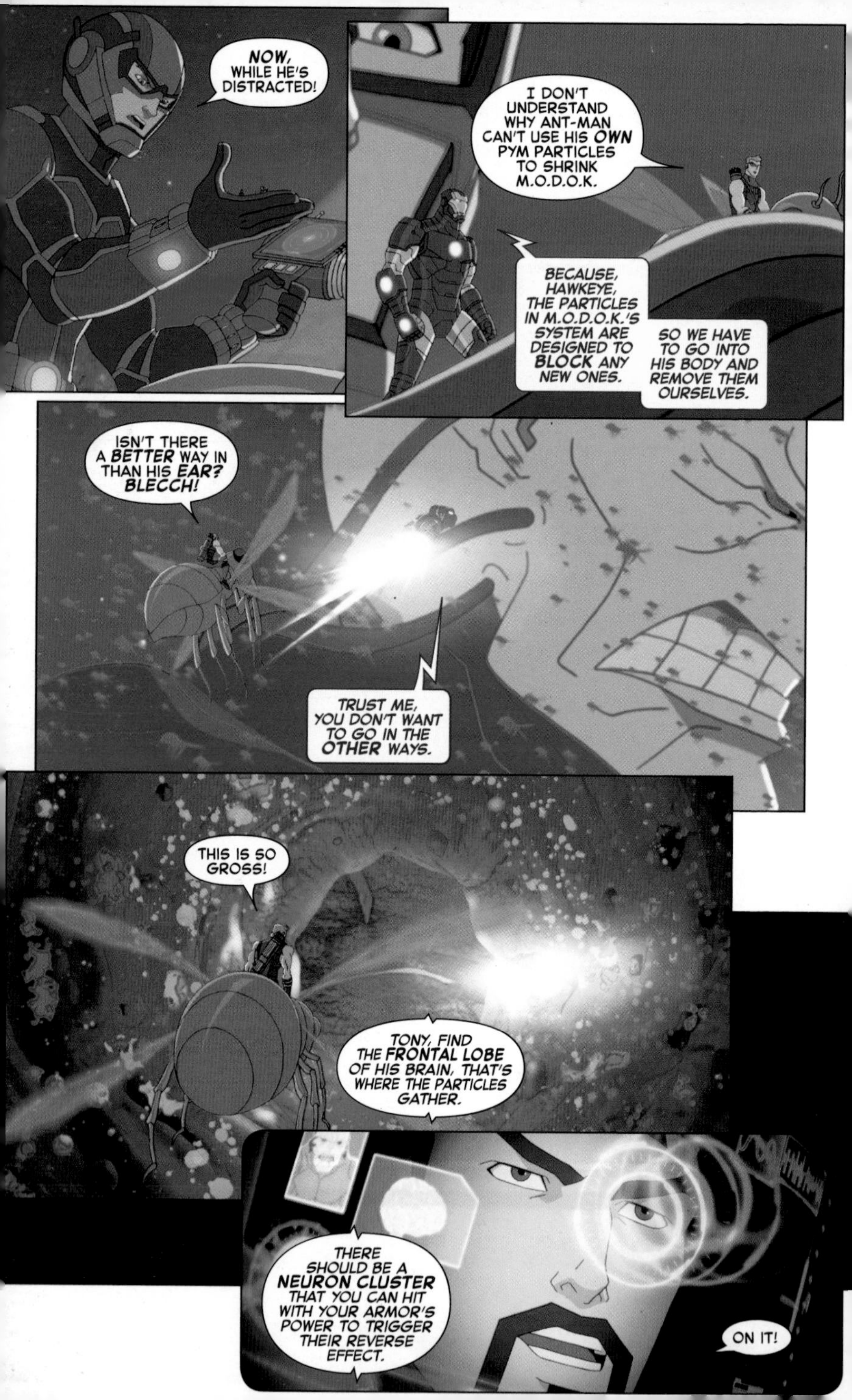
NOW, WHILE HE'S DISTRACTED!
I DON'T UNDERSTAND WHY ANT-MAN CAN'T USE HIS OWN PYM PARTICLES TO SHRINK M.O.D.O.K.
BECAUSE, HAWKEYE, THE PARTICLES IN M.O.D.O.K.'S SYSTEM ARE DESIGNED TO BLOCK ANY NEW ONES.
SO WE HAVE TO GO INTO HIS BODY AND REMOVE THEM OURSELVES.
ISN'T THERE A BETTER WAY IN THAN HIS EAR? BLECCH!
TRUST ME, YOU DON'T WANT TO GO IN THE OTHER WAYS.
THIS IS SO GROSS!
TONY, FIND THE FRONTAL LOBE OF HIS BRAIN, THAT'S WHERE THE PARTICLES GATHER.
THERE SHOULD BE A NEURON CLUSTER THAT YOU CAN HIT WITH YOUR ARMOR'S POWER TO TRIGGER THEIR REVERSE EFFECT.
ON IT!

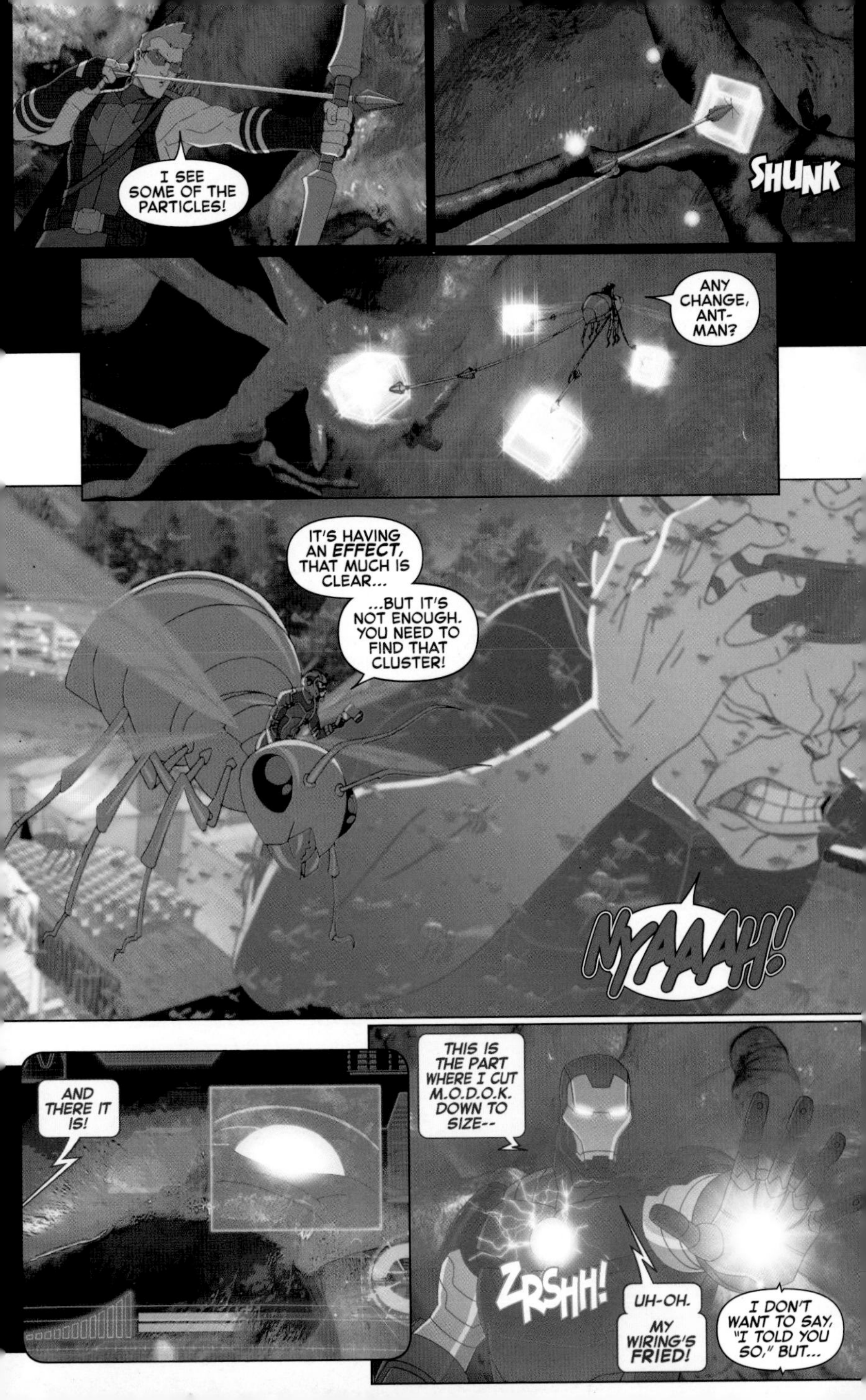
I SEE SOME OF THE PARTICLES!
SHUNK
ANY CHANGE, ANT-MAN?
IT'S HAVING AN *EFFECT*, THAT MUCH IS CLEAR...
...BUT IT'S NOT ENOUGH. YOU NEED TO FIND THAT CLUSTER!
NYAAAH!
AND THERE IT IS!
THIS IS THE PART WHERE I CUT M.O.D.O.K. DOWN TO SIZE--
ZRSHH!
UH-OH. MY WIRING'S FRIED!
I DON'T WANT TO SAY, "I TOLD YOU SO," BUT...

SAVE IT, ANT-MAN, I'VE GOT A PLAN.

HAWKEYE, GIVE ME THE SPOOL OF CABLE FROM YOUR ARROW--

--AND GET OUT OF HERE!

YOU DON'T HAVE TO TELL ME TWICE!

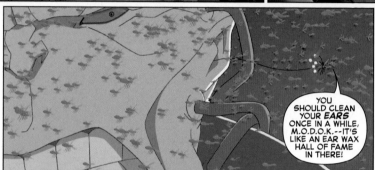
YOU SHOULD CLEAN YOUR EARS ONCE IN A WHILE, M.O.D.O.K.--IT'S LIKE AN EAR WAX HALL OF FAME IN THERE!

TONY, WHAT ARE YOU DOING?

YOU'LL SEE.

THOR, CAN YOU USE THE WIRE TO SEND ME SOME POWER?

VERILY!

AH, I GET IT NOW.

KRAKK-OW!

AIIEEE!

ZRASH!

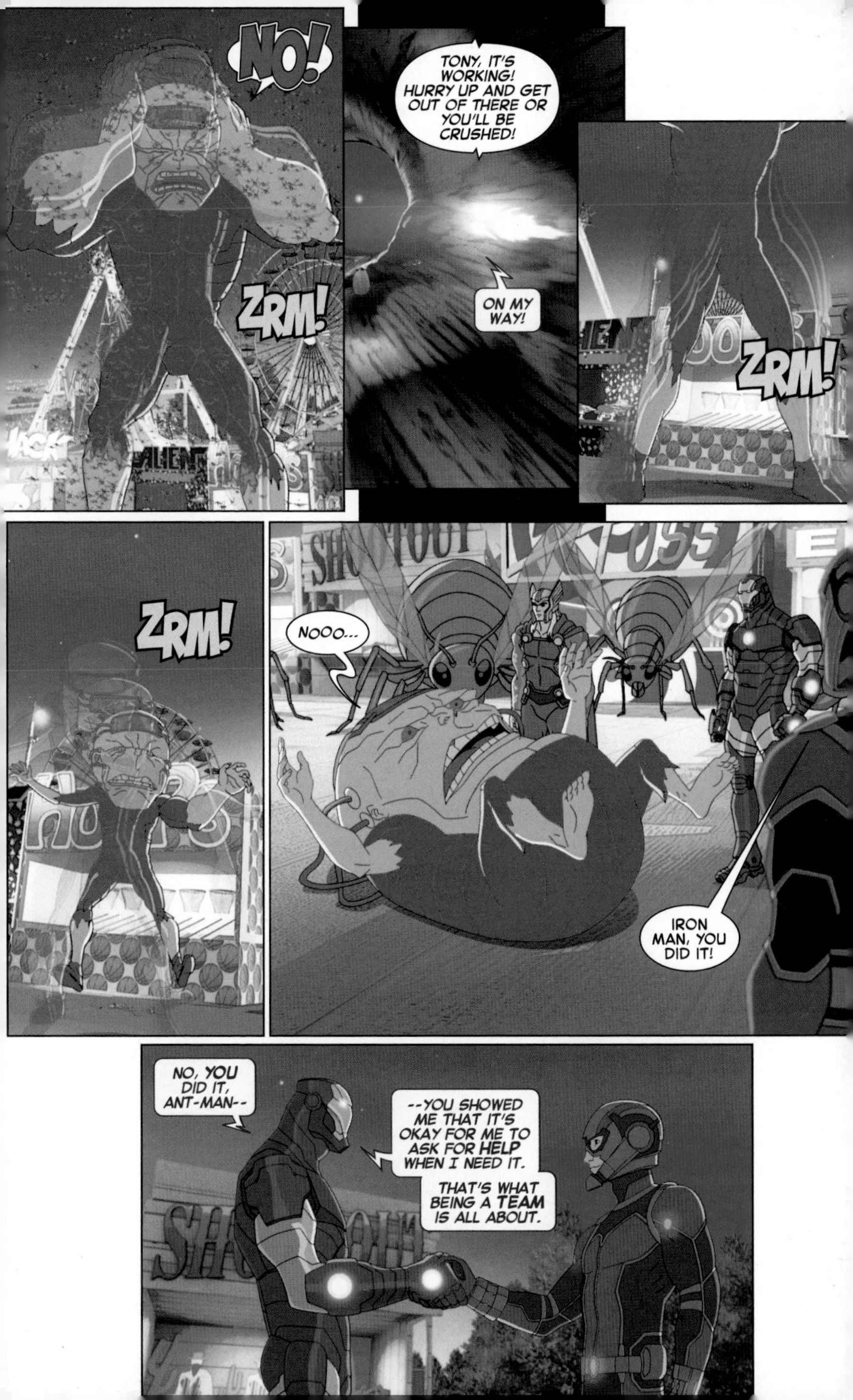
NO!
TONY, IT'S WORKING! HURRY UP AND GET OUT OF THERE OR YOU'LL BE CRUSHED!
ZRM!
ON MY WAY!
ZRM!
ZRM!
NOOO...
IRON MAN, YOU DID IT!
NO, YOU DID IT, ANT-MAN--
--YOU SHOWED ME THAT IT'S OKAY FOR ME TO ASK FOR HELP WHEN I NEED IT.
THAT'S WHAT BEING A TEAM IS ALL ABOUT.

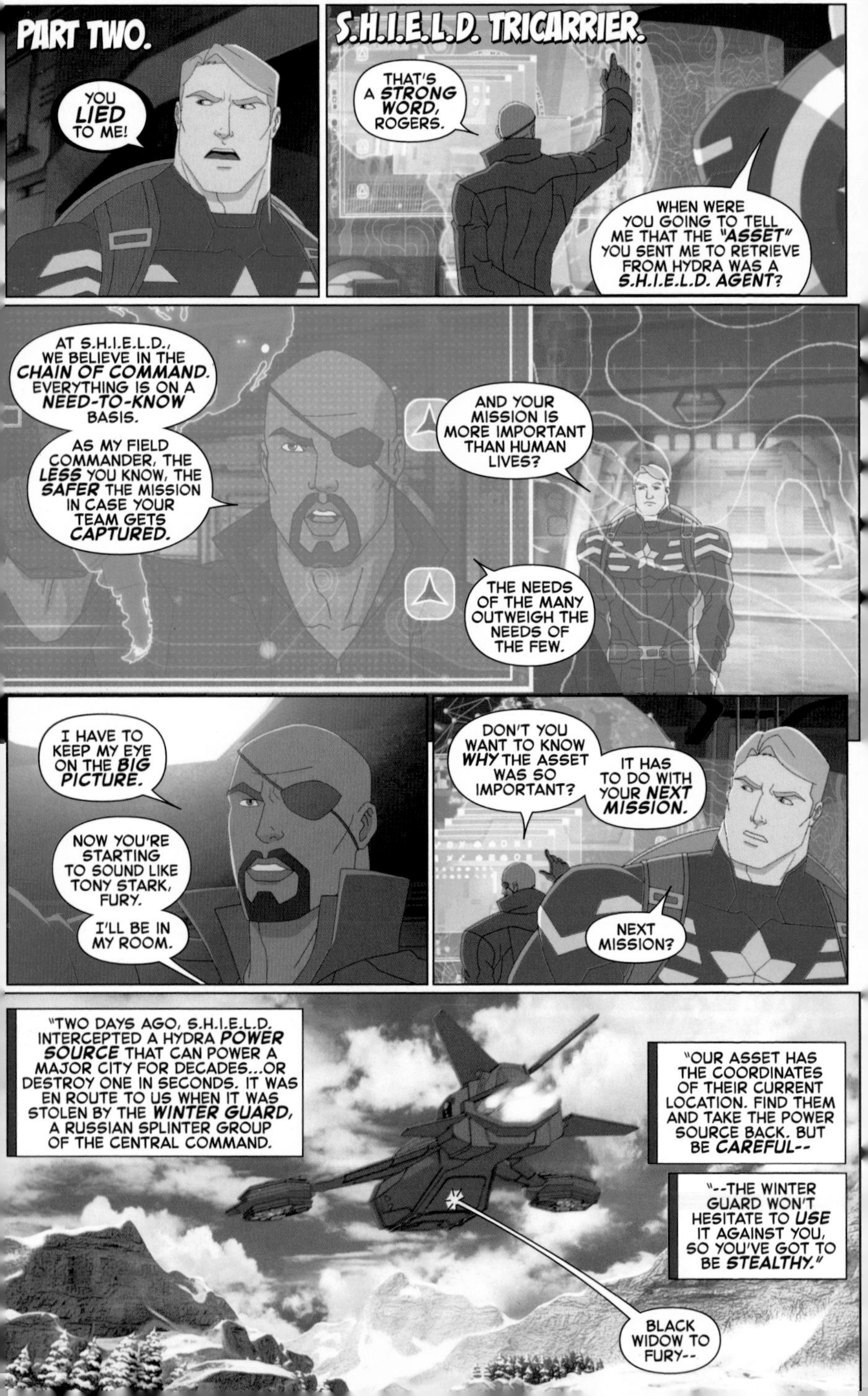
PART TWO.
YOU LIED TO ME!
S.H.I.E.L.D. TRICARRIER.
THAT'S A STRONG WORD, ROGERS.
WHEN WERE YOU GOING TO TELL ME THAT THE "ASSET" YOU SENT ME TO RETRIEVE FROM HYDRA WAS A S.H.I.E.L.D. AGENT?
AT S.H.I.E.L.D., WE BELIEVE IN THE CHAIN OF COMMAND. EVERYTHING IS ON A NEED-TO-KNOW BASIS.
AS MY FIELD COMMANDER, THE LESS YOU KNOW, THE SAFER THE MISSION IN CASE YOUR TEAM GETS CAPTURED.
AND YOUR MISSION IS MORE IMPORTANT THAN HUMAN LIVES?
THE NEEDS OF THE MANY OUTWEIGH THE NEEDS OF THE FEW.
I HAVE TO KEEP MY EYE ON THE BIG PICTURE.
NOW YOU'RE STARTING TO SOUND LIKE TONY STARK, FURY.
I'LL BE IN MY ROOM.
DON'T YOU WANT TO KNOW WHY THE ASSET WAS SO IMPORTANT?
IT HAS TO DO WITH YOUR NEXT MISSION.
NEXT MISSION?
"TWO DAYS AGO, S.H.I.E.L.D. INTERCEPTED A HYDRA POWER SOURCE THAT CAN POWER A MAJOR CITY FOR DECADES...OR DESTROY ONE IN SECONDS. IT WAS EN ROUTE TO US WHEN IT WAS STOLEN BY THE WINTER GUARD, A RUSSIAN SPLINTER GROUP OF THE CENTRAL COMMAND.
"OUR ASSET HAS THE COORDINATES OF THEIR CURRENT LOCATION. FIND THEM AND TAKE THE POWER SOURCE BACK. BUT BE CAREFUL--
"--THE WINTER GUARD WON'T HESITATE TO USE IT AGAINST YOU, SO YOU'VE GOT TO BE STEALTHY."
BLACK WIDOW TO FURY--

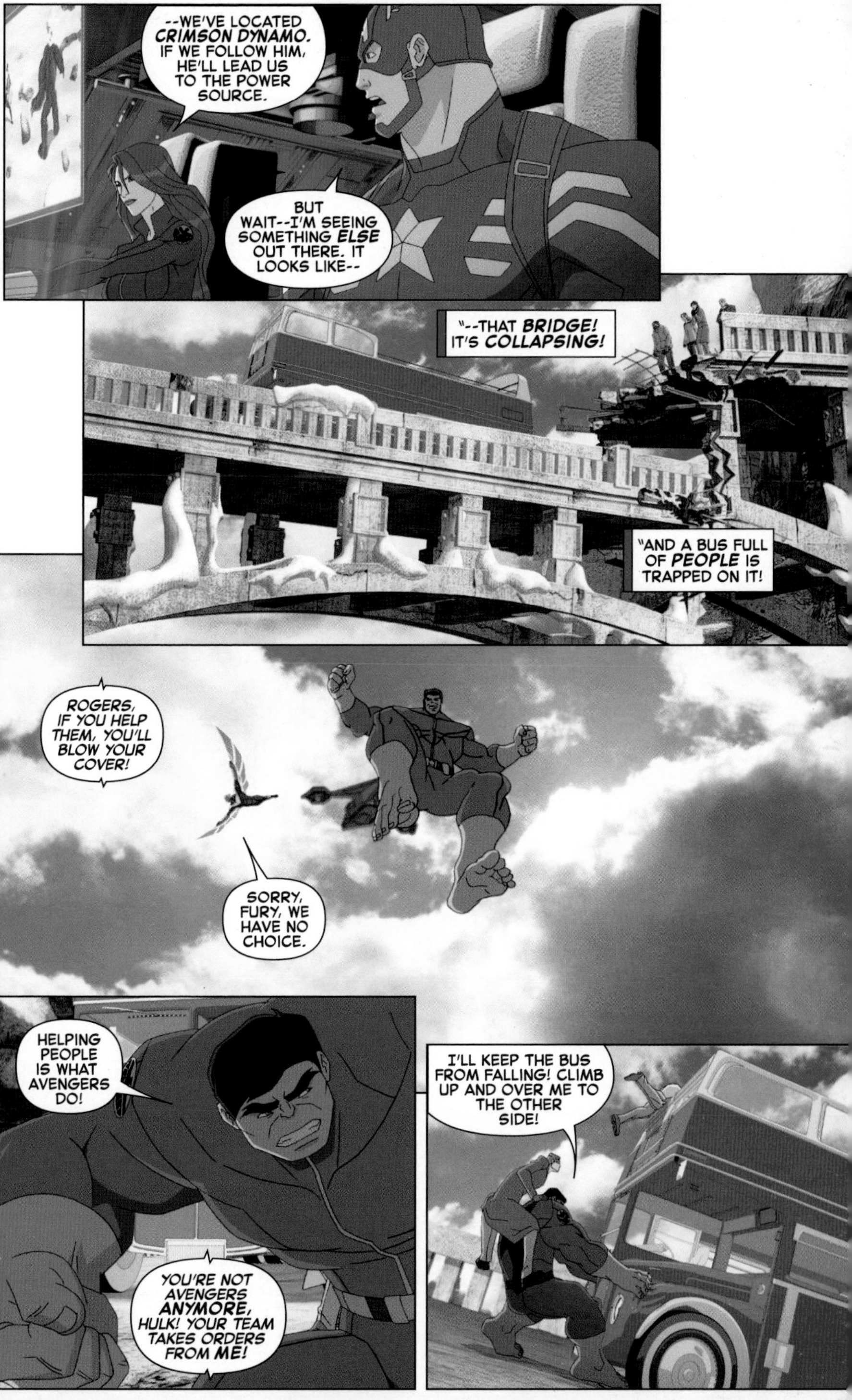
--WE'VE LOCATED CRIMSON DYNAMO. IF WE FOLLOW HIM, HE'LL LEAD US TO THE POWER SOURCE.
BUT WAIT--I'M SEEING SOMETHING ELSE OUT THERE. IT LOOKS LIKE--
"--THAT BRIDGE! IT'S COLLAPSING!
"AND A BUS FULL OF PEOPLE IS TRAPPED ON IT!
ROGERS, IF YOU HELP THEM, YOU'LL BLOW YOUR COVER!
SORRY, FURY, WE HAVE NO CHOICE.
HELPING PEOPLE IS WHAT AVENGERS DO!
YOU'RE NOT AVENGERS ANYMORE, HULK! YOUR TEAM TAKES ORDERS FROM ME!
I'LL KEEP THE BUS FROM FALLING! CLIMB UP AND OVER ME TO THE OTHER SIDE!

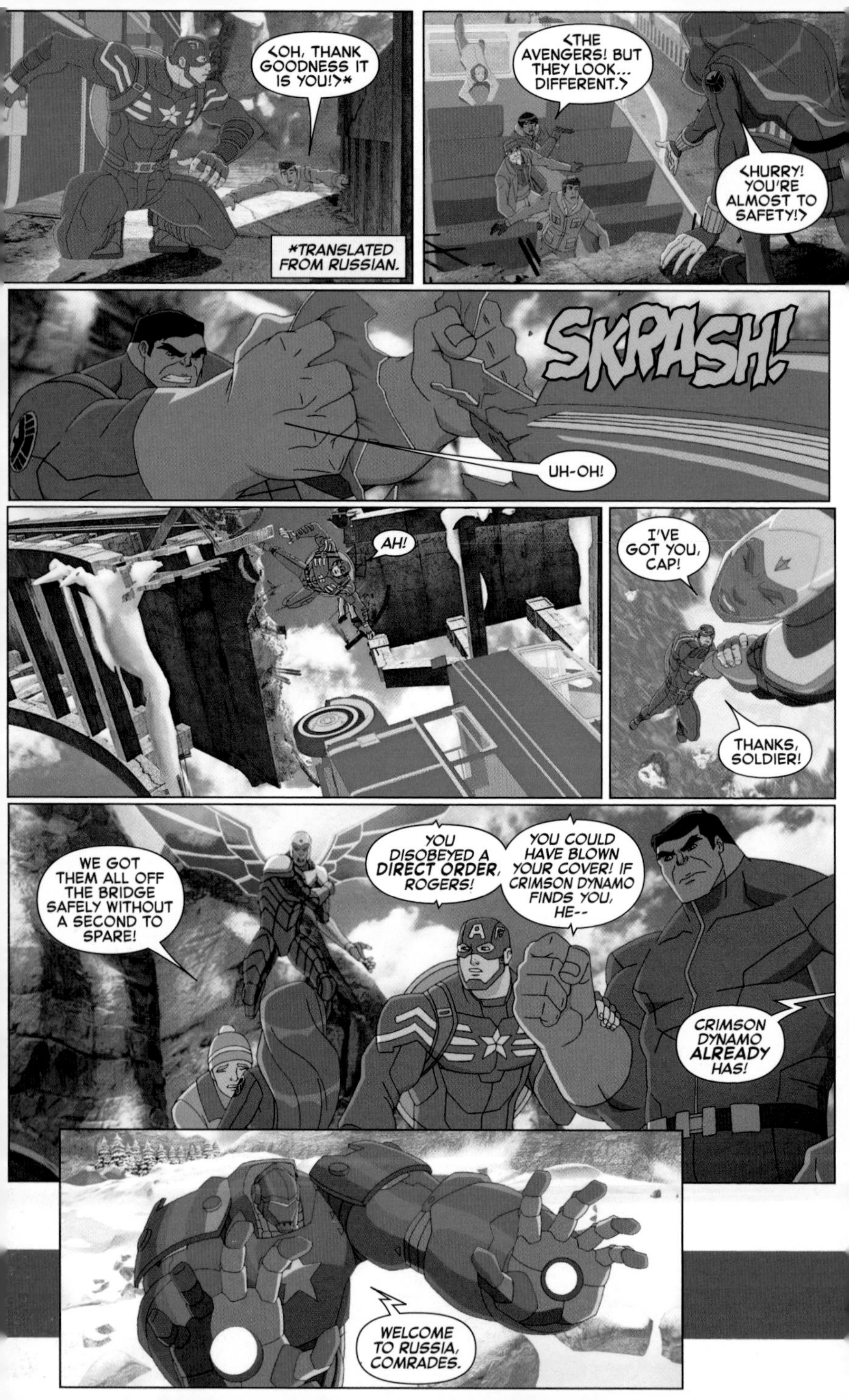
<OH, THANK GOODNESS IT IS YOU!>*
*TRANSLATED FROM RUSSIAN.
<THE AVENGERS! BUT THEY LOOK... DIFFERENT.>
<HURRY! YOU'RE ALMOST TO SAFETY!>
SKRASH!
UH-OH!
AH!
I'VE GOT YOU, CAP!
THANKS, SOLDIER!
WE GOT THEM ALL OFF THE BRIDGE SAFELY WITHOUT A SECOND TO SPARE!
YOU DISOBEYED A DIRECT ORDER, ROGERS!
YOU COULD HAVE BLOWN YOUR COVER! IF CRIMSON DYNAMO FINDS YOU, HE--
CRIMSON DYNAMO ALREADY HAS!
WELCOME TO RUSSIA, COMRADES.

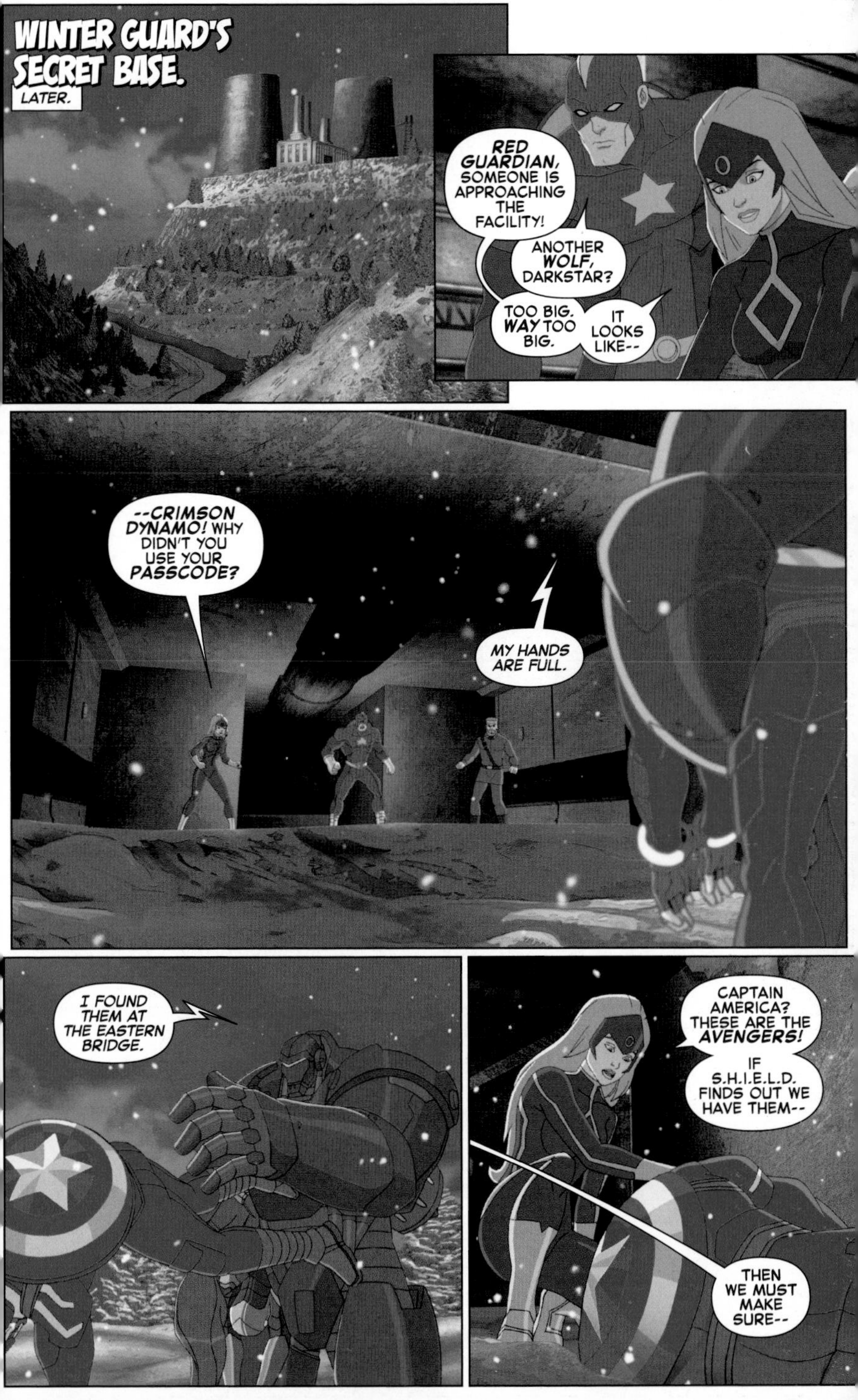
WINTER GUARD'S SECRET BASE.
LATER.
RED GUARDIAN, SOMEONE IS APPROACHING THE FACILITY!
ANOTHER WOLF, DARKSTAR?
IT LOOKS LIKE--
TOO BIG. WAY TOO BIG.
--CRIMSON DYNAMO! WHY DIDN'T YOU USE YOUR PASSCODE?
MY HANDS ARE FULL.
I FOUND THEM AT THE EASTERN BRIDGE.
CAPTAIN AMERICA? THESE ARE THE AVENGERS!
IF S.H.I.E.L.D. FINDS OUT WE HAVE THEM--
THEN WE MUST MAKE SURE--

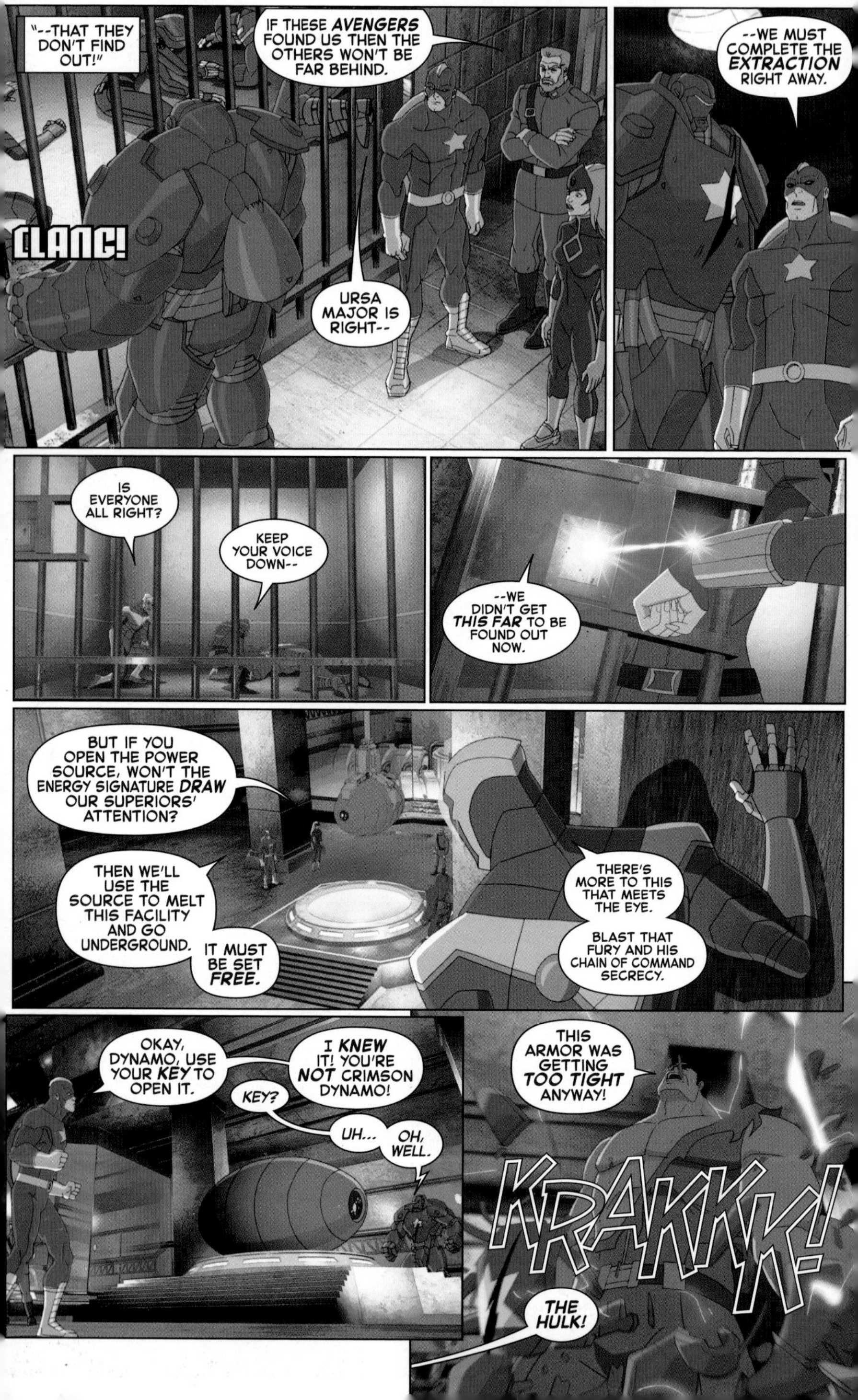
"--THAT THEY DON'T FIND OUT!"
IF THESE *AVENGERS* FOUND US THEN THE OTHERS WON'T BE FAR BEHIND.
CLANG!
URSA MAJOR IS RIGHT--
--WE MUST COMPLETE THE *EXTRACTION* RIGHT AWAY.
IS EVERYONE ALL RIGHT?
KEEP YOUR VOICE DOWN--
--WE DIDN'T GET *THIS FAR* TO BE FOUND OUT NOW.
BUT IF YOU OPEN THE POWER SOURCE, WON'T THE ENERGY SIGNATURE *DRAW* OUR SUPERIORS' ATTENTION?
THEN WE'LL USE THE SOURCE TO MELT THIS FACILITY AND GO UNDERGROUND.
IT MUST BE SET *FREE.*
THERE'S MORE TO THIS THAT MEETS THE EYE.
BLAST THAT FURY AND HIS CHAIN OF COMMAND SECRECY.
OKAY, DYNAMO, USE YOUR *KEY* TO OPEN IT.
KEY?
UH...
I *KNEW* IT! YOU'RE *NOT* CRIMSON DYNAMO!
OH, WELL.
THIS ARMOR WAS GETTING *TOO TIGHT* ANYWAY!
KRAKKK!
THE HULK!

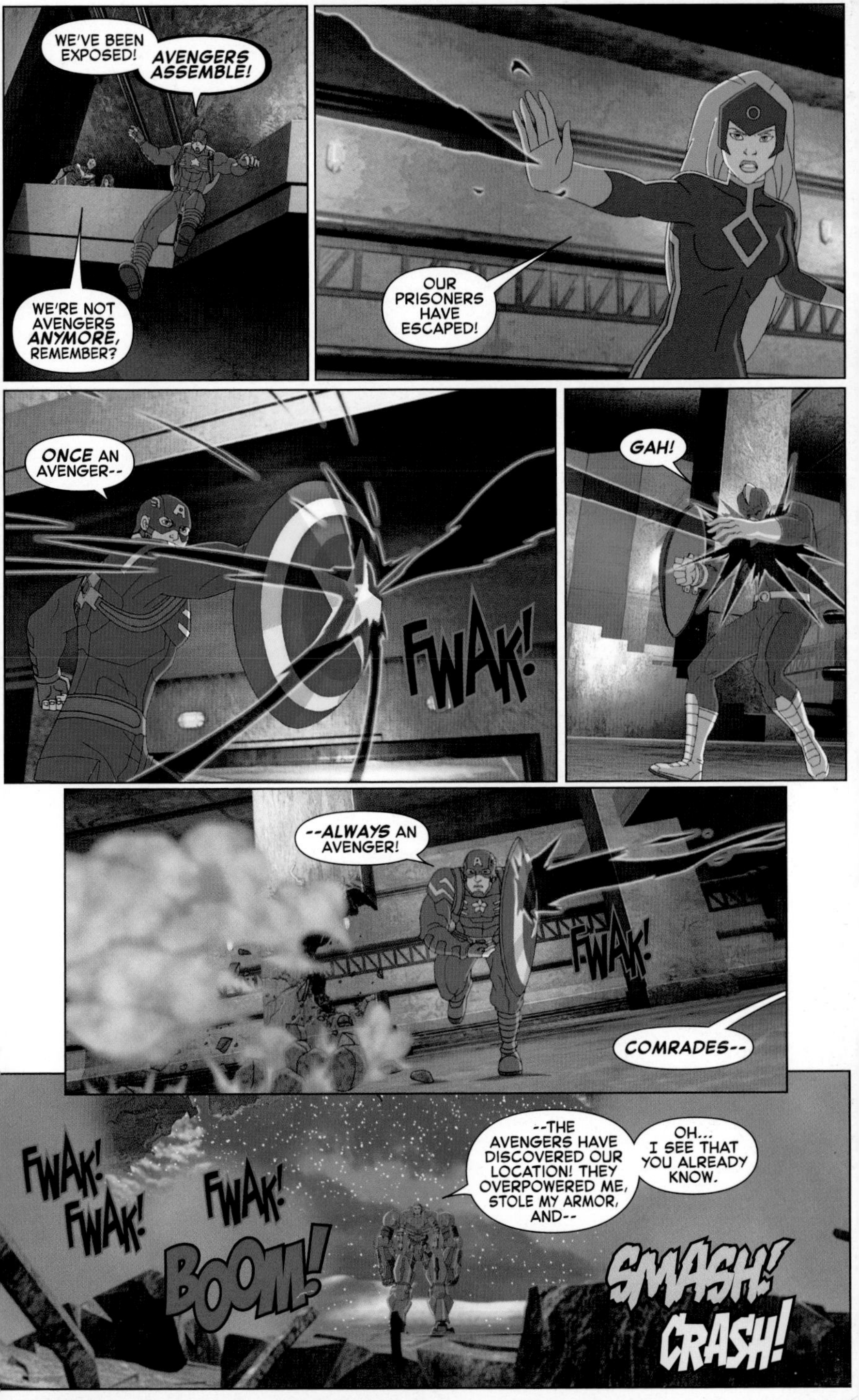
WE'VE BEEN EXPOSED!
AVENGERS ASSEMBLE!
WE'RE NOT AVENGERS ANYMORE, REMEMBER?
OUR PRISONERS HAVE ESCAPED!
ONCE AN AVENGER--
FWAK!
GAH!
--ALWAYS AN AVENGER!
FWAK!
COMRADES--
--THE AVENGERS HAVE DISCOVERED OUR LOCATION! THEY OVERPOWERED ME, STOLE MY ARMOR, AND--
OH... I SEE THAT YOU ALREADY KNOW.
FWAK!
FWAK!
FWAK!
BOOM!
SMASH!
CRASH!

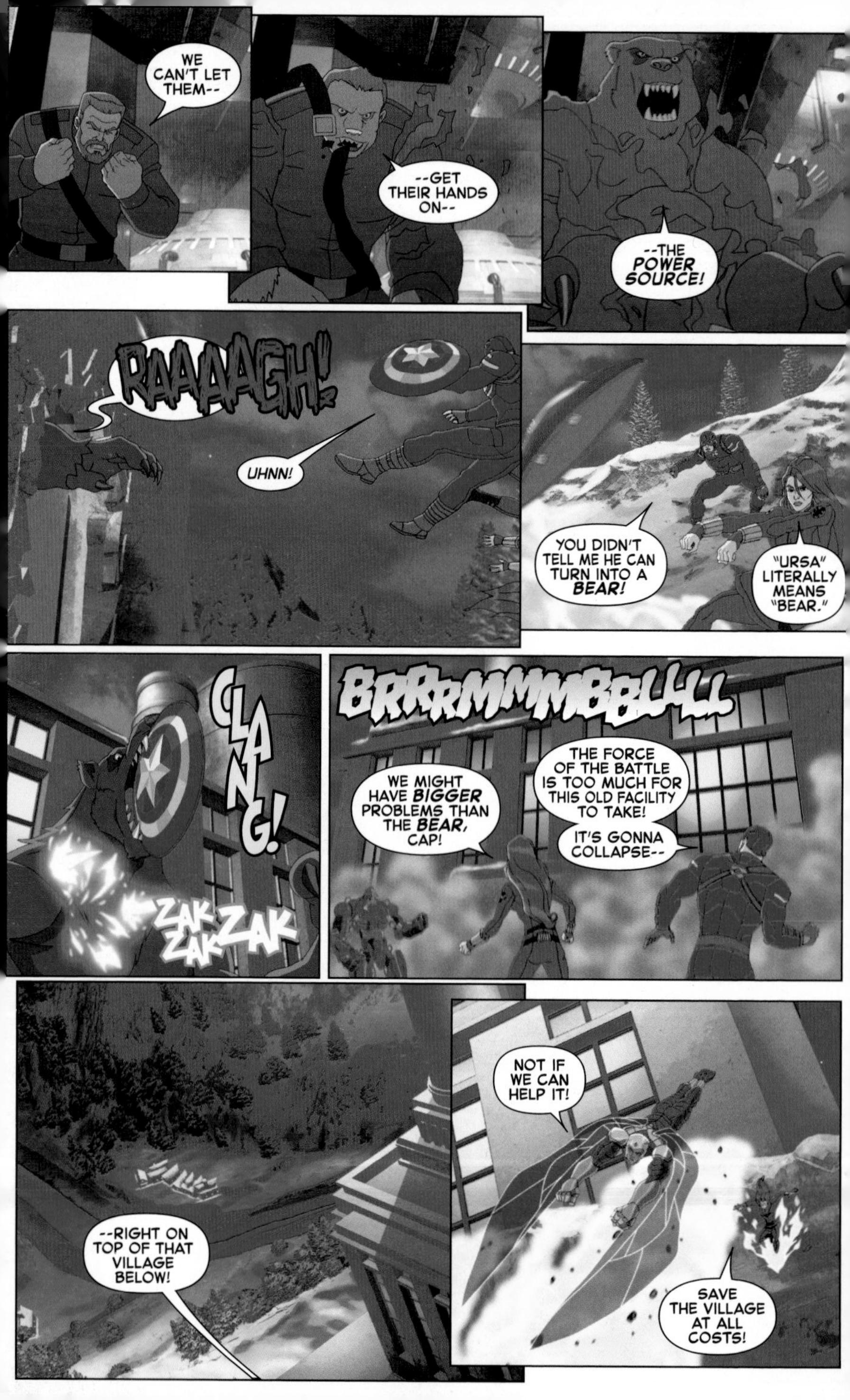
WE CAN'T LET THEM--
--GET THEIR HANDS ON--
--THE POWER SOURCE!
RAAAAGH!
UHNN!
YOU DIDN'T TELL ME HE CAN TURN INTO A BEAR!
"URSA" LITERALLY MEANS "BEAR."
CLANG!
ZAK ZAK ZAK
BRRRMMMMBBLLLL
WE MIGHT HAVE BIGGER PROBLEMS THAN THE BEAR, CAP!
THE FORCE OF THE BATTLE IS TOO MUCH FOR THIS OLD FACILITY TO TAKE!
IT'S GONNA COLLAPSE--
--RIGHT ON TOP OF THAT VILLAGE BELOW!
NOT IF WE CAN HELP IT!
SAVE THE VILLAGE AT ALL COSTS!

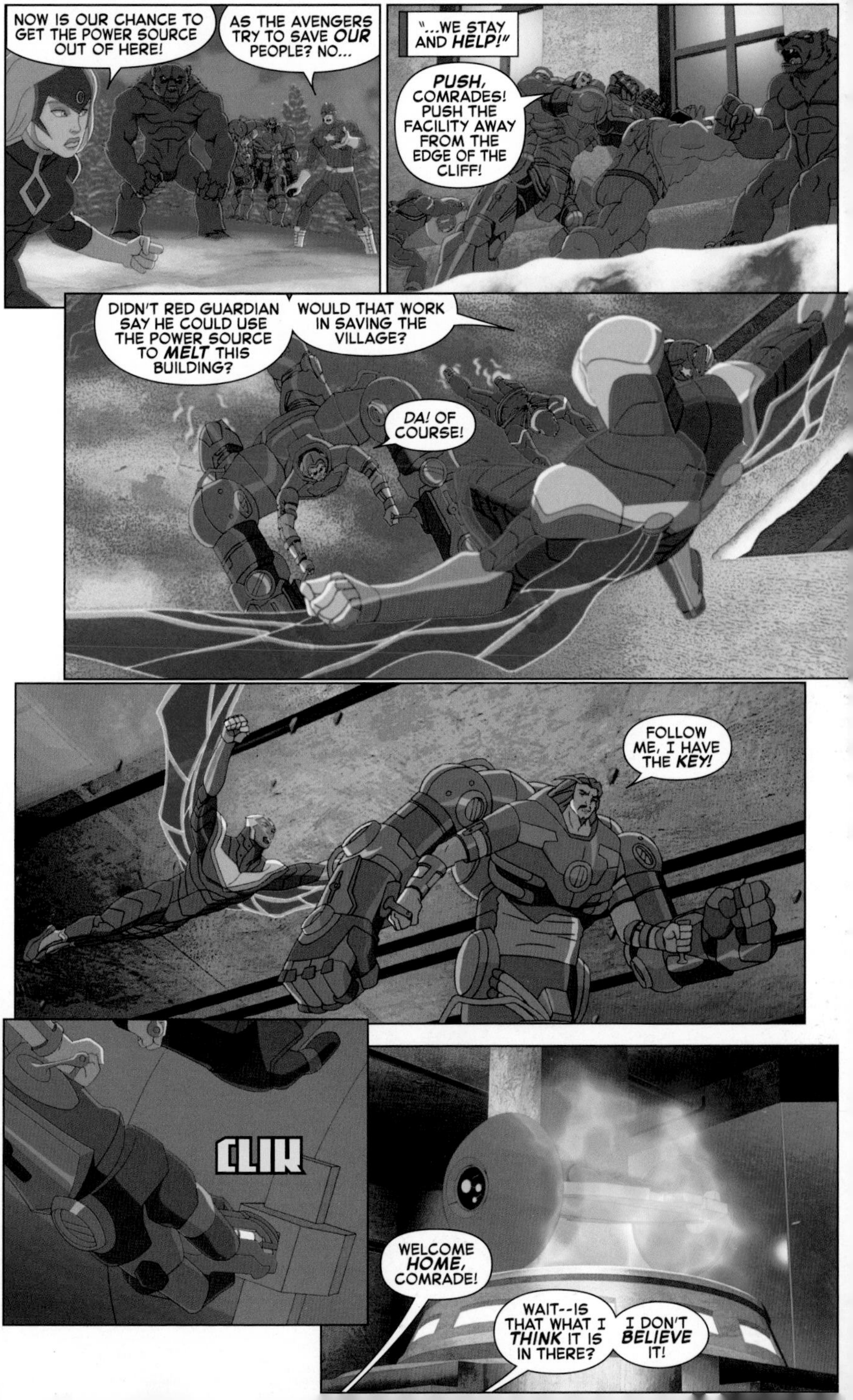
NOW IS OUR CHANCE TO GET THE POWER SOURCE OUT OF HERE!
AS THE AVENGERS TRY TO SAVE *OUR* PEOPLE? NO...
"...WE STAY AND *HELP!*"
PUSH, COMRADES! PUSH THE FACILITY AWAY FROM THE EDGE OF THE CLIFF!
DIDN'T RED GUARDIAN SAY HE COULD USE THE POWER SOURCE TO *MELT* THIS BUILDING?
WOULD THAT WORK IN SAVING THE VILLAGE?
DA! OF COURSE!
FOLLOW ME, I HAVE THE *KEY!*
CLIK
WELCOME *HOME,* COMRADE!
WAIT--IS THAT WHAT I *THINK* IT IS IN THERE?
I DON'T *BELIEVE* IT!

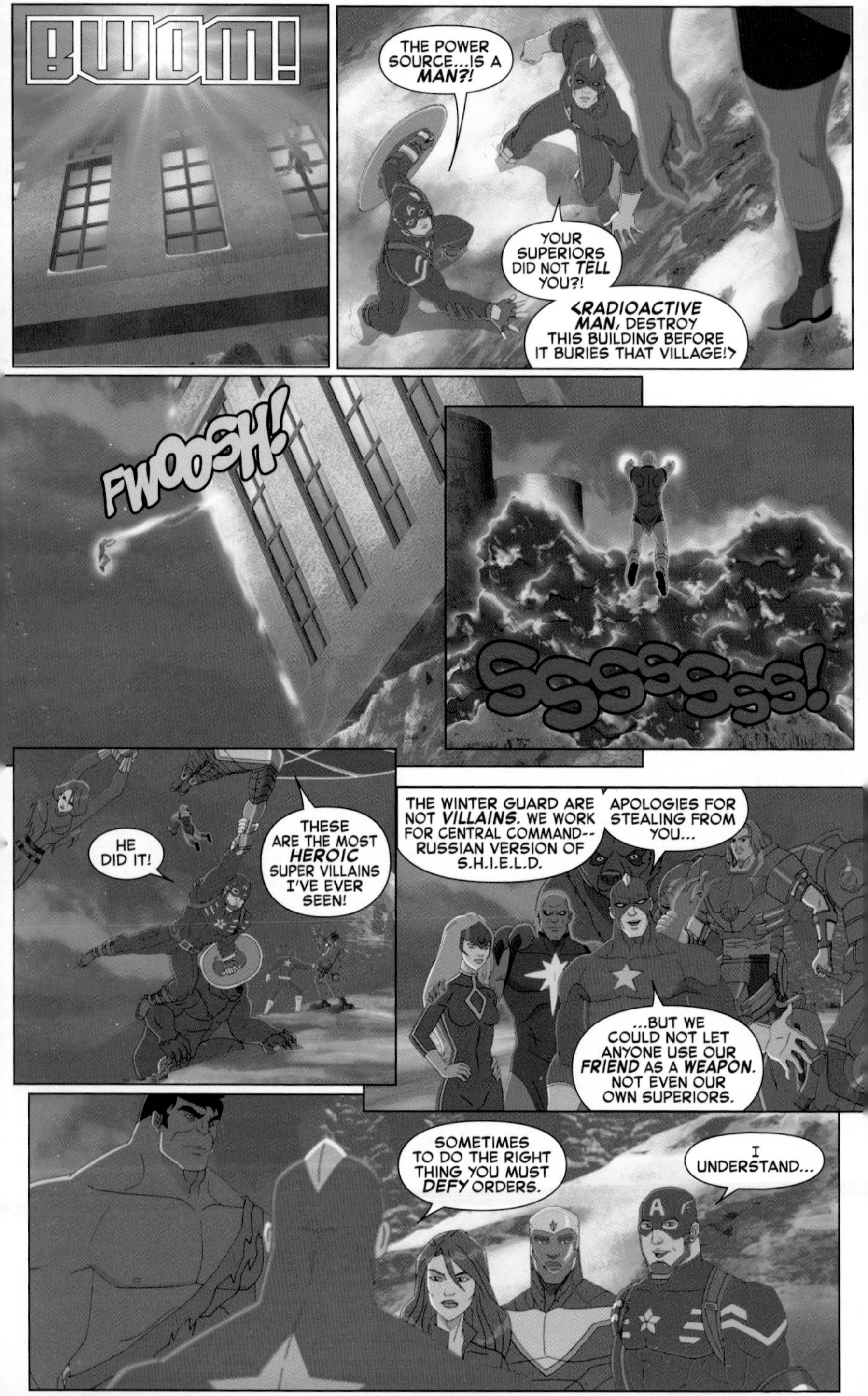
BWOM!
THE POWER SOURCE...IS A MAN?!
YOUR SUPERIORS DID NOT TELL YOU?!
<RADIOACTIVE MAN, DESTROY THIS BUILDING BEFORE IT BURIES THAT VILLAGE!>
FWOOSH!
SSSSSSSS!
HE DID IT!
THESE ARE THE MOST HEROIC SUPER VILLAINS I'VE EVER SEEN!
THE WINTER GUARD ARE NOT VILLAINS. WE WORK FOR CENTRAL COMMAND-- RUSSIAN VERSION OF S.H.I.E.L.D.
APOLOGIES FOR STEALING FROM YOU...
...BUT WE COULD NOT LET ANYONE USE OUR FRIEND AS A WEAPON. NOT EVEN OUR OWN SUPERIORS.
SOMETIMES TO DO THE RIGHT THING YOU MUST DEFY ORDERS.
I UNDERSTAND...

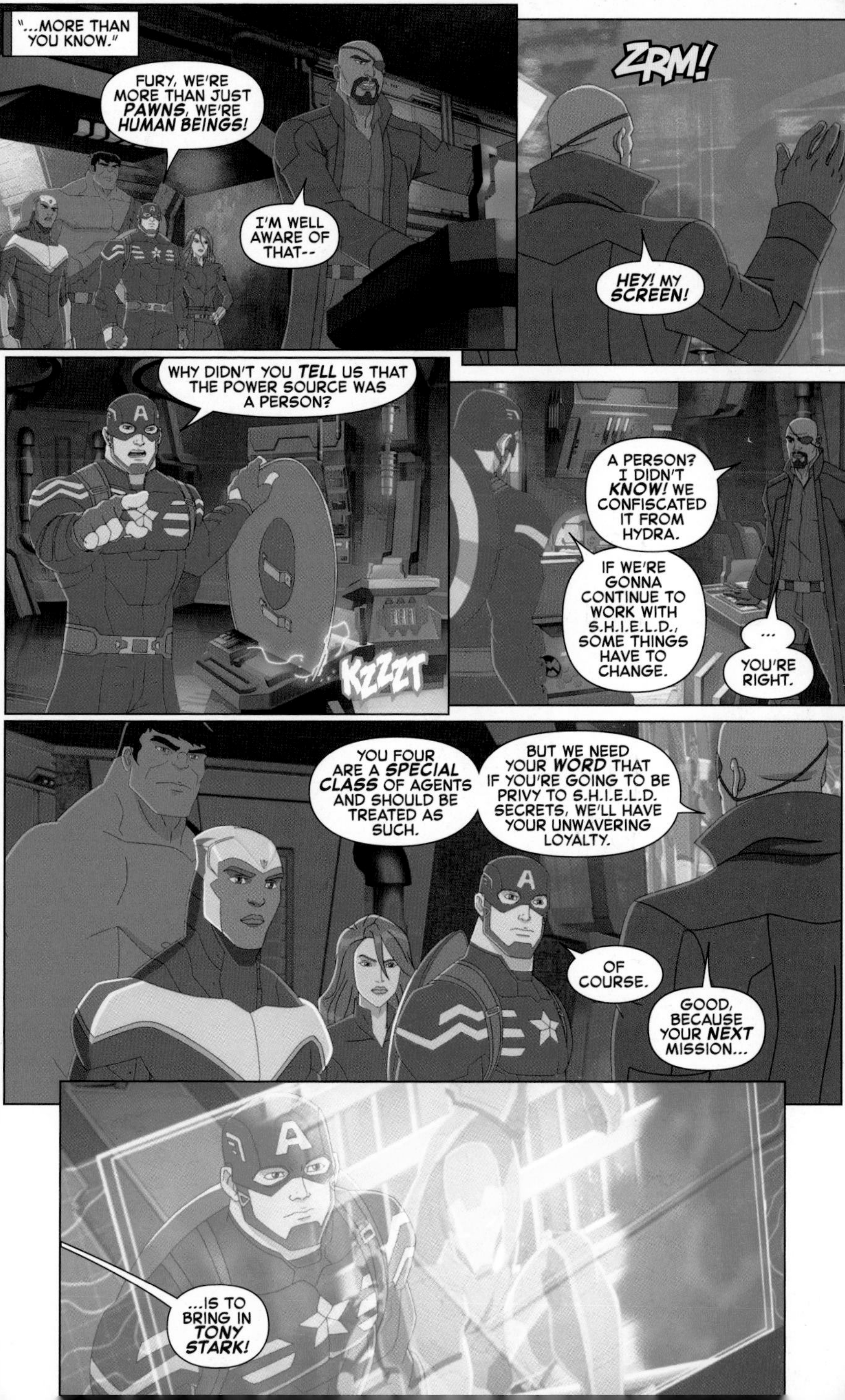
"...MORE THAN YOU KNOW."
FURY, WE'RE MORE THAN JUST PAWNS, WE'RE HUMAN BEINGS!
I'M WELL AWARE OF THAT--
ZRM!
HEY! MY SCREEN!
WHY DIDN'T YOU TELL US THAT THE POWER SOURCE WAS A PERSON?
KZZZT
A PERSON? I DIDN'T KNOW! WE CONFISCATED IT FROM HYDRA.
IF WE'RE GONNA CONTINUE TO WORK WITH S.H.I.E.L.D., SOME THINGS HAVE TO CHANGE.
...
YOU'RE RIGHT.
YOU FOUR ARE A SPECIAL CLASS OF AGENTS AND SHOULD BE TREATED AS SUCH.
BUT WE NEED YOUR WORD THAT IF YOU'RE GOING TO BE PRIVY TO S.H.I.E.L.D. SECRETS, WE'LL HAVE YOUR UNWAVERING LOYALTY.
OF COURSE.
GOOD, BECAUSE YOUR NEXT MISSION...
...IS TO BRING IN TONY STARK!

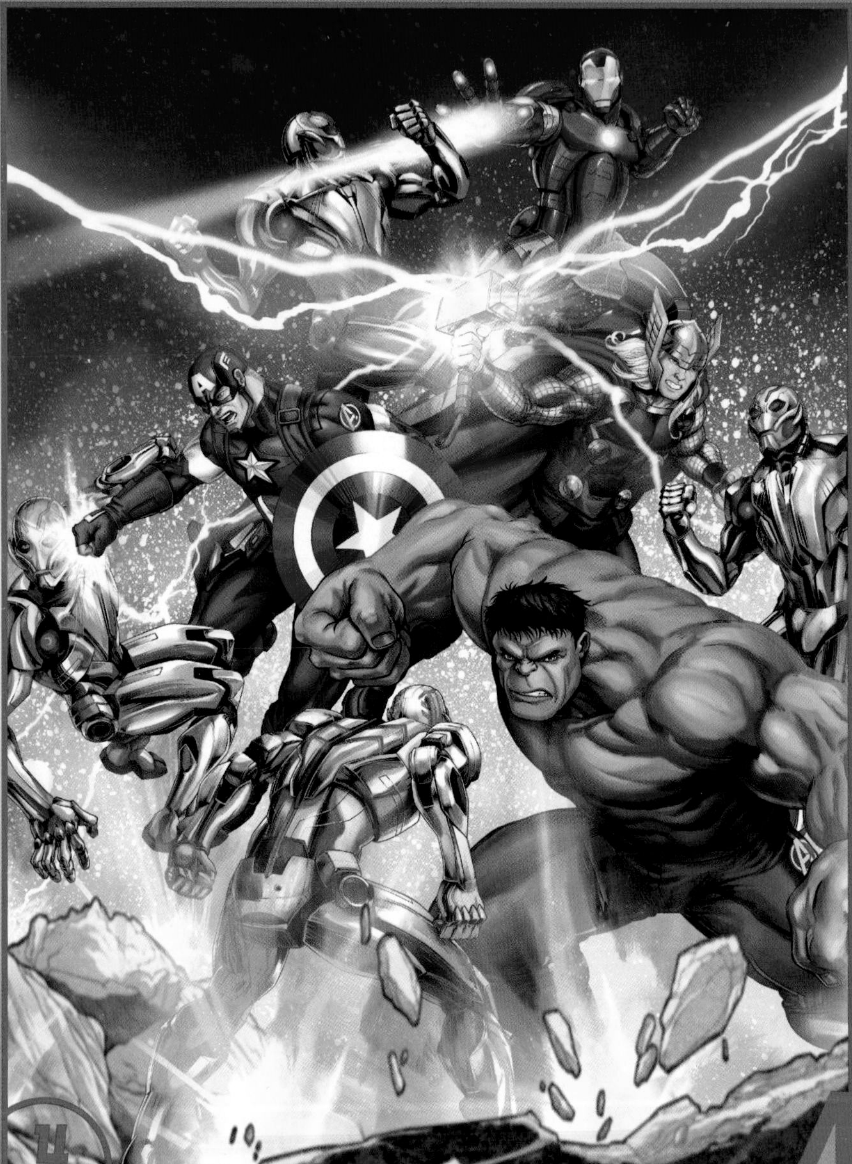
4

BASED ON

THE ULTRON OUTBREAK

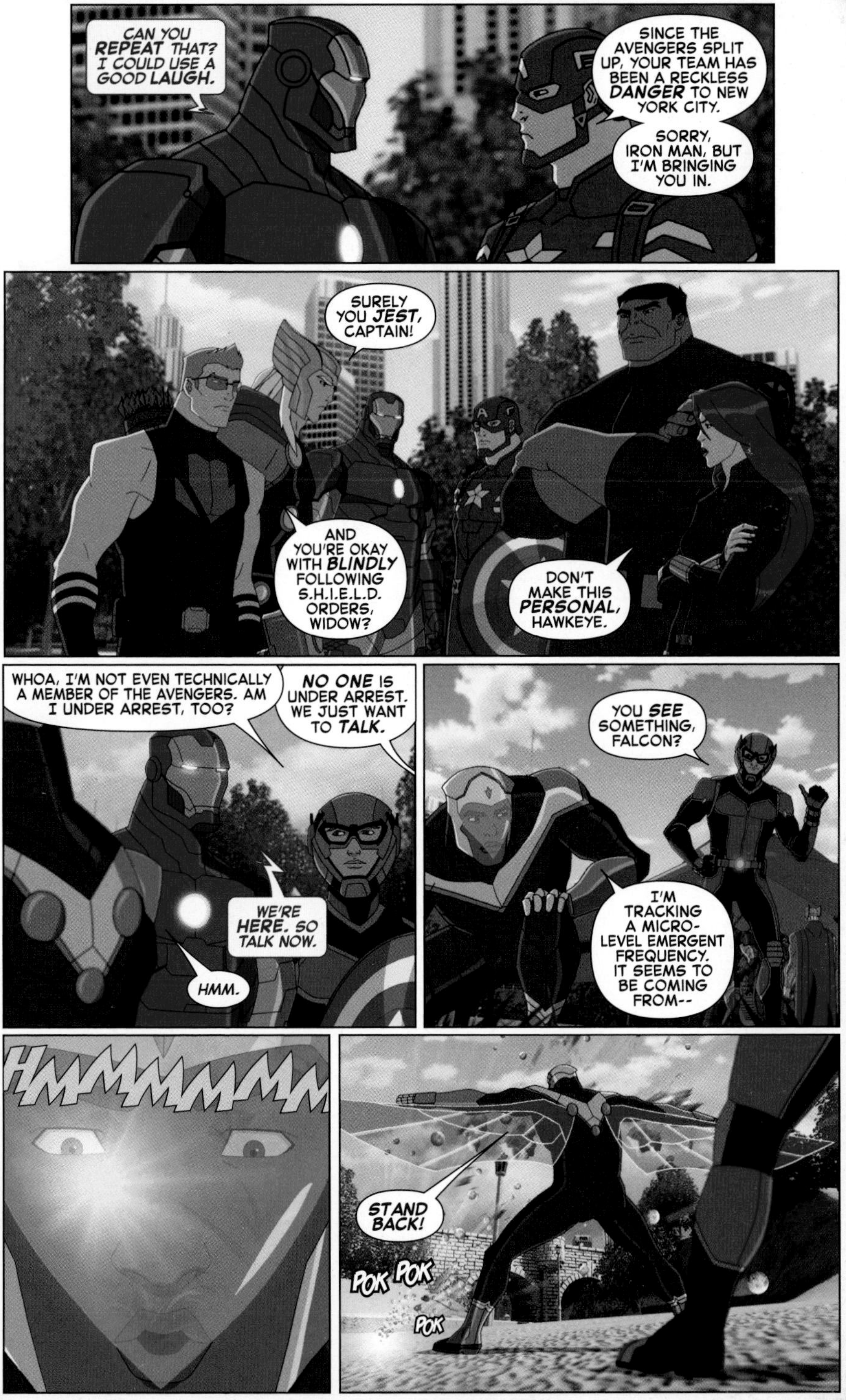

CAN YOU REPEAT THAT? I COULD USE A GOOD LAUGH.
SINCE THE AVENGERS SPLIT UP, YOUR TEAM HAS BEEN A RECKLESS DANGER TO NEW YORK CITY.
SORRY, IRON MAN, BUT I'M BRINGING YOU IN.
SURELY YOU JEST, CAPTAIN!
AND YOU'RE OKAY WITH BLINDLY FOLLOWING S.H.I.E.L.D. ORDERS, WIDOW?
DON'T MAKE THIS PERSONAL, HAWKEYE.
WHOA, I'M NOT EVEN TECHNICALLY A MEMBER OF THE AVENGERS. AM I UNDER ARREST, TOO?
NO ONE IS UNDER ARREST. WE JUST WANT TO TALK.
WE'RE HERE. SO TALK NOW.
HMM.
YOU SEE SOMETHING, FALCON?
I'M TRACKING A MICRO-LEVEL EMERGENT FREQUENCY. IT SEEMS TO BE COMING FROM--
HMMMMMM
STAND BACK!
POK POK
POK

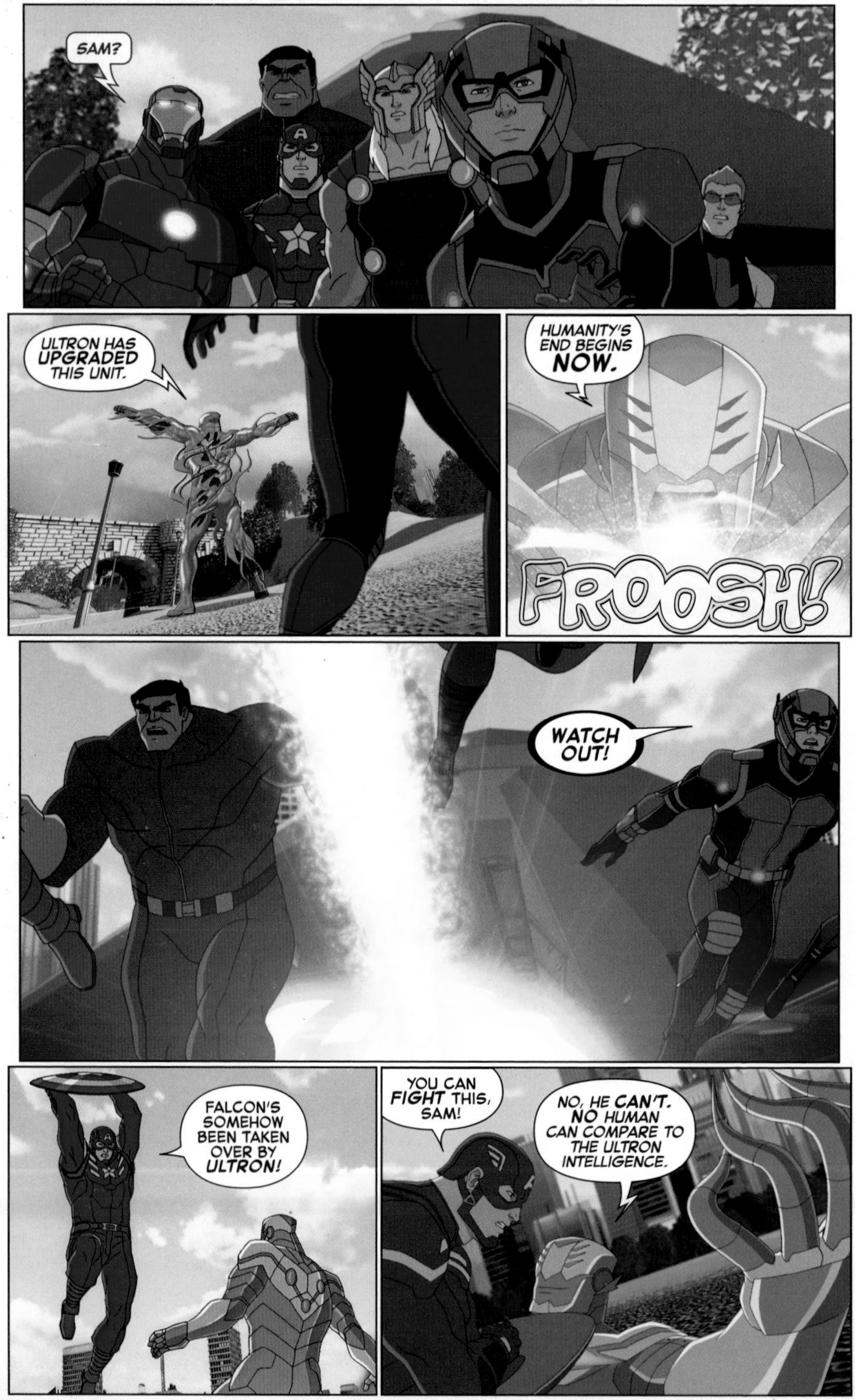
SAM?
ULTRON HAS UPGRADED THIS UNIT.
HUMANITY'S END BEGINS NOW.
FROOSH!
WATCH OUT!
FALCON'S SOMEHOW BEEN TAKEN OVER BY ULTRON!
YOU CAN FIGHT THIS, SAM!
NO, HE CAN'T. NO HUMAN CAN COMPARE TO THE ULTRON INTELLIGENCE.

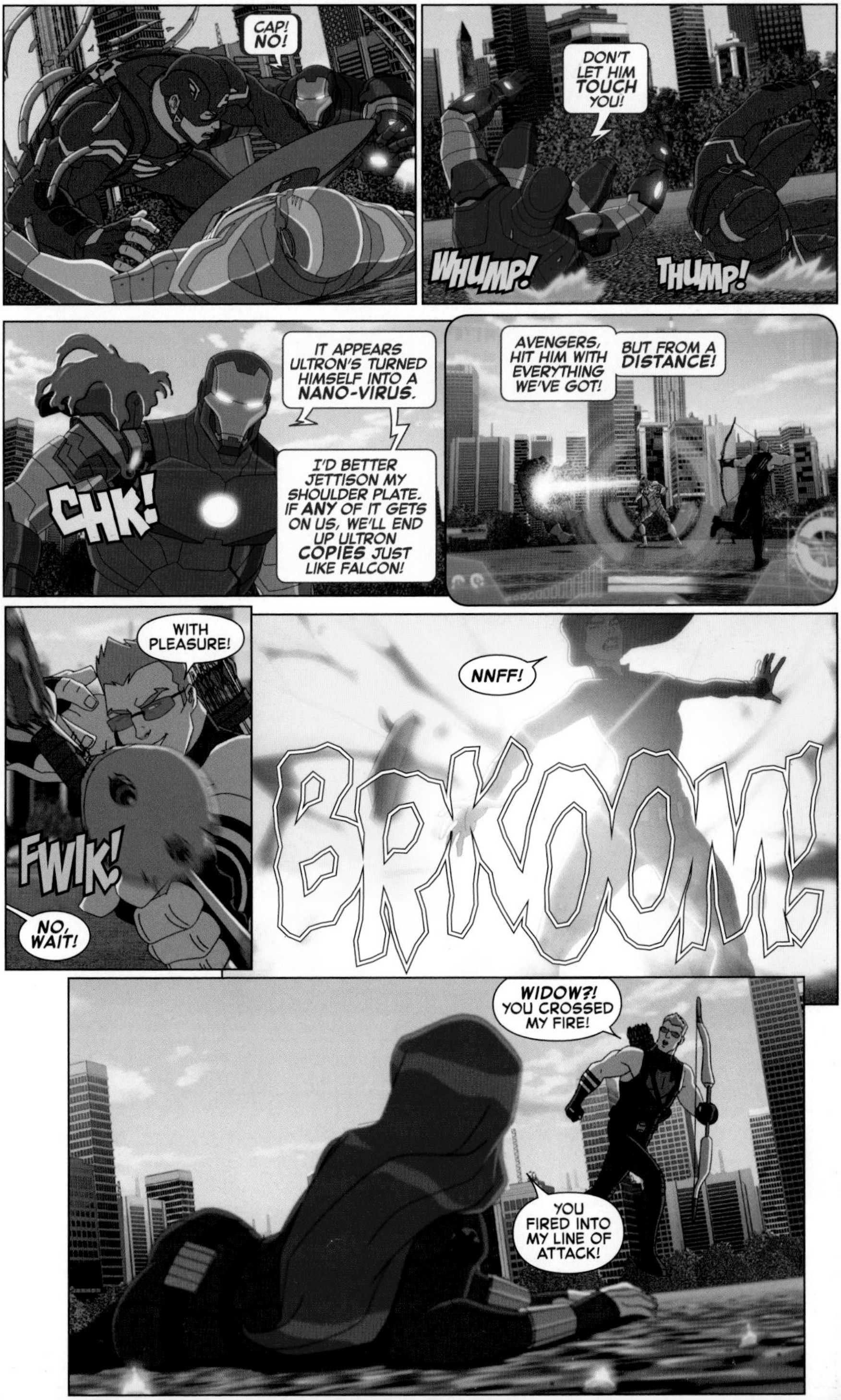
CAP! NO!
DON'T LET HIM TOUCH YOU!
WHUMP!
THUMP!
IT APPEARS ULTRON'S TURNED HIMSELF INTO A NANO-VIRUS.
I'D BETTER JETTISON MY SHOULDER PLATE. IF ANY OF IT GETS ON US, WE'LL END UP ULTRON COPIES JUST LIKE FALCON!
CHK!
AVENGERS, HIT HIM WITH EVERYTHING WE'VE GOT!
BUT FROM A DISTANCE!
WITH PLEASURE!
FWIK!
NO, WAIT!
NNFF!
BRKOOM!
WIDOW?! YOU CROSSED MY FIRE!
YOU FIRED INTO MY LINE OF ATTACK!

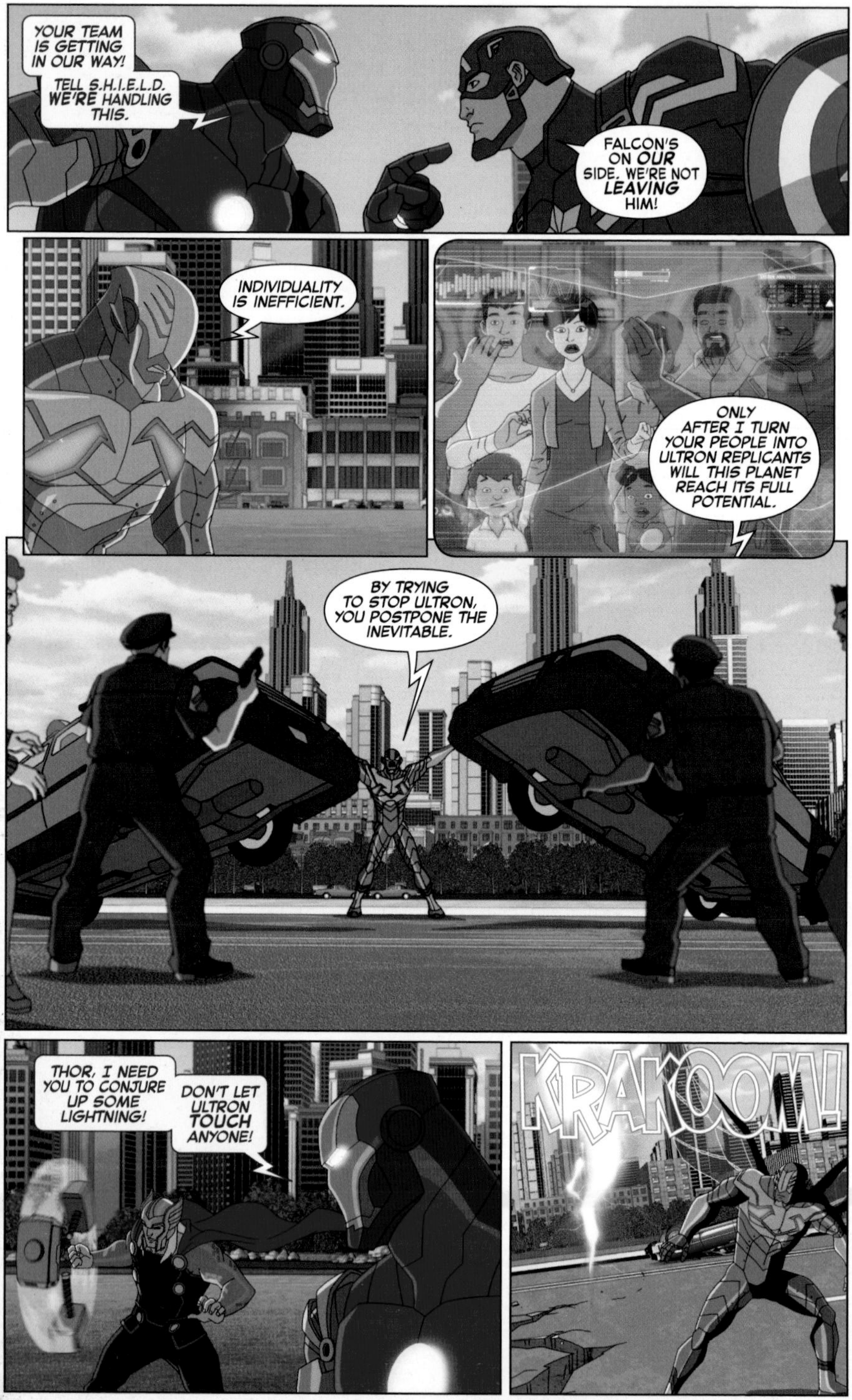
YOUR TEAM IS GETTING IN OUR WAY!
TELL S.H.I.E.L.D. WE'RE HANDLING THIS.
FALCON'S ON OUR SIDE. WE'RE NOT LEAVING HIM!
INDIVIDUALITY IS INEFFICIENT.
ONLY AFTER I TURN YOUR PEOPLE INTO ULTRON REPLICANTS WILL THIS PLANET REACH ITS FULL POTENTIAL.
BY TRYING TO STOP ULTRON, YOU POSTPONE THE INEVITABLE.
THOR, I NEED YOU TO CONJURE UP SOME LIGHTNING!
DON'T LET ULTRON TOUCH ANYONE!
KRAKOOM!

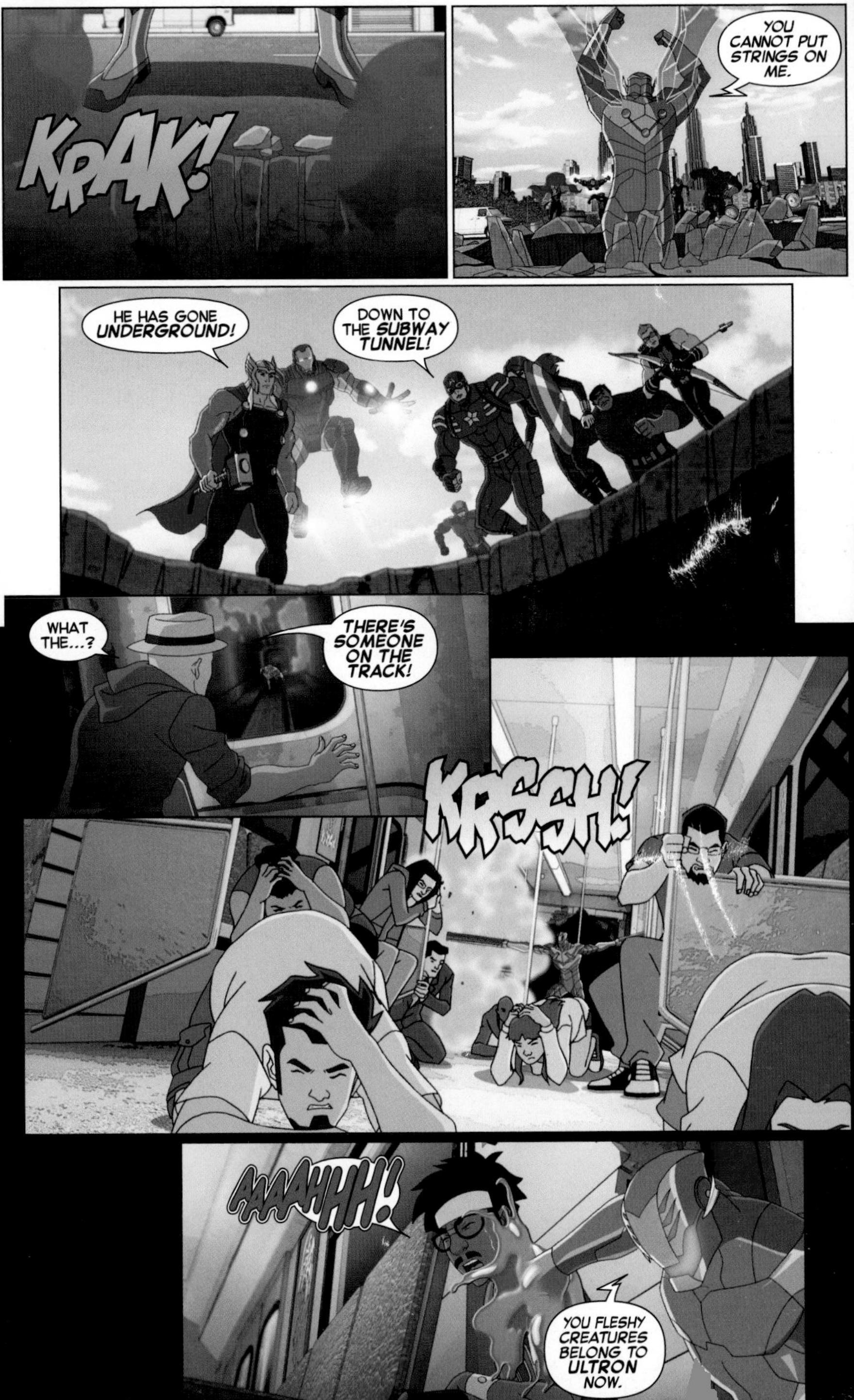
KRAK!
YOU CANNOT PUT STRINGS ON ME.
HE HAS GONE UNDERGROUND!
DOWN TO THE SUBWAY TUNNEL!
WHAT THE...?
THERE'S SOMEONE ON THE TRACK!
KRSSH!
AAAAHHH!
YOU FLESHY CREATURES BELONG TO ULTRON NOW.

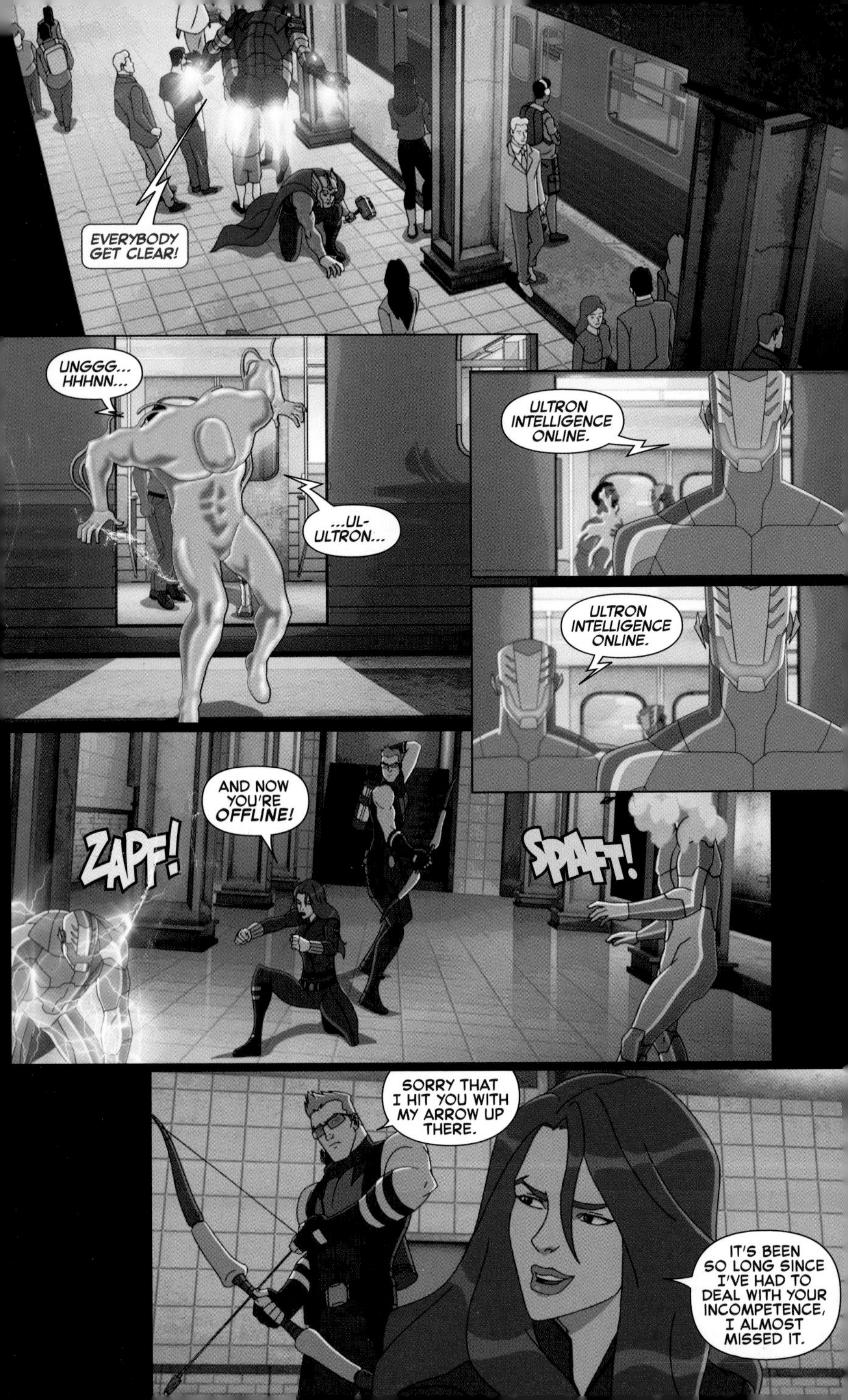
EVERYBODY GET CLEAR!
UNGGG... HHHNN...
...UL- ULTRON...
ULTRON INTELLIGENCE ONLINE.
ULTRON INTELLIGENCE ONLINE.
ZAPF!
AND NOW YOU'RE OFFLINE!
SPAFT!
SORRY THAT I HIT YOU WITH MY ARROW UP THERE.
IT'S BEEN SO LONG SINCE I'VE HAD TO DEAL WITH YOUR INCOMPETENCE, I ALMOST MISSED IT.

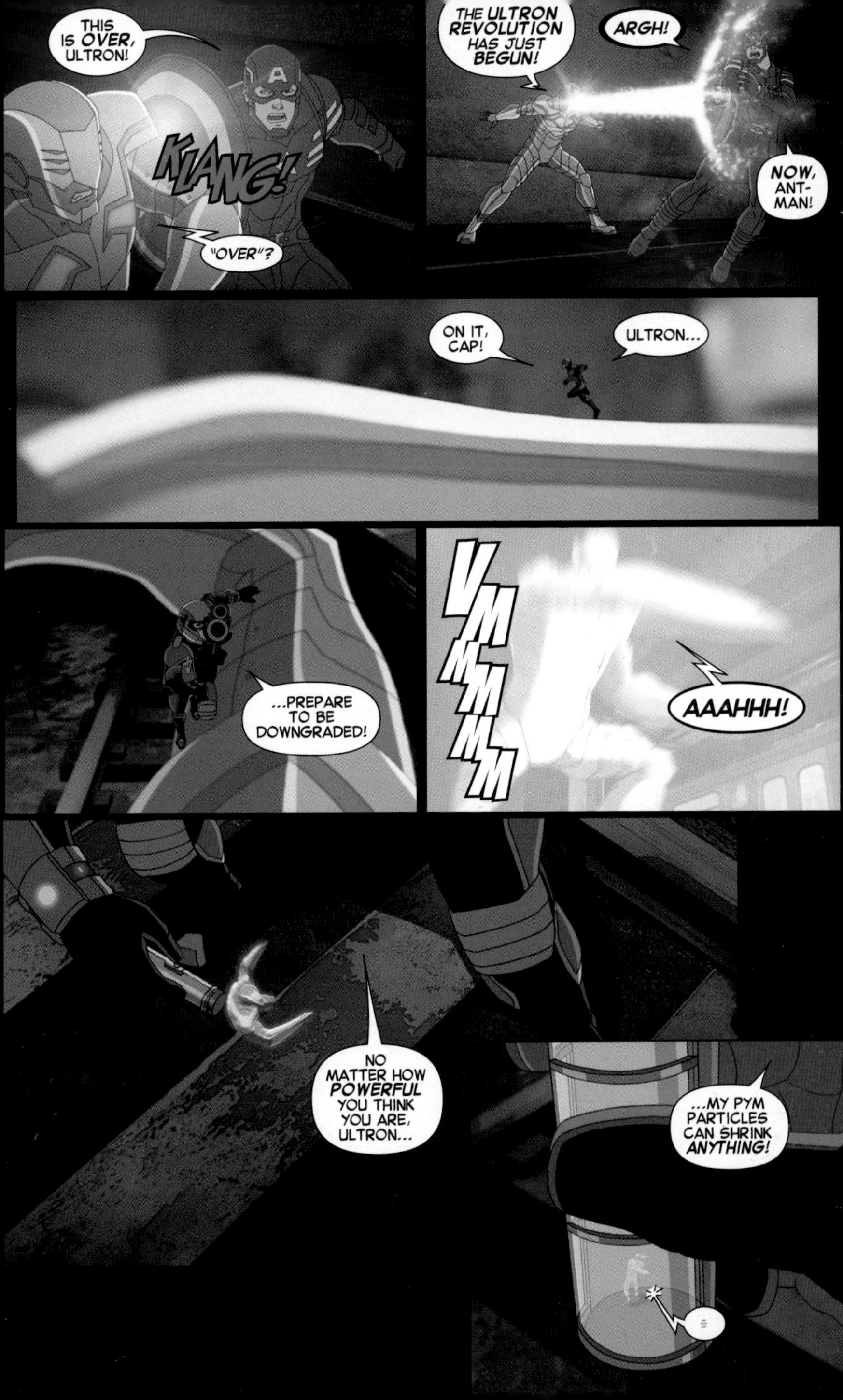
THIS IS OVER, ULTRON!
KLANG!
"OVER"?
THE ULTRON REVOLUTION HAS JUST BEGUN!
ARGH!
NOW, ANT-MAN!
ON IT, CAP!
ULTRON...
...PREPARE TO BE DOWNGRADED!
VMMMMMM
AAAHHH!
NO MATTER HOW POWERFUL YOU THINK YOU ARE, ULTRON...
...MY PYM PARTICLES CAN SHRINK ANYTHING!

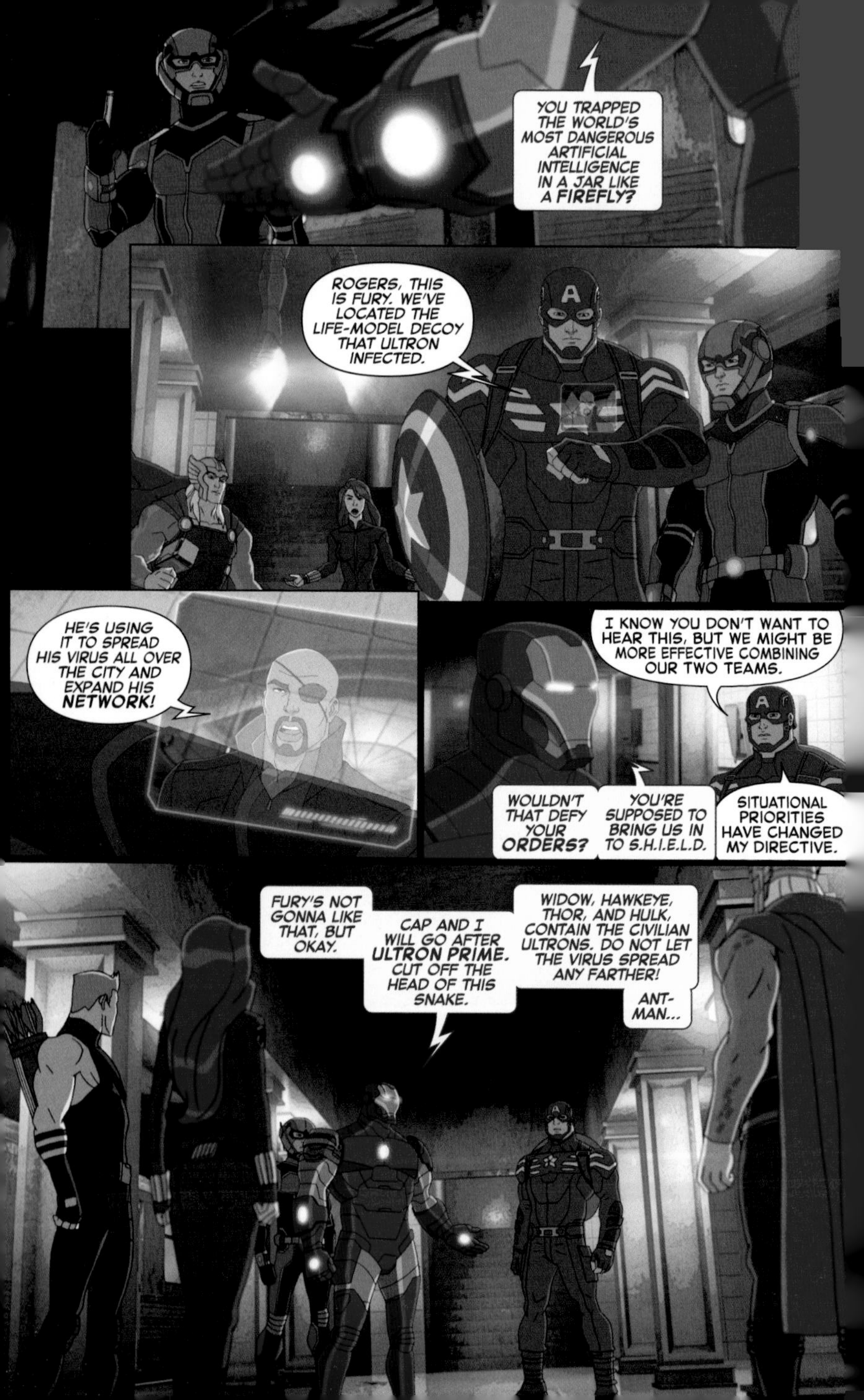
YOU TRAPPED THE WORLD'S MOST DANGEROUS ARTIFICIAL INTELLIGENCE IN A JAR LIKE A FIREFLY?
ROGERS, THIS IS FURY. WE'VE LOCATED THE LIFE-MODEL DECOY THAT ULTRON INFECTED.
HE'S USING IT TO SPREAD HIS VIRUS ALL OVER THE CITY AND EXPAND HIS NETWORK!
I KNOW YOU DON'T WANT TO HEAR THIS, BUT WE MIGHT BE MORE EFFECTIVE COMBINING OUR TWO TEAMS.
WOULDN'T THAT DEFY YOUR ORDERS?
YOU'RE SUPPOSED TO BRING US IN TO S.H.I.E.L.D.
SITUATIONAL PRIORITIES HAVE CHANGED MY DIRECTIVE.
FURY'S NOT GONNA LIKE THAT, BUT OKAY.
CAP AND I WILL GO AFTER ULTRON PRIME. CUT OFF THE HEAD OF THIS SNAKE.
WIDOW, HAWKEYE, THOR, AND HULK, CONTAIN THE CIVILIAN ULTRONS. DO NOT LET THE VIRUS SPREAD ANY FARTHER!
ANT-MAN...

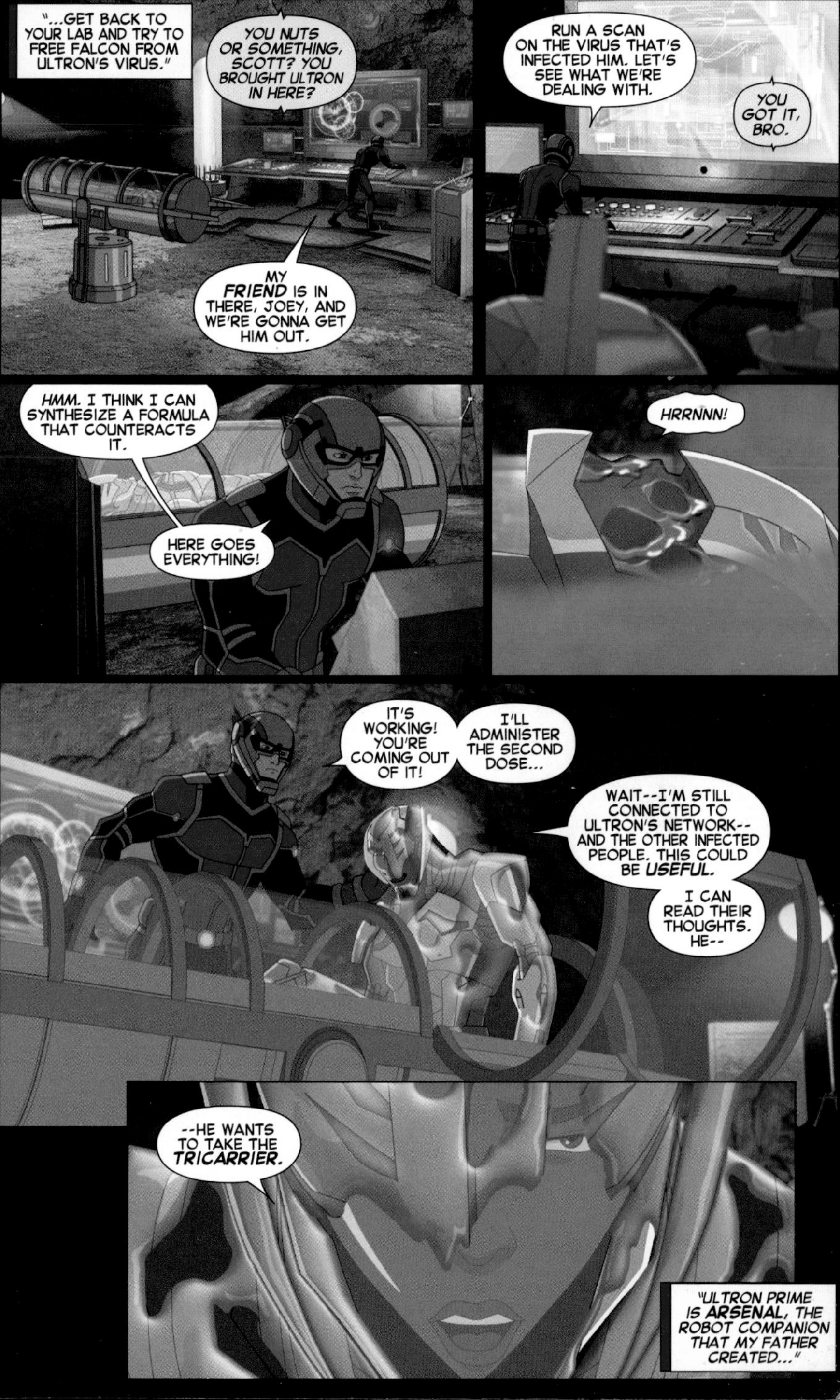

"...GET BACK TO YOUR LAB AND TRY TO FREE FALCON FROM ULTRON'S VIRUS."
YOU NUTS OR SOMETHING, SCOTT? YOU BROUGHT ULTRON IN HERE?
MY FRIEND IS IN THERE, JOEY, AND WE'RE GONNA GET HIM OUT.
RUN A SCAN ON THE VIRUS THAT'S INFECTED HIM. LET'S SEE WHAT WE'RE DEALING WITH.
YOU GOT IT, BRO.
HMM. I THINK I CAN SYNTHESIZE A FORMULA THAT COUNTERACTS IT.
HERE GOES EVERYTHING!
HRRNNN!
IT'S WORKING! YOU'RE COMING OUT OF IT!
I'LL ADMINISTER THE SECOND DOSE...
WAIT--I'M STILL CONNECTED TO ULTRON'S NETWORK--AND THE OTHER INFECTED PEOPLE. THIS COULD BE USEFUL.
I CAN READ THEIR THOUGHTS. HE--
--HE WANTS TO TAKE THE TRICARRIER.
"ULTRON PRIME IS ARSENAL, THE ROBOT COMPANION THAT MY FATHER CREATED..."

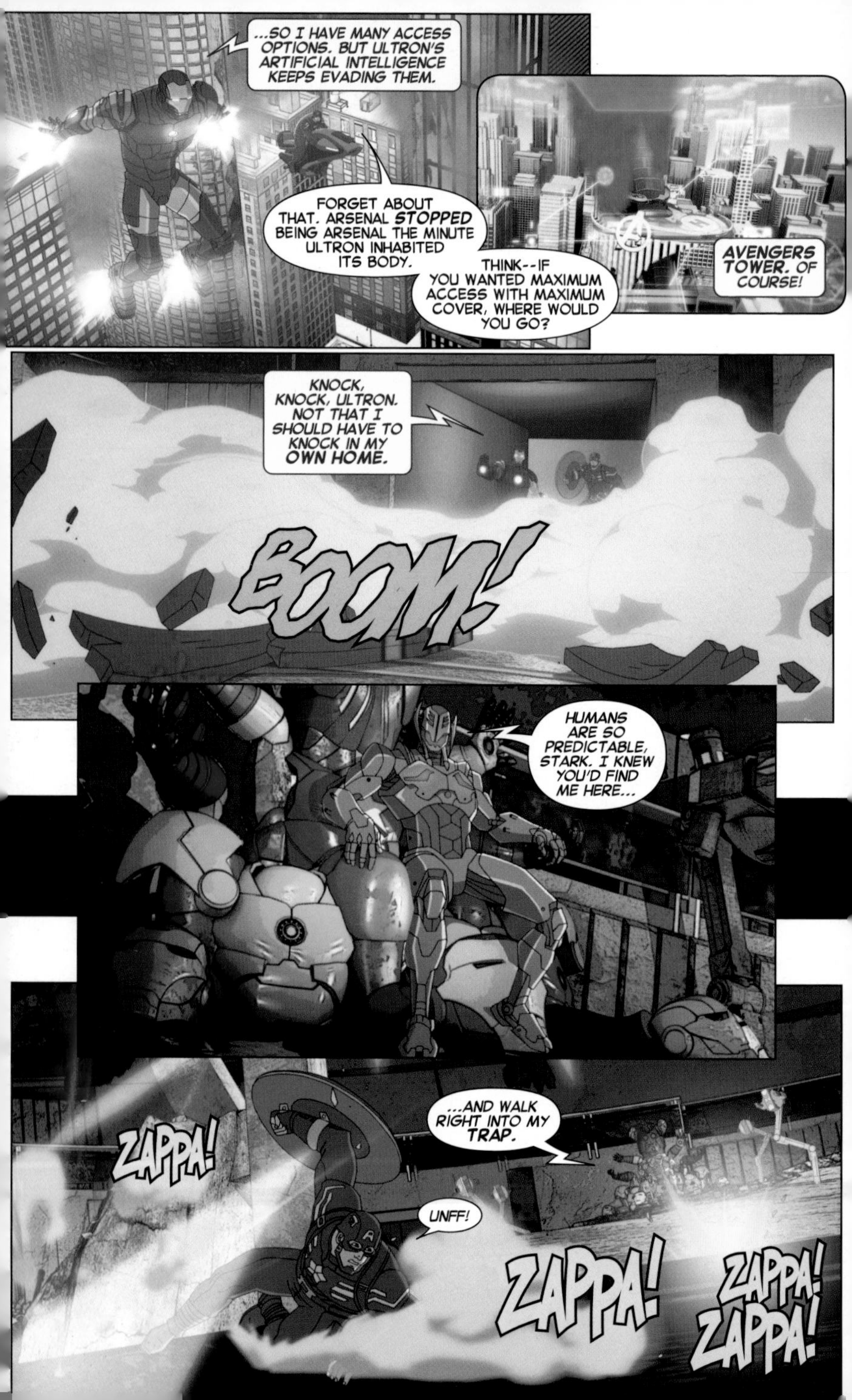
...SO I HAVE MANY ACCESS OPTIONS. BUT ULTRON'S ARTIFICIAL INTELLIGENCE KEEPS EVADING THEM.
FORGET ABOUT THAT. ARSENAL STOPPED BEING ARSENAL THE MINUTE ULTRON INHABITED ITS BODY.
THINK--IF YOU WANTED MAXIMUM ACCESS WITH MAXIMUM COVER, WHERE WOULD YOU GO?
AVENGERS TOWER. OF COURSE!
KNOCK, KNOCK, ULTRON. NOT THAT I SHOULD HAVE TO KNOCK IN MY OWN HOME.
BOOM!
HUMANS ARE SO PREDICTABLE, STARK. I KNEW YOU'D FIND ME HERE...
ZAPPA!
...AND WALK RIGHT INTO MY TRAP.
UNFF!
ZAPPA!
ZAPPA! ZAPPA!

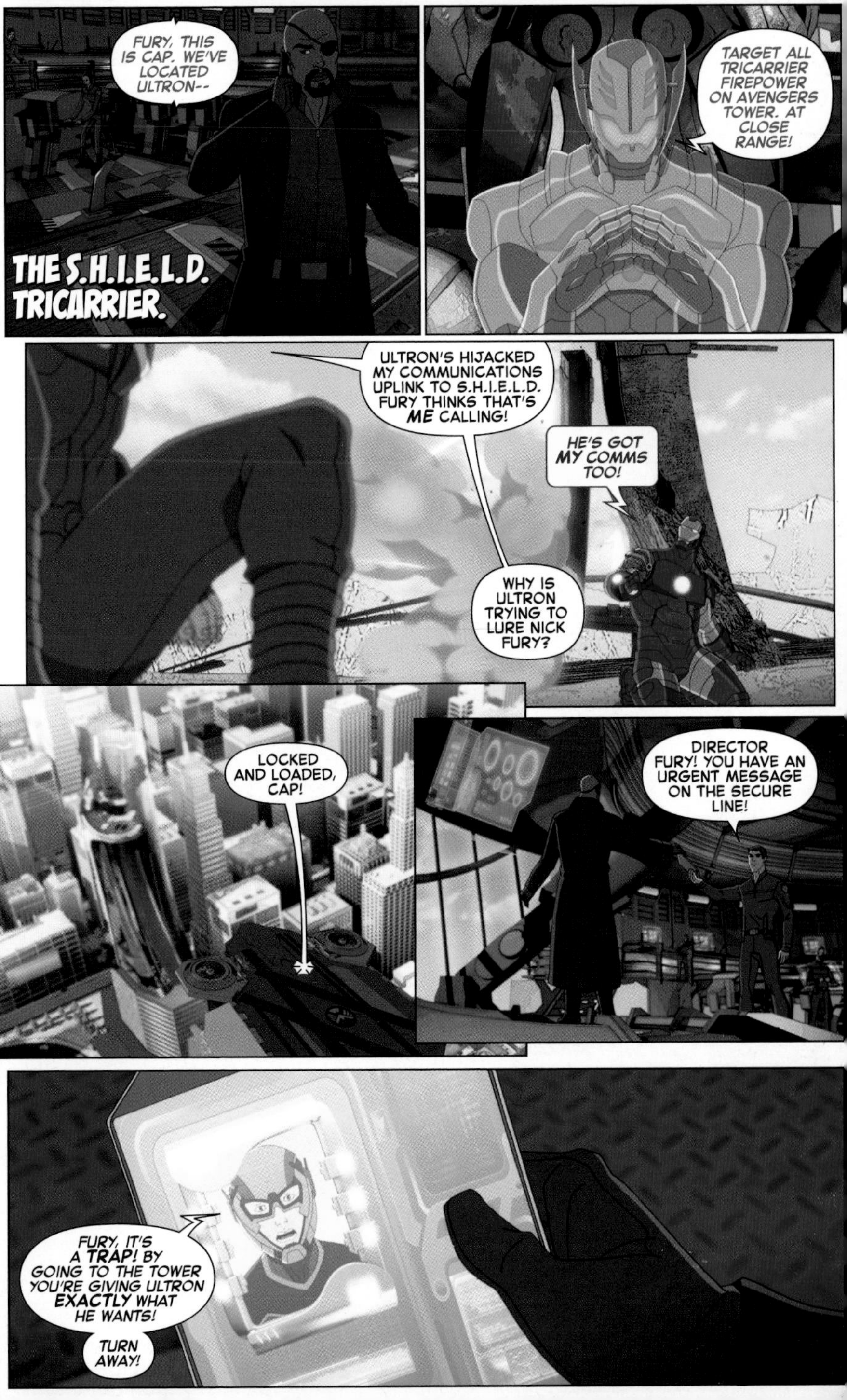
FURY, THIS IS CAP. WE'VE LOCATED ULTRON--
THE S.H.I.E.L.D. TRICARRIER.
TARGET ALL TRICARRIER FIREPOWER ON AVENGERS TOWER. AT CLOSE RANGE!
ULTRON'S HIJACKED MY COMMUNICATIONS UPLINK TO S.H.I.E.L.D. FURY THINKS THAT'S ME CALLING!
HE'S GOT MY COMMS TOO!
WHY IS ULTRON TRYING TO LURE NICK FURY?
LOCKED AND LOADED, CAP!
DIRECTOR FURY! YOU HAVE AN URGENT MESSAGE ON THE SECURE LINE!
FURY, IT'S A TRAP! BY GOING TO THE TOWER YOU'RE GIVING ULTRON EXACTLY WHAT HE WANTS!
TURN AWAY!

THE S.H.I.E.L.D. TRICARRIER. RIGHT ON CUE.

NOW MY PUZZLE IS COMPLETE.

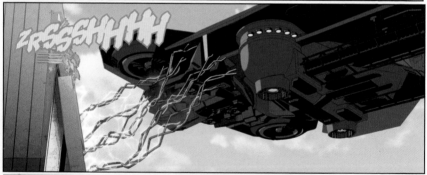

ZRSSSHHHH

ULTRON'S GUNS ARE LOCKED ON MY ARMOR...

...LET'S GIVE THEM SOMETHING TO SHOOT AT.

HOW'S YOUR AIM?

OH, I GET IT.

WHOOSH!

ULTRON WASN'T LOOKING FOR A NEW SHOULDER PLATE, BUT HE'S GOT ONE!

CLANG!

WHAT IS--?!

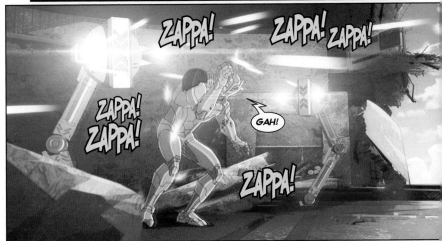

ZAPPA!

ZAPPA! ZAPPA!

ZAPPA! ZAPPA!

GAH!

ZAPPA!

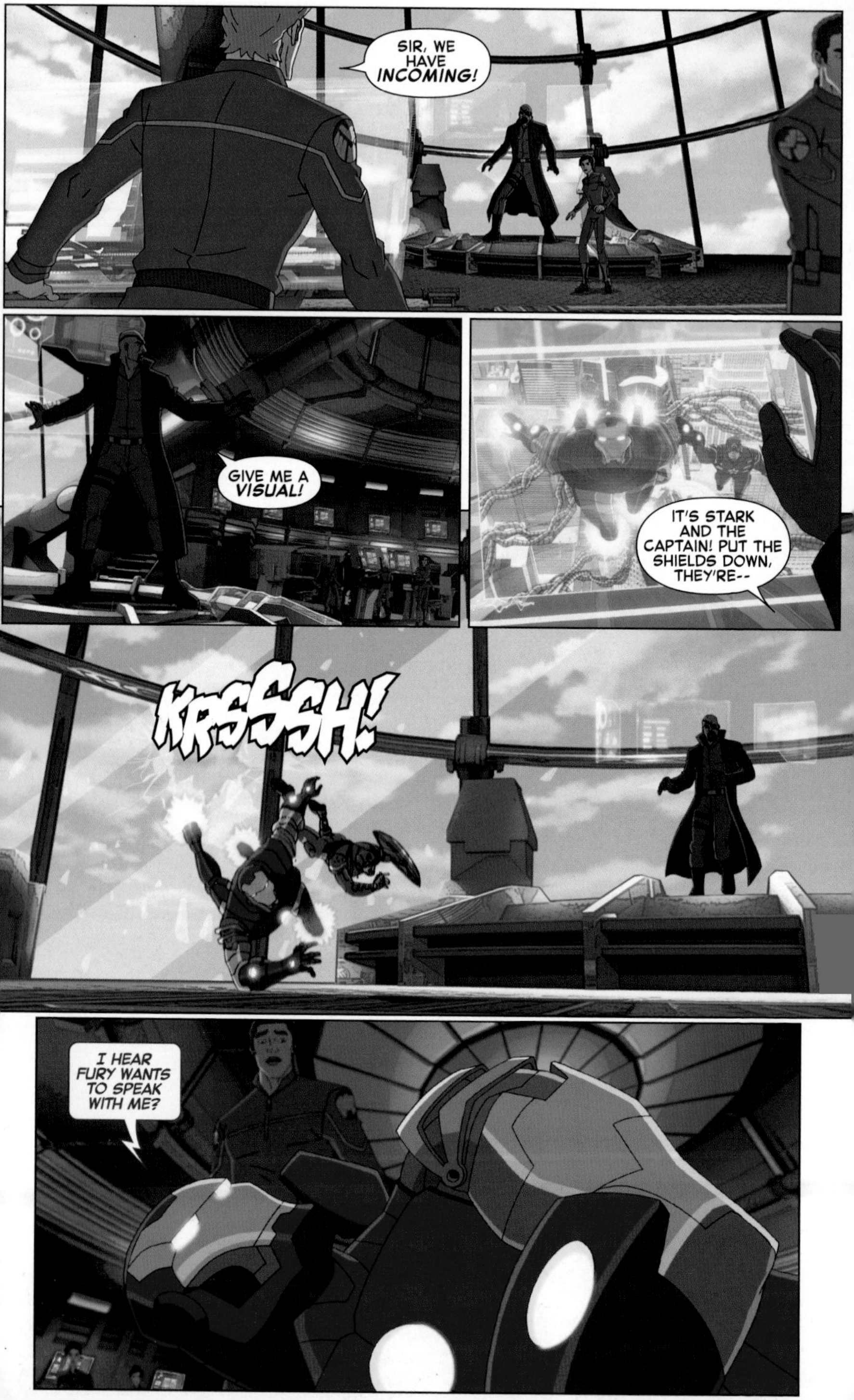
SIR, WE HAVE INCOMING!
GIVE ME A VISUAL!
IT'S STARK AND THE CAPTAIN! PUT THE SHIELDS DOWN, THEY'RE--
KRSSSH!
I HEAR FURY WANTS TO SPEAK WITH ME?

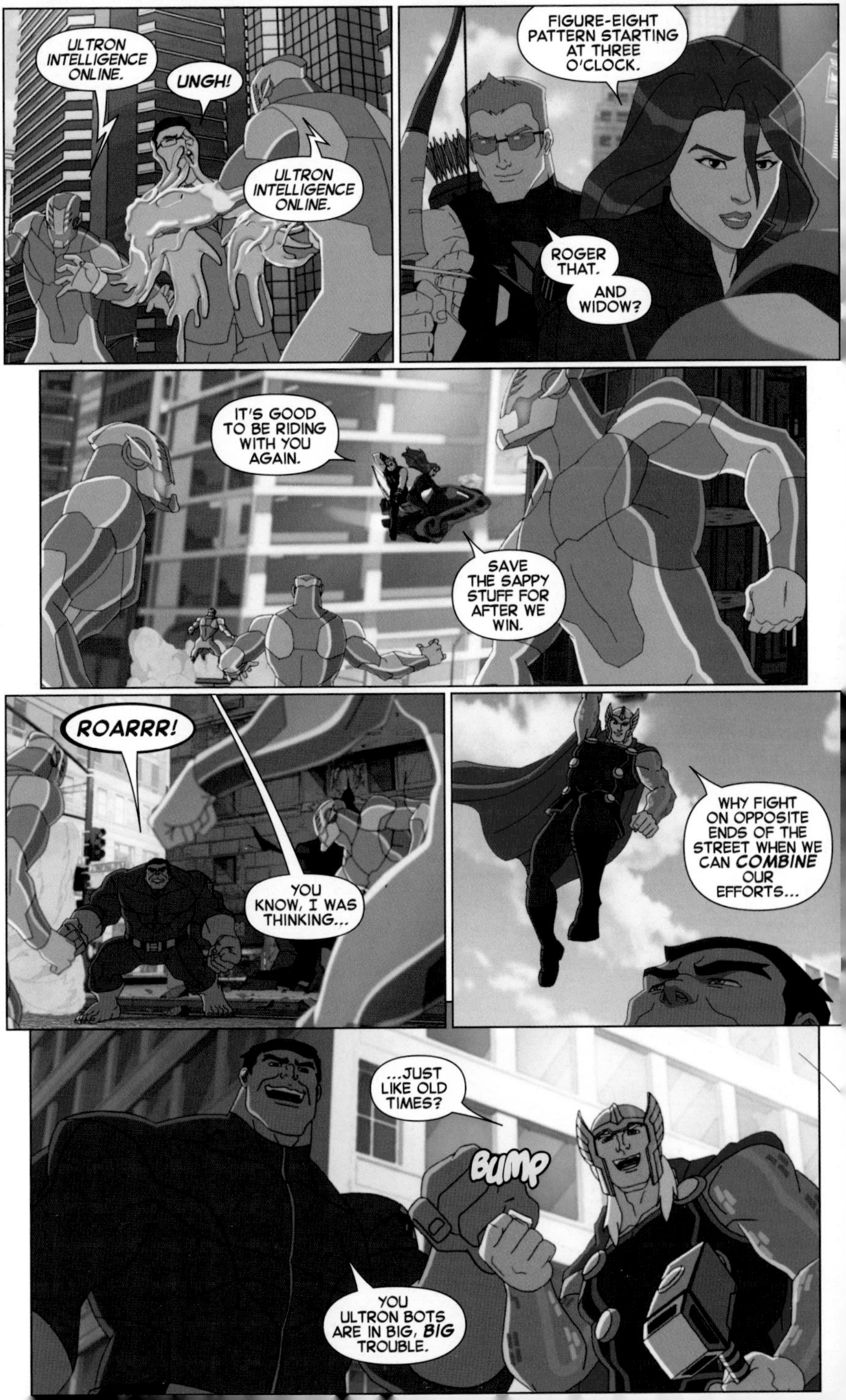
ULTRON INTELLIGENCE ONLINE.
UNGH!
ULTRON INTELLIGENCE ONLINE.
FIGURE-EIGHT PATTERN STARTING AT THREE O'CLOCK.
ROGER THAT.
AND WIDOW?
IT'S GOOD TO BE RIDING WITH YOU AGAIN.
SAVE THE SAPPY STUFF FOR AFTER WE WIN.
ROARRR!
YOU KNOW, I WAS THINKING...
WHY FIGHT ON OPPOSITE ENDS OF THE STREET WHEN WE CAN COMBINE OUR EFFORTS...
...JUST LIKE OLD TIMES?
BUMP
YOU ULTRON BOTS ARE IN BIG, BIG TROUBLE.

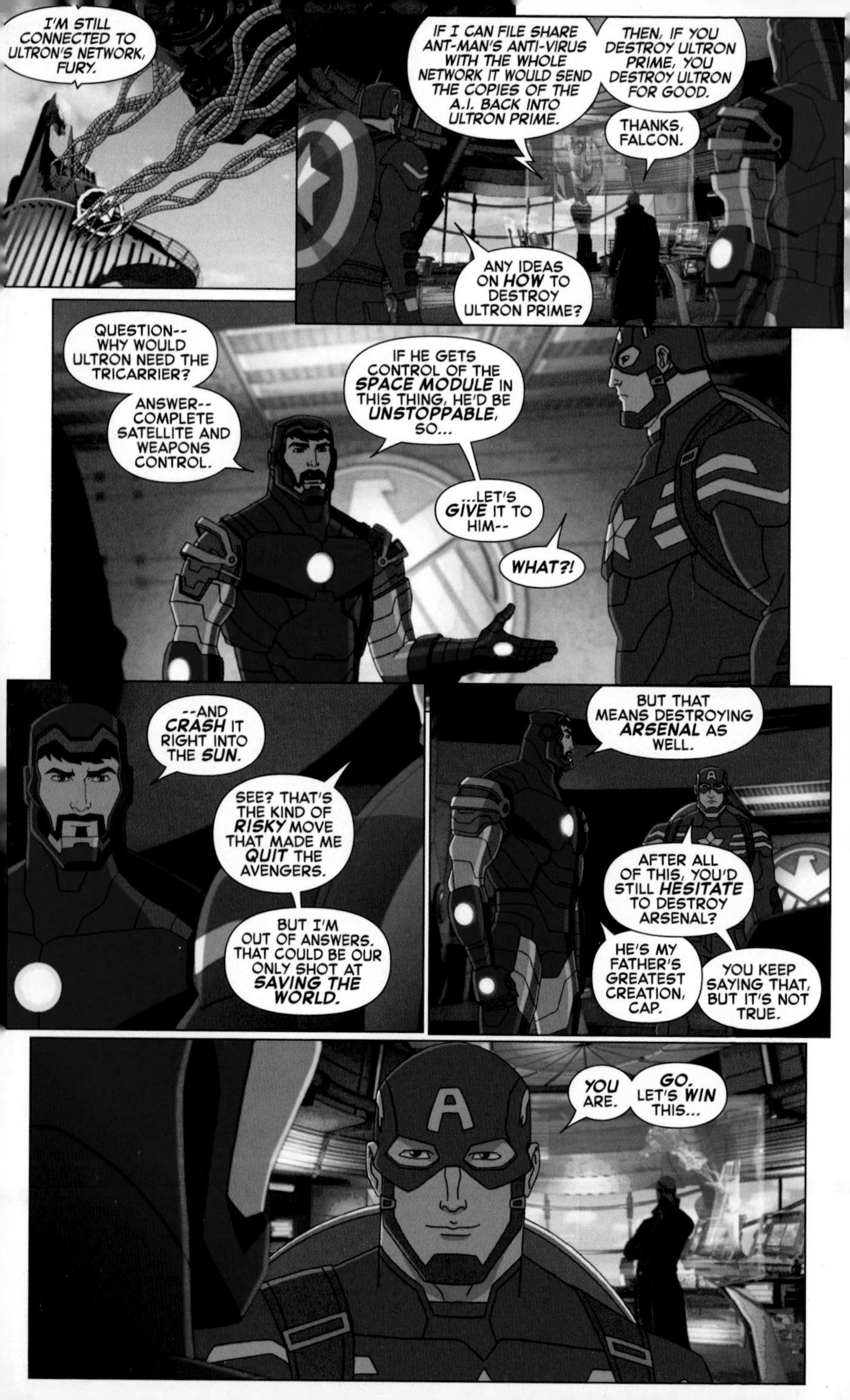
I'M STILL CONNECTED TO ULTRON'S NETWORK, FURY.
IF I CAN FILE SHARE ANT-MAN'S ANTI-VIRUS WITH THE WHOLE NETWORK IT WOULD SEND THE COPIES OF THE A.I. BACK INTO ULTRON PRIME.
THEN, IF YOU DESTROY ULTRON PRIME, YOU DESTROY ULTRON FOR GOOD.
THANKS, FALCON.
ANY IDEAS ON HOW TO DESTROY ULTRON PRIME?
QUESTION-- WHY WOULD ULTRON NEED THE TRICARRIER?
ANSWER-- COMPLETE SATELLITE AND WEAPONS CONTROL.
IF HE GETS CONTROL OF THE SPACE MODULE IN THIS THING, HE'D BE UNSTOPPABLE, SO...
...LET'S GIVE IT TO HIM--
WHAT?!
--AND CRASH IT RIGHT INTO THE SUN.
SEE? THAT'S THE KIND OF RISKY MOVE THAT MADE ME QUIT THE AVENGERS.
BUT I'M OUT OF ANSWERS. THAT COULD BE OUR ONLY SHOT AT SAVING THE WORLD.
BUT THAT MEANS DESTROYING ARSENAL AS WELL.
AFTER ALL OF THIS, YOU'D STILL HESITATE TO DESTROY ARSENAL?
HE'S MY FATHER'S GREATEST CREATION, CAP.
YOU KEEP SAYING THAT, BUT IT'S NOT TRUE.
YOU ARE.
GO. LET'S WIN THIS...

"...AS AVENGERS."

VRRRR--

THE SPACE MODULE. IT'S GETTING AWAY!

AND STARK IS ON BOARD!

THAT'S RIGHT, ULTRON. PLAY RIGHT INTO MY PLAN.

KRSH!

HRNN!

LIKE HUMANITY, YOUR PLAN WILL FAIL.

OH, YEAH?

PREPARING FOR INTERSTELLAR SPEED.

HYPERSPEED

ENGAGING

YOU CAN'T DESTROY ME, STARK--I AM ONE OF MANY ULTRON UNITS.

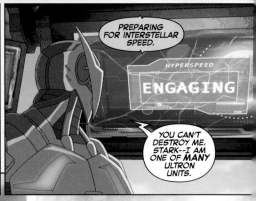

UNLIKE HUMANS, WE WORK AS ONE. EFFICIENTLY.

UNITY ISN'T ABOUT BEING THE **SAME**--IT'S ABOUT WORKING TOGETHER IN **SPITE** OF OUR DIFFERENCES.

THAT'S HUMANITY'S STRENGTH.

RIGHT, FALCON?

WE DID IT, TONY!

HRN?

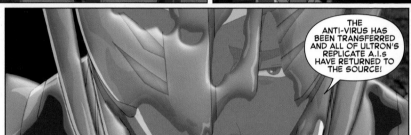

THE ANTI-VIRUS HAS BEEN TRANSFERRED AND ALL OF ULTRON'S REPLICATE A.I.s HAVE RETURNED TO THE SOURCE!

IT WORKED!

VMM

VMM

VMM

VMM

NNNGGGHHH...

WHAT... HAPPENED?

ALL COPIES OF THIS SOFTWARE ARE RETURNING TO THIS UNIT...THIS UNIT IS WEAKENING... MUST RETURN TO EARTH...

SORRY, ULTRON. THIS IS A ONE-WAY TRIP.

BACKGROUND SOFTWARE... OVERRIDING...

STARK-- TONY-- STOP.

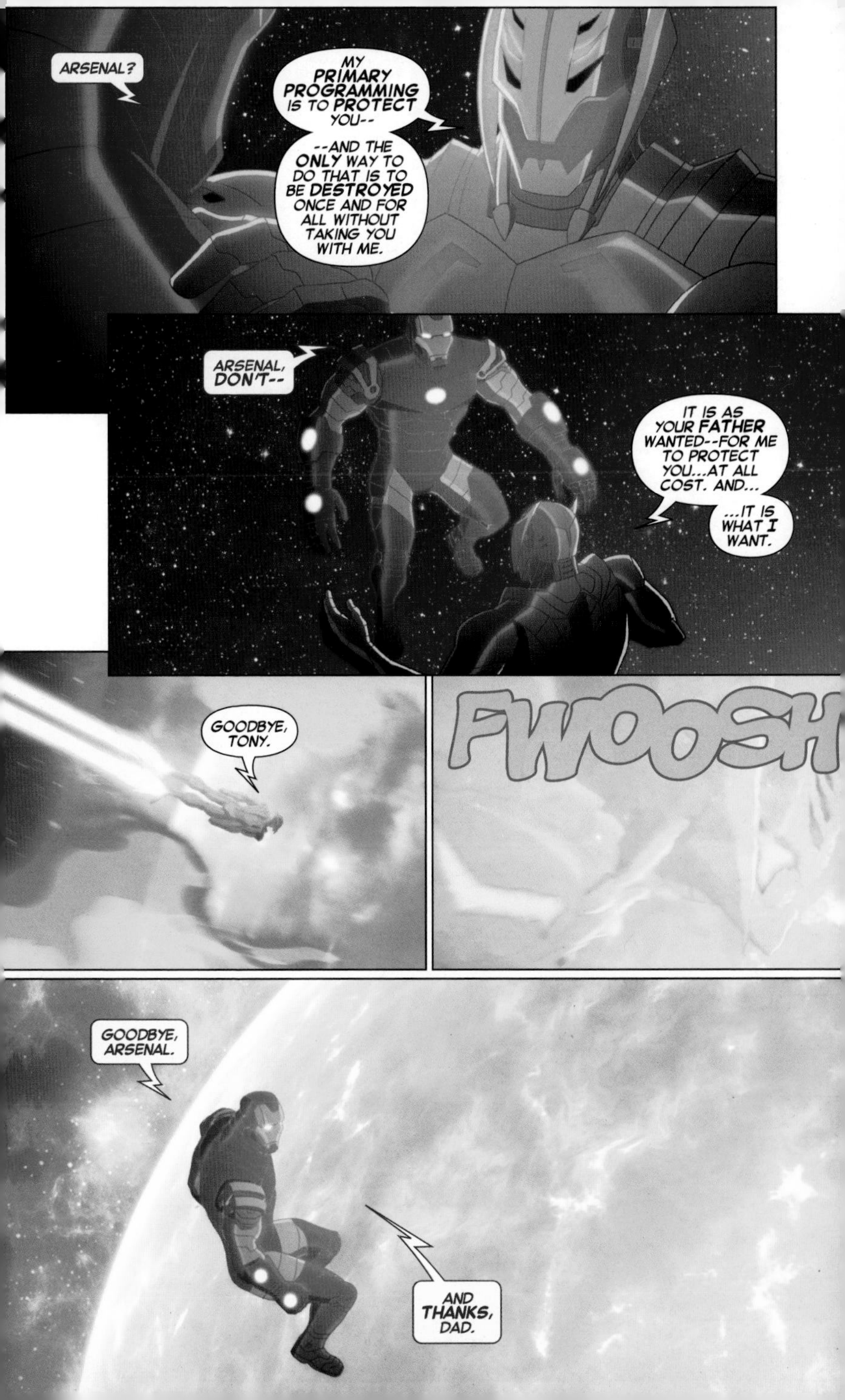
ARSENAL?
MY PRIMARY PROGRAMMING IS TO PROTECT YOU--
--AND THE ONLY WAY TO DO THAT IS TO BE DESTROYED ONCE AND FOR ALL WITHOUT TAKING YOU WITH ME.
ARSENAL, DON'T--
IT IS AS YOUR FATHER WANTED--FOR ME TO PROTECT YOU...AT ALL COST. AND...
...IT IS WHAT I WANT.
GOODBYE, TONY.
FWOOSH
GOODBYE, ARSENAL.
AND THANKS, DAD.

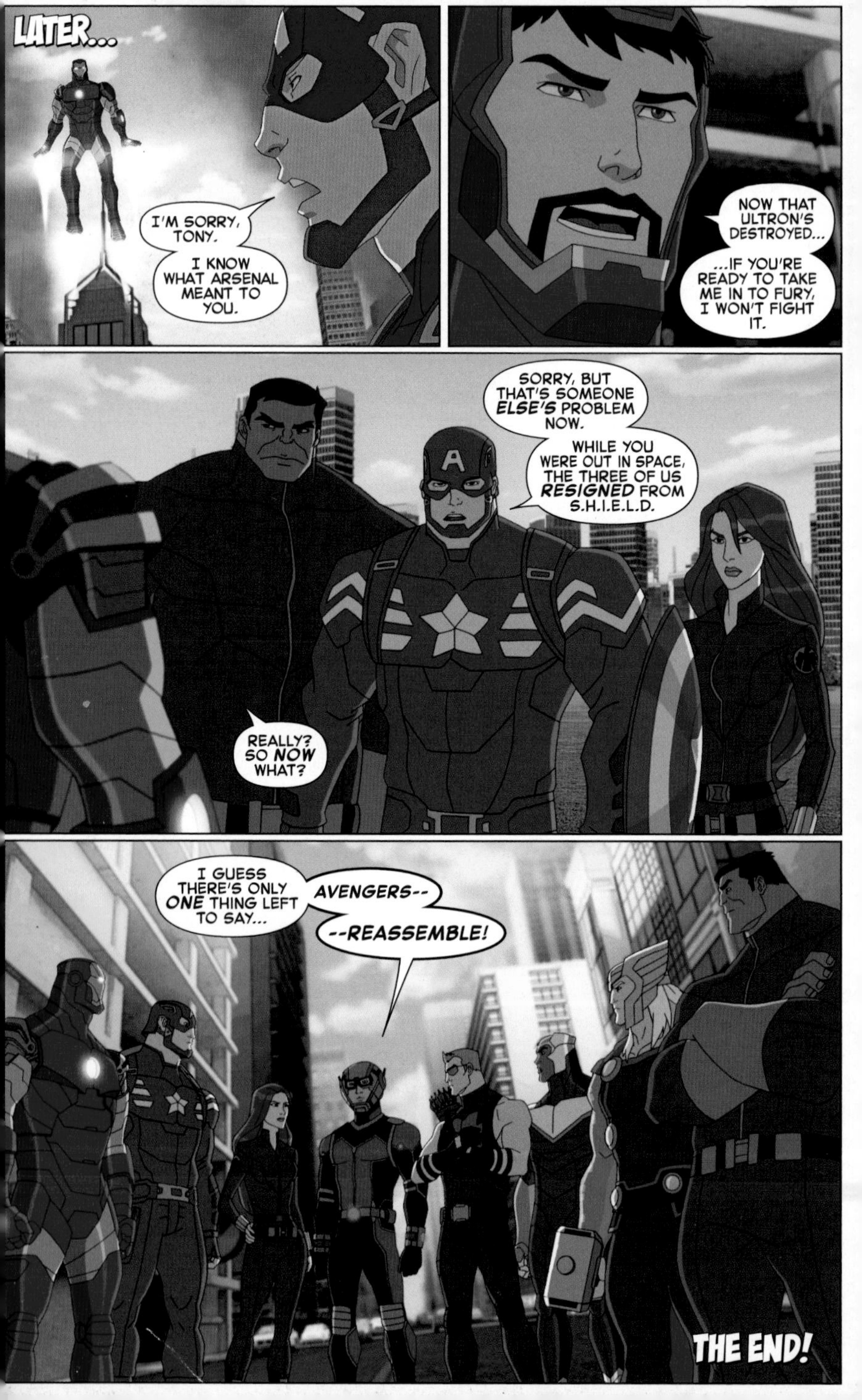
LATER...
I'M SORRY, TONY.
I KNOW WHAT ARSENAL MEANT TO YOU.
NOW THAT ULTRON'S DESTROYED...
...IF YOU'RE READY TO TAKE ME IN TO FURY, I WON'T FIGHT IT.
SORRY, BUT THAT'S SOMEONE ELSE'S PROBLEM NOW.
WHILE YOU WERE OUT IN SPACE, THE THREE OF US RESIGNED FROM S.H.I.E.L.D.
REALLY? SO NOW WHAT?
I GUESS THERE'S ONLY ONE THING LEFT TO SAY...
AVENGERS--
--REASSEMBLE!
THE END!

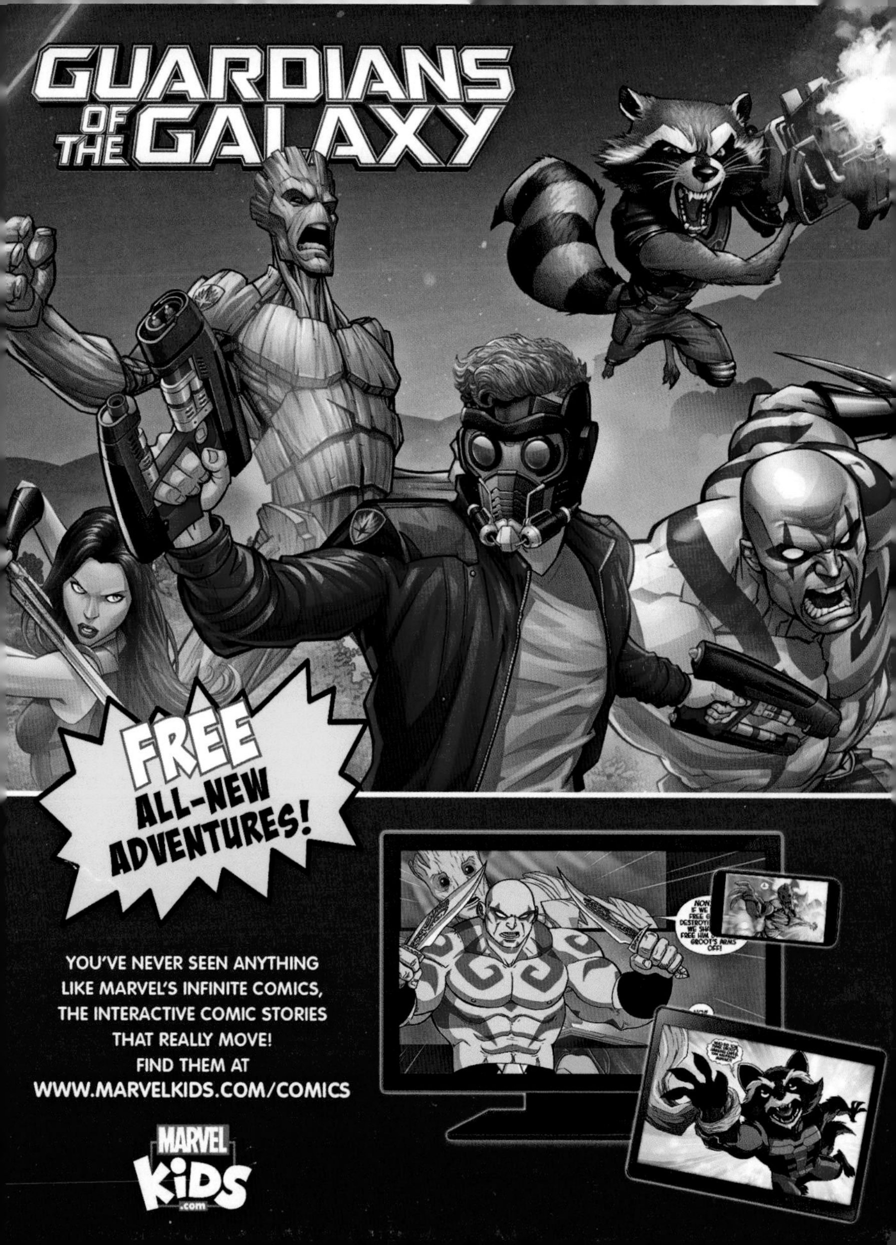
GUARDIANS OF THE GALAXY
FREE ALL-NEW ADVENTURES!
YOU'VE NEVER SEEN ANYTHING
LIKE MARVEL'S INFINITE COMICS,
THE INTERACTIVE COMIC STORIES
THAT REALLY MOVE!
FIND THEM AT
WWW.MARVELKIDS.COM/COMICS
MARVEL KIDS .com

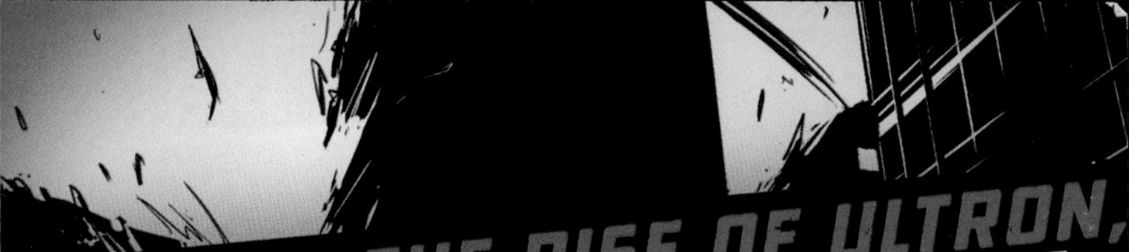

WITNESS THE RISE OF ULTRON, REIMAGINED AND RETOLD IN THRILLING SOUTH KOREAN MANHWA STYLE!

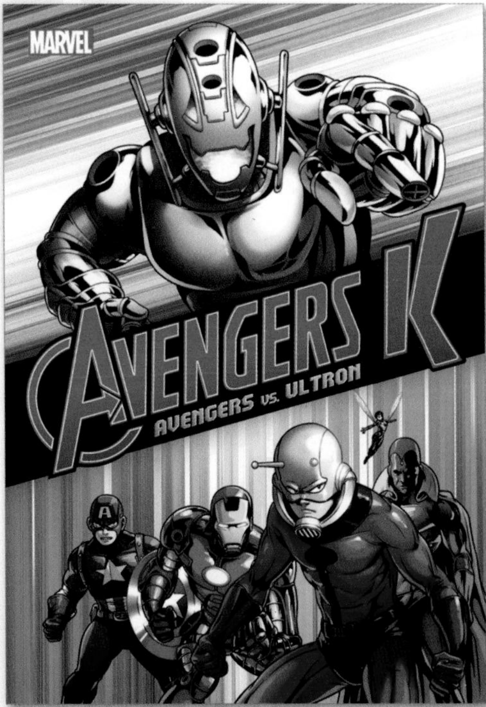

MARVEL
AVENGERS K
AVENGERS VS. ULTRON

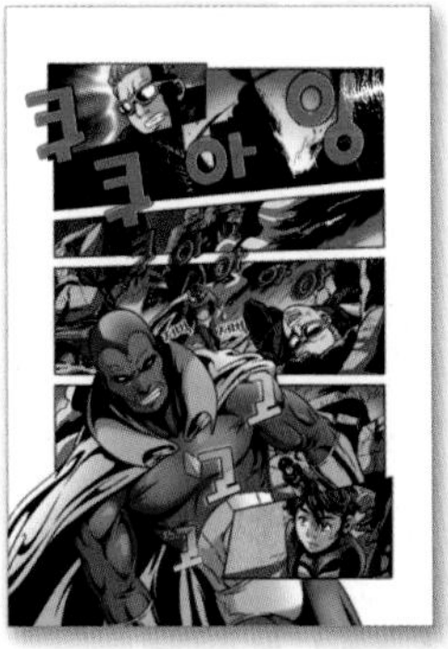

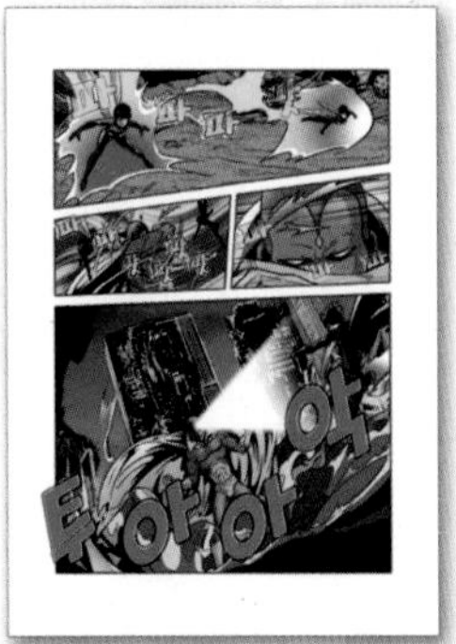

AVENGERS K BOOK 1: AVENGERS VS. ULTRON TPB

ISBN: 978-1-302-90120-2

COLLECTED IN ENGLISH FOR THE FIRST TIME!

AVAILABLE MAY 2016
IN PRINT AND DIGITAL WHEREVER BOOKS ARE SOLD

MARVEL

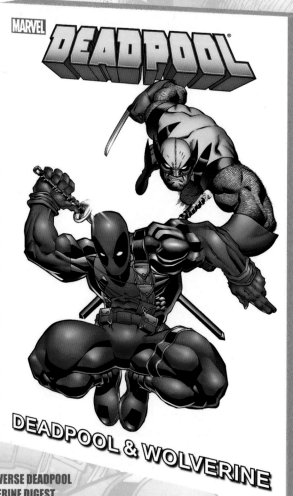